The Saboteur

OTHER AXEL BRAND MYSTERIES

(available in print and electronic editions)

The Hotel Dick

"The plot is as devious as any of Donald Westlake's and hard-boiled enough to please Bill Pronzini fans. The end result is pure entertainment." –*Library Journal*

The Dead Genius

"...Where to begin with a man whose background is a mystery? Well, for one thing, too many people want the cops to think they're barking up the wrong tree....This is historical fiction done well, with steady pacing and bullpen humor. Think of Sheldon Russell's *The Yard Dog* for time period and sense of place. Highly recommended." –*Library Journal*

Night Medicine

The Saboteur

A Joe Sonntag Mystery

Axel Brand

This is a work of fiction. The characters and events portrayed in this novel do not represent any real person, living or dead.

ISBN 13: 978-1477634097
ISBN 10: 1477634096

Book design by Get It Together Productions
(www.awritersaide.com)
Yellow rose image by Tamara Kulikova

Printed in The United States of America

Chapter One

Joe Sonntag knew who was calling in the middle of the night. It would be Lammers, the night dispatcher. He flipped on the kitchen light and headed for the upright phone and yanked the receiver off the black stalk.

"Sonntag, get over to Allis Chalmers, south gate. There's a body."

"What's there?"

"A mob, and a few cops."

"Tell me more."

"A scab. They shot him as he was coming off the night shift."

"Who shot him?"

"Go find out." The line went dead.

He studied the kitchen clock. It was ten minutes before one on a summer's night. The shift got off at twelve-thirty. The entire shift was scabs. The Machinists Union had been on strike for six weeks, and it hadn't been pretty. The tractor plant had been limping along with temporary labor, and this was the end of the second shift.

He hated this. He struggled back to the bedroom and tried to rustle up some clothing without awakening Lizbeth, but she snapped the light on the bedside table.

"What?" she asked.

"Scab got killed at the Allis-Chalmers plant."

"Serves him right," she said, and snapped the light off.

"You could leave it on until I get into my sox," he said.

But she had turned away, her back to him.

That wasn't like her at all.

He yawned and dressed, and fumbled out the door, envying his wife. Allis-Chalmers wasn't far away, in the small industrial suburb of West Allis. The town had only a few cops, and they had been borrowing Milwaukee cops wholesale during the brutal strike, in a hopeless attempt to maintain order.

Now there was a killing. It was inevitable. And there might be many more. Day by day, the papers tolled the damage: shots fired, rocks thrown, chanting protesters, fistfights, brawls, kicking fallen mortals until every rib was busted, language unfit for delicate ears, big tough men smashing fists into smaller men. Small men jabbing boots into big men. Shrill headlines, bitter denunciations, condemnations from mayors and bishops and chiefs of police. Paddy wagons hauling away load after load of hard men who hadn't any sense that they had committed crimes. Crimes against other men, against property, against the peace.

Lieutenant Joe Sonntag was head of the investigations unit of the Milwaukee Police Department and did a lot of the legwork himself because there never were enough detectives to find who did what to whom. And he got called into every case. Like now.

He ran a hand over the stubble on his chin, noted it, and for some absurd reason felt pleased with it. He wouldn't need to lather up his jaw with a brush, and scrape it off with his straight-edge. Not this night.

He slipped into the dark, finding the air pleasant but heavy with the smell of hops from the breweries. That was a Milwaukee trademark. If you didn't smell smoke, you smelled hops.

He fired up the old Hudson coupe, pushed the choke back, and eased the car out of the narrow garage. The prewar car was burning oil, and now it offended his nostrils. He got out, closed the shuddering door, and then drove west and south, to the homely suburb where a giant plant was surrounded by bungalows and small shops–and the

Wisconsin State Fairgrounds. How that dreary hinterland got that plum he'd never know. But maybe he did know. Wisconsin was a People's State. The humbler the people, the better they were treated by the politicians.

The streetlights, few and far between, marched west on Wells, but at 60th he turned south and then west, and arrived at last at a badly lit factory gate, where a silent handful of spectators stood watching. The strikers had fled.

There were a few West Allis and Milwaukee cops, an ambulance, and two black and whites, one of which had its red light whirling. Darkness clawed at the place, trying to snuff out the two small lights that lit the gate. The brick ramparts of the factory stretched into the darkness at either side. That was Milwaukee for you. Build everything to last forever. He parked the coupe and approached, only to have a cop block the way. "You can't go over there," he said.

"I'm Lieutenant Sonntag. You want my badge?"

The West Allis cop backed off and nodded him through. Ahead lay a body, a sheet thrown over it by an ambulance man. Sonntag wondered why they hadn't taken the body away; why it was still lying there, waiting for him. In the shadows, people stared at him, at the body, at the ambulance men.

"Who do I talk to?" Sonntag said.

"I'm the one," an old sergeant said. "Not much of a story. He's a temporary. His social security card reads Joseph L. Ginger. No drivers license. Someone got him coming out."

"Why's he here? Why wasn't he taken to a hospital?"

For an answer, the sergeant led him to the body and pulled the sheet back. The man's face was obliterated where a large-caliber bullet had shattered septum and bone and vanished into the skull. It was a fast and brutal way to die.

"No exit wound," the officer said. "It's in there."

"Have we an address? Relatives? Have you contacted the plant?"

"The foreman identified him. He's been working two weeks. He said we could get the address and all that in the morning. It was all locked up in a room where they keep a few files on the temporaries."

"I think we want that information right now," Sonntag said. "Even if we have to wake up a manager to get it. Now, why were you waiting for me?"

"We have a death; a murder. You're the man, they said. Too bad we have to go through all this crappola."

"Have you talked to these people?"

"By the time we got here, there weren't any people. Only some of the scabs who came out with the dead man."

"I want their names."

"Yeah, we'll get them for you. Scabs, you know how that is."

"No, how is it?"

"Mostly crackers up from the South; nothing much to them. They sooner this is over and they're gone, the better."

"Have you checked the ground? A weapon?'

"Yeah, with flashlights. You want to bring in floodlights for this?"

"A gun anywhere?"

"Lots of stuff. Mostly strike posters, lunch junk, sticks."

"A gun anywhere?"

"Something eating you, lieutenant?"

The West Allis sergeant wasn't going to help any. Especially help a Milwaukee detective. Sonntag headed toward a group of spectators, shadowy people in the dim light, herded behind an invisible line by two or three uniforms.

"Any of you see the shooting?" he asked.

They stared back.

"Any of you a striker?"

No response.

"Any of you a temporary at the plant?"

No response. He singled out an older man.

"You there. Why are you here at two in the morning?"

"Just enjoying the show," the man said. "We don't see a good killing very often, not even here."

"You saw the killing?"

"I did. I knew it was gonna happen one of these times. The union's tired of throwing rocks and punching noses. Time to get real serious."

"You with the Machinists' Union?"

"Used to be; retired."

"Who shot this man there?"

The old guy stared. "I think maybe someone inside, with a rifle. Wasn't no one around here."

The old buzzard was grinning.

"Now tell me who shot that man?"

"Well, my theory is that them two scabs were fighting over the same woman, and one scab shot the other."

There were some chuckles. These two-in-the-morning visitors to the plant gate were enjoying the show.

"You got a name and address for me?" Sonntag said.

"I think I forgot it," the man said.

"One more time," Sonntag said.

"Babe Ruth? That do?"

Sonntag found a Milwaukee cop. "Hold that one until you get a name and address off a drivers license."

The cop reached for the man, but the whole vulture lot of them raced into the night.

"Hey!" the cop yelled, and started after the scattering flock. But he was a lumbering two hundred fifty pounds, and fell behind. Sonntag watched the show, knew at once that he had stepped into scab-killing headquarters, and knew that putting a name to the killer of the man lying dead in the wan light was going to be as tough a task as he'd ever tackled.

The forlorn silence engulfed him. There were red lights rotating on a couple of Ford black and whites, a few uniforms standing around, two ambulance guys waiting for instructions, and the body under a sheet. Two dim lights turned the scene into a layer of hell.

Sonntag headed for the ambulance guys. "I want one last look, and then you can take him," he said.

They pulled back the sheet until the sickly light caught the man's worn denim shirt, his frayed dungarees, and busted shoes.

"Do you find any other injury?" Sonntag asked.

"Nope, just that sucker in the face," one said.

The pair lifted the dead man and set him down on his stomach. There were no rear-entry or exit injuries visible. But in the miserable light, it was hard to tell. A coroner's report would make it official.

"All right," Sonntag said.

They lifted the body to a stretcher, carried it to the yawning rear doors of the ambulance, and closed the doors. They clanked shut with a great finality. Moments later the meat wagon rattled away. Then there were only the West Allis and Milwaukee cops.

"Which of you were here?" Sonntag asked.

"Gill and me," said a young West Allis cop. One was beet-faced and forty, the other dark and twenty five.

"How does it work?"

"We drive here a few minutes before the shift ends. When the scabs come busting out, we keep them apart from any strikers, and try to keep missiles from flying around, and when they all are gone, we're gone."

"Only tonight things were different. One of you want to tell me?"

The young guy, cheerful for a change, volunteered. "It's not like the day shift. That's when the trouble happens. Two hundred, three hundred Machinists Union men with rocks and sticks and bullhorns and even whips, and some skinny scabs trying to get in and out. Not like that now, the end of the second shift, the scabs hurrying to get away, and maybe just a few union guys, always a few, just a token few, but someone, anyway."

"Any trouble before?"

"Nah, usually just some yelling. Those guys, they sure got some colorful words to toss at the scabs. It's sort of the usual, right? Tell 'em they're pricks."

"Any threats?"

"Always. You're gonna die. You're gonna croak. You're going to get your balls cut off. You ain't ever going back to where you came from."

"And the scabs?"

"They don't yell back. They just want to get in and out, get paid for as long as the strike lasts, and get away."

"What do they throw at the scabs?"

"Rocks mostly. Also shit. Any kind, dog, horse, people. Acid sometimes. That's bad stuff, burn a hole through the flesh in no time. Bleach, anything that they can lay their hands on."

"What are your duties?"

"Duties?"

"What line do you draw?"

"It's all assault. We just got to go after the worst of it, and knock heads. Billy club stuff. If it's just words and yells, we just stay put. They throw something and we wade in."

"Okay, what happened tonight?"

"Usual exit, bunches of scabs coming out, they're tired, want to sleep. There wasn't any shouting, and I thought maybe this wouldn't be so rough, but then the shot. Just one, bang, a scab falls, and the machinists, they're gone. It's dark, and they're gone in a minute. We get over to the scab, and he's dead on the spot, bullet ruined his face, and the rest of the scabs hurrying by. They don't know each other. They're from all over, not like the union guys that work side by side every day; the scabs, they're all loners, and they see the dead man and all they want is to get as far as they can from that gate."

"Did you detain any, question any?"

"We're looking after the dead man, calling for an ambulance, getting help."

"You're the only two people I have who witnessed it?"

"There's a gatekeeper at the plant; maybe he saw it."

"The rest ran?"

"You bet they ran."

"Then what?"

"We tried some first aid on the dead man. There wasn't much blood. We waited for help. We asked the gateman to send the foreman out."

"And when help came, then what?"

The young cop sighed. "Then we stood around and waited for you."

Chapter Two

It sure was forlorn there, three in the morning, two dim lights, no cops any more. Sonntag headed for the gate, now shut tight. He spotted the old gatekeeper inside a little shack, reading a Captain Marvel comic. Sonntag waved at him, with no effect.

"Hey! Mind if we talk?"

The old guy stuck his head out the door of the gate-house.

"You can't come in. We open the gate at six-thirty, next shift."

"Milwaukee police."

"Sorry, my orders are to keep her shut."

"I'm investigating that shooting. You want to come out and talk?"

"I didn't see it. I'm busy watching the temps leave, hear something, some shouts, and there's some cops out there and someone down."

"That's it? Any of your temporaries shouting? Causing trouble?"

"They just took one look and got the hell away, scared half to death."

"You want to steer me to the boss?"

"Night supervisor. That's a long way around. You'd do better at the main entrance, around that way. This is one big place, and you'd just get lost."

"So I get there, and is that door locked at night?"

"Oh, all right, goddamn it, I'll take you. Probably get fired for it."

The man stepped out, freed the gate, motioned Sonntag in, and locked.

"It's the strike," he said. "We hardly ever lock during regular times. But now we lock up. Vandals, you know. Wreckers. Let some vandal in, and they pour sand in the works, and shut down all the lines."

"There much of that?"

"Not this time. We've got a couple of armed guards, and the Machinists know it."

The old guy limped ahead, going so fast that Sonntag marveled. He entered one long building that proved to be a tractor assembly line, now silent and smoky in dim light. Sonntag didn't see a soul. They exited that line and entered another where farm implements were built and another where Allis-Chalmers assembled hydroelectric turbines. And finally, the duffer turned into a broad interior street and pointed at a lit office building.

"In there," he said. "Second floor."

"How do I get out of here?"

"Wait for the dawn's early light. The gates open at six-thirty."

The duffer had a certain malicious gleam in his eyes.

Sonntag headed for the offices, which were utilitarian. The company didn't waste money on executive perks. Except for corridor lights, it was dark as hell in there.

"You going somewhere, pal?" someone asked from the shadows.

"I'm wanting the night supervisor. Milwaukee police."

A shotgun-armed man in blue materialized. "You got a badge?"

Sonntag flipped his. "You mind taking me there?"

"We got to be on the watch," the man said. "Death threats."

"I saw them in the papers. There's two of you here?"

"I'm not supposed to talk."

"You do police work?"

"No, not like that. Plant security. Started with Pinkerton; now I'm on my own."

"There was a killing outside the tractor gate."

"Heard about it."

"Know anything about it?"

"Nah. I was over here. That's two city blocks away."

They climbed some terrazzo stairs and the guard pointed to the only lit office. "In there."

"How do I get out of here later?"

"I will see you on the first floor."

The guard left him, so Sonntag knocked on the lit office door, which had a pebbled glass window, and entered.

"Sonntag, Milwaukee police," Sonntag said.

The supervisor stared.

"Milwaukee police. I'm here about the shooting."

"Temporary employee."

"Whatever. He's dead, and I need information. Home address, family contact, local address. Your employment records."

The supervisor slowly settled back in his seat.

"You are?"

"Hannigan."

"A man was shot to death at the tractor gate, and I need to find out about him, Mr. Hannigan. You're the night supervisor, right?"

"I wouldn't know anything about him, officer."

"I don't expect you to. What I need is some records. His name was Ginger, Joseph L. Ginger. I need his address, his home, his relatives, next of kin."

"We don't have any of that for temporaries, officer."

"What do you have?"

"Personnel's locked; come back at eight."

"How about you unlock it and help me find what's on file?"

"That would be a waste of time, sir. There'd be nothing there."

"Tell me how it works, Mr. Hannigan."

"These people are working for us only a few days or weeks, or months. They get rooms by the week or day; we advertise for help, and they come up by Greyhound. They don't have bank accounts here, and want pay in cash, so they get it weekly in manila envelopes.

They're here until the strike's over and then they're gone. They know that, live cheap, make good money on the line, and get their last pay the moment we come to terms with the union."

"You must have some sort of records. You withhold money for social security, and maybe other taxes."

"Sure, if they've got a social security number it'll be on file. They record names and addresses in a ledger. There's no point in running a file. They're here and gone."

"How about you taking me there and showing me the ledger?"

"There's five or six hundred temporaries, officer. I'd suggest you come back during business hours and doing it right."

"There's a dead man who worked here, and there's relatives somewhere, and we need to know who he was, and why he was shot if it wasn't random. So let's go."

Hannigan looked at his watch. "Officer, it's approaching four. At eight, there'll be people who can help you. I can't."

Sonntag backed off. "All right, tell me about these people," he said.

Hannigan relaxed a little. The man was big, had scarred hands, and looked like he had worked his way up the ladder.

"We put ads in help wanted, temporary employment for metal workers. They come. They got it figured out. They're going to take a lot of crap coming and going, and they're going to take home some good pay, especially if they're up from down south, and the one's worth the other to them. They get seventy-five cents down there; they get two dollars up here. It adds up."

"Down there is where?"

"I shouldn't use that term, officer. They come from out there, not down there. They come off farms, they come up from Chicago. They come out of the north woods."

"Wisconsin?"

"Sure. Small town, country. Not like West Allis."

"Where do they stay?"

"Who knows? They don't know one another. One'll rent a flat and they sub rent it to a dozen, and they get some bedrolls and move in."

"So who shot Ginger?"

Hannigan laughed. "Always the cop, right? Does it matter?"

"Scab, right?"

"Temporary employee."

"Union guy shot Ginger?"

"Communist probably."

"Explain that, all right?"

"Machinist Union's pinko. They take orders from Uncle Joe."

"What's that got to do with it?"

"Communists shoot anyone in their way."

"You want to tell me who's the Communists in the union?"

"Nah, one day they all are, the next day they're pledging allegiance to the flag."

"So who shot Ginger?"

"I wouldn't know until after we get a new contract with the union, okay?"

"After that you'll know?"

"We're sweethearts, officer. We woo the Machinists and they woo Allis Chalmers, right?"

"So who shot Ginger?"

But Hannigan was reaching for some Alka-Seltzer.

It went downhill from there.

"We'll be back at eight," Sonntag said.

"We'll hire a replacement," Hannigan said.

"How do I get out of here?"

"Go to the front door here. A guard'll open. Walk around the plant to the tractor gate. It's six or seven blocks."

Hannigan was busy watching his medicine fizz in a tumbler.

Joe Sonntag retreated, hiked down the echoing stairwell, and the night guard let him out. It wasn't far to sunrise. He started hiking, not sure which way to walk, but he figured he'd get to his old coupe eventually. The night air was gentle. He thought he'd be walking through deserted streets, but there were knots of men standing around. They left him alone, and he was glad of it. They looked like they'd kill him with a tire iron if he didn't keep on moving. He hadn't come armed.

When he finally got to the right gate, and went to collect his car and get out, he realized something was wrong. The Hudson had four flat tires, barely visible in the dull light. He crouched, studying the tires. Each one had been ripped open with something. The tires were history. A rage built in him. The goddamned Communist union.

He stalked the dark, looking for the strikers. It had to be the strikers. They saw the guard let him in. They thought he was management. They butchered four tires.

But there was no one around. He hiked over to the gatehouse, but there was no one in it now. No West Allis cops, not for a while, not until the plant opened up for the day shift. It was the damndest thing. He studied the gate, wondering if he could open it without getting shot by those security men. Maybe the old boy had gone to the bathroom. He decided to wait a bit. He kept a flashlight in the dashboard of his coupe, so he got it, studied the tires, and concluded that they had all been stabbed with a double-edged knife; something like a bowie. They were pretty new, and he was ticked off. The department had better pay up.

The grounds outside the gate were littered with strike debris. He focused the beam of light on the signs. United Machine Workers On Strike. Pay, Not Profits, Fair Wage. Broken sticks. Torn cardboard. There had been some brawls around there. He found lunch bucket waste; wax paper, apple cores. The beam caught something shiny, and he plucked it up. A cartridge case, forty-five caliber. He eyed the distance from there to the gate, where the scabs were racing out and one got killed. Not an easy shot. Twenty yards, maybe. He pocketed the cartridge.

That's when he saw half a dozen men moving his way, rising out of the dark. A swift glance indicated he was surrounded. There were more behind him.

They had sticks or clubs of some sort.

"Milwaukee police," he said.

He reached for his badge, but it was too late. They rushed him, six, seven, he didn't know how many, but they grabbed him from all sides. His badge wallet was ripped out of his hands. They yanked him down, landed on him, started pounding on him with those sticks. He felt one crack across his arms, felt a boot hit his ribs, felt the sticks hit his face, and then break over his shins. They pinned him. Pain shot out of his side. Something in there was grinding. A boot caught his head, spinning him. A stick landed on his leg, shooting hot hurt up it.

He struggled, but there were six, seven men jamming him down. One dug into Sonntag's shirt pocket and pulled the brass casing.

"Copper, don't come back. The scab's dead. You're next," a big guy said. The man's face was invisible in shadow. "Get out, all you Milwaukee cops. This ain't your town. Don't come back. Don't mess with the union. You put big city cops on this, and cops will die."

At some signal, they pulled away from him, leaving him in the filth. They slipped into the night as silently as they had come out of it.

He ached in more places than he could count. His head stung. His ribs hurt so badly he couldn't breathe right. He got to his knees, forced himself to stand, stood up slowly, checking himself for busted bones. He had his wallet. They had his badge. He cussed himself for poking around alone, without backup, in the dark, without any way to defend himself. Captain Ackerman, his immediate superior back at the station house, was going to ream him out. He stared at the forbidding plant, the no-man's land outside the gate, the two dim lights and their sickly glow. He wiped blood off his face.

He limped toward his coupe; there might be a little safety in it if the doors were locked. Then he saw that the gateman was back. It was the old man, all right. Still reading comics. Sonntag rapped on the window.

"Gate opens at six-thirty," the man yelled.

"It's the police."

The gateman looked him over, and smiled. "I'm Superman," he said.

"Could you phone for help?"

"Beat it," he said.

"I need help. Right now."

"Sleep it off, buddy."

"I've been beaten. I'm a cop. I need help. Get the West Allis police here."

The gateman yawned and returned to his comics.

Sonntag shook the gate, shook it until the hot pain in his side stopped him.

It was a hell of a night. He was hurting. He didn't think he could walk back to the offices and get help. He limped to the old Hudson, climbed in, and waited. At least he didn't hurt so much sitting in there. But it would be a long time before daylight.

Chapter Three

He must have dozed. Next he knew, a West Allis sergeant was rapping on the window with his night stick. The day was quickening.

Sonntag rolled down the window.

"Now what have we here, some joker sleeping off a drunk, with four flat tires, on company property," the cop said.

"I'm Lieutenant Sonntag, Milwaukee PD."

"Sure you are, fella, in an old Hudson, four flats, and trespassing."

"Sergeant, I was sent here to look at that killing last night. My dispatcher sent me, after one in the morning. I live on the west side."

"Sure you do, and you came in your own jalopy. You got a badge?"

"I was jumped and it was stolen."

"Sure you were, fella. You got a drivers license?"

Sonntag pulled out his wallet and gave the cop the license. "Now will you get ahold of my department? I'm stuck here."

"Oh, friend, West Allis isn't a place to be stuck in. You stay right there. I'm keeping this license. I got other stuff to do and I'll deal with you later."

"Look, call my superior, Captain Ackerman, downtown station."

"Sure, and do you know it's illegal to impersonate a cop?"

"I'm not; I'm on duty."

"And that's a black-and-white you're sitting in, right?"

"Have you got any Milwaukee cops here?"

"Oh, a few."

"Send one over."

"My boy, you just sit right there. I got other business here."

Sonntag opened the door, started to get out, only to have the sergeant's night stick jam into his chest and shove him back in.

Sonntag raged. He needed a trip to a bathroom. He needed a lot of things.

The tractor gate was boiling with union men, swiftly gathering at the start of the shift. They were silent now. None of the shouting and chanting and placard-waving that had marked previous radio broadcasts. They collected in knots, waiting for the scabs, the strikebreakers keeping the plant operating. There were a lot of leather jackets, bomber jackets from the war, and some sport coats. They were oddly well dressed, as if this was a sacred ritual not to be profaned by grubby clothing. There was a palpable tension there, men waiting, waiting, quietly, a mob with its claws showing.

The cops, both Milwaukee and West Allis, casually formed a double line. But not very far apart. Not so far that a Machinists Union man could not slip a few punches or kicks to the scabs when they came.

Sonntag realized that this was how it went at the start of every shift, and at the end of the day shift. There was a foreboding, even though the cops seemed uncommonly cheerful. They'd get to knock a few heads together, maybe haul a few off to the paddy wagon. It was an entertainment. The strikers arrived steadily, more and more, until they were five or six deep, forming a long gauntlet that the temporary workers had to run. They were enjoying the summer dawn, old friends waiting for some action. A few had sticks. Others were carrying brown paper bags of something, probably excrement.

Sonntag spotted Matt Dugan, top reporter for the *Milwaukee Journal*, steno pad in hand.

"Hey, Matt!" he yelled.

The reporter, surprised, walked over.

"Matt, get me out of here."

"Four flat tires, eh? Tell me."

"My dispatcher sent me last night to look at that killing. I got jumped. I'm being held here."

Dugan was grinning.

But then the scabs showed up. They did their own organizing, just beyond the gauntlet they would run. They had their lunch pails in hand, but nothing else. Their safety would depend on speed, and they knew it. They also knew they'd get no help from the cops.

"Look at that, Sonntag. It's war," Dugan said.

The temporaries made a run for it, straight into the throat of the picketers, and even as they barged in, they took hits; rocks, sticks, fists on the shoulders, and threats.

"You're gonna die, scab," yelled one.

"You're dead meat," yelled another.

A punch flattened a scab. He crawled away even as strikers' boots caught him. A cop waded in, drove the strikers back with his night stick. The scab staggered to his feet and limped toward the gate, reeling from several more punches.

The cops sure weren't trying very hard to let the scabs through.

The brooding morning exploded into life, as two or three hundred temporary employees ducked blows, dodged, lifted up the fallen, and finally made it through the gate and into the tractor works. There was a low howl rising from the strikers, something animal and dark. But the scabs were in, and heading for their work stations.

The strikers spotted a press photographer with a big Speed Graflex, and started waving their signs and picketing.

"Hey, lieutenant, this is a good story. I'll see what I can do," Dugan said.

Sonntag watched Dugan head for the sergeant, grinning away. It didn't take long. The sergeant returned. "You looked like a drunk," he said.

"Where's a can?"

"You can wet a flat tire," he said.

Sonntag decided not to. He got out, hurting plenty.

"I'll take you downtown," Dugan said.

"I have to report."

"This is the best story I've had in weeks. I told him he'd collared one of the top cops in the force and I was going to write a big fat story. Boy, did he back off."

"Thanks for springing me. I'll find a black and white around here."

"These are Southside cops. They ain't gonna believe you. Especially if you've lost your badge."

"Okay, take me downtown," Sonntag said. He was exhausted, hurting, and needed to find a men's room fast. He was also unshaven, grubby, his clothing stained, and he felt some caked blood on his neck.

Dugan didn't tarry. Sonntag gave him the whole story, from the dispatcher's call to the visit to the supervisor to getting jumped and beaten.

"And no one cares about the scabs," Dugan said. "A man's killed and it's a shrug of the shoulders."

"That's your story, Matt. But there's one exception. Me."

"Yeah, and you'll give it your best. Even if the dead was a piece of work. That's what I like about you, Sonntag."

Dugan dropped off Sonntag downtown, and Sonntag steered immediately toward the men's room, only to discover Captain Ackerman in there.

"Where the hell have you been?" Ackerman asked, buttoning up.

"Held by the West Allis cops."

"Do you know we've a missing person bulletin out on you? Your car, blood on the seat, tires slashed."

"It's a long story," Sonntag as he relieved himself.

The captain stared at him. "You're going to the emergency room," he said. "I'll call Lizbeth. She's worried sick."

Once Sonntag was out of there, a black and white was waiting to take him away. He clambered into the rear of the cruiser and got driven out to Deaconess.

By the time he was processed and they were patching up his cuts and checking him out, he had an audience of three: Captain

Ackerman, and Sonntag's two best investigators, young Frank Silva, and silver-haired Eddy Walsh.

It was a complex story, and Sonntag wasn't telling it well, and they kept asking him to back up and retell it, even while a doc and a nurse gave him a tetanus shot and some sulfa.

"You've got two cracked ribs," the doctor said. "We'll just tape them up."

"Feels like I have a dozen cracked ribs."

"Don't try hugging your wife," the doctor said.

"You don't know his wife," Ackerman said. "She'll crack the rest."

"They knocked you down and went for the brass you found?" Walsh asked.

"Yeah, in my shirt pocket."

"They must have been watching you. Maybe they were looking for it themselves.

"Forty-five," Sonntag said. "Like in a military automatic."

"We haven't got the report from the morgue yet. So we don't know what hit the scab."

"Not much left of his face," Sonntag said.

"You see these people that jumped you?"

"Dark, a long way from the gate lights. No."

"What's this guy's name again?" Silva asked.

"Joseph L. Ginger. They keep sketchy records on temporaries. They told me to come back when the personnel office opens at eight."

"I'll do it. I'd like to see where all those scabs come from, and send them back there," Silva said. "Maybe in a coffin, like Ginger."

Sonntag said nothing. Silva was the lefty on the force. His father had been a socialist alderman. Silva was an activist before he joined up. Scabs were near the bottom of his totem pole. Scabs and the southern subversive hunters in the House of Representatives.

"We'll do for Ginger what we do for everyone else," Ackerman said. "He's been killed and we're going to find the killer."

Silva went silent.

"I'll try for new tires," Ackerman said. "They don't like it, using a personal vehicle on duty. They'll do one of two things: put a set of used tires on, or get you the cheapest new ones they can find. You ain't going to get a set of whitewall Firestones, that's for sure. That's the accounting office for you."

"My tires were almost new."

"That almost isn't going to help you much." Ackerman patted Sonntag's shoulder. "I'll make it good."

He would, too, Sonntag thought. Ackerman had his ways. And sometimes, like now, he wasn't even smoking one of his dogturd-colored five cent cigars.

A uniformed officer he knew, Mark Johnson, drove him out to his place on 57thth St. Lizbeth was waiting, her face pinched. They helped him inside.

"Anything more I can do, lieutenant?"

"Shut down the pain machine," Sonntag said. He was hurting a lot more now, in the middle of the morning, than he had been after the beating.

Johnson looked worried. "We're all with you, lieutenant."

"I'm glad of it, Mister Johnson."

The driver left, and he and Lizbeth stared at each other. There was always that thing about being a cop. It was always there, every day of their lives together. She was not crying. He was not trying to make light of it.

Lizbeth helped him out of his stained clothing and got him into bed.

"You want something to eat?"

He hadn't had a bite since last evening, but he didn't feel like one now, so he shook his head.

"You want to sleep, then?"

"Just rest. I need some rest."

She was being tugged by two things; a concern for him, and her hunger for the story. She lived for his stories. All through their long marriage, she had wanted to know everything, and sometimes that had helped him. Sometimes just talking with her had brought new angles to mind. And sometimes she had come up with some insight that proved to be the key to unlocking one of his cases.

"No one likes strikebreakers," he said. "Someone in the machinists union killed one, and he's ready to kill more."

"What do you know about the scab?"

"He's barely a name right now. I couldn't even get his employment file last night. In fact, they don't keep files. Ledgers. Strikebreakers are names on their ledger. We haven't even found any relatives yet."

"You were in there?"

"They have a night supervisor; he's the man in charge. When I found him, he looked like he was about to pull a weapon out of a desk drawer."

"It's been a very bad strike."

"But this was the first killing."

"What was the man's name?"

"Joseph Ginger."

"Is that southern?"

"Who knows? They crawl out of the woodwork, it seems. The supervisor, Hannigan, gave me a run-down. They hire on, live in rooming houses or share some dump like an auto court, keep to themselves, risk running through the picket line twice a day. For what?"

" Hate the unions, or something."

"No one cares. "

"But you care."

"About Ginger? No. But he had a right to life. I care about that. He was killed."

"I wonder who'll grieve," she said.

And that was the last thing he remembered that worn-out morning.

Chapter Four

The next dawn Sonntag dragged himself out of bed.

"I knew you would," Lizbeth said.

He was decorated with purple and red bruises, and ribs that made it hard to get a breath, and some lumps here and there.

He struggled into some clean clothing; Lizbeth had condemned the wrecked pants and shirt to gardening. She had a whole drawer of his ruined clothing that she had relegated to gardening, even though he didn't garden. It was there if he ever decided to garden.

She eyed him as he fumbled into the kitchen. "I don't know why you're going in," she said. She didn't wait for a response, but poured his coffee and then stuffed his sandwich in his black lunch bucket, along with two Oreos and an apple.

"I don't either," he said. He hurt. He could have nursed his aching body instead of playing the iron man.

"What are you going to do today?" he asked.

"Worry about you."

He didn't like that. She was probably right; he should have stayed in bed. She would have enjoyed that. She'd prefer to worry about him in bed than worry about him at the station house.

He picked up his bucket and hobbled to her, and she accepted a kiss, and then he was out the door. She had her mending club, six or eight friends with sewing baskets and darning eggs and a lot of gossip. There'd be plenty of gossip this time, all about him.

He waited patiently for the Wells Street car, the Number Ten line, that would take him downtown, almost to the station. The orange car ground to a halt, the folding door cranked open, he handed his monthly pass to the motorman, who punched it, and he headed down the isle to one of the wicker seats near the rear. He always sat as far back as he could, so he might live a second or two longer when the car fell off the Menomonee River Viaduct, a two-thousand-foot trestle that spanned the river valley, and carried the car over an industrial sprawl, and a Miller Brewery warehouse.

That twice-a-day ordeal was reason enough to move some day to some other part of the city where you didn't have to sit in a street car and see no earth, no streets, nothing but a sinister sprawl of buildings a hundred feet below. The cars always slowed to ten miles an hour while crossing; the streetcar company knew. The motormen knew. The city knew. Some day the fragile Viaduct would collapse and take a streetcar or two or three to their doom. He knew he'd be on one of those cars. He'd bet on it.

By the time the earth slid away and the car was riding through space, his palms were moist; by the time the earth leapt upward and the car was on solid ground again, his hands dripped. It was like that twice daily, winter and summer. When he reached safety he was always astonished to be alive. After that, the car traversed the seedy neighborhoods that got poorer and more cramped as Wells Street penetrated into the heart of Milwaukee. He got off, winced his way to the station, climbed the grimy steps, and reported for duty. He wasn't a uniformed cop. Detectives got to wear suits. He got his off the pipe racks of Irv the Workingman's Friend, on the south side. That's where most of the detectives got theirs. Irv made a deal for cops.

"Go back to bed," Captain Ackerman said.

Sonntag ignored him. He found a new badge on his desk, encased in a leather wallet, and slid it into his breast pocket.

"What are you trying to prove?" Ackerman said, firing up one of his dogturd colored five-cent stogies. That was Ackerman, for you. The captain should be giving Sonntag a medal.

"Who's doing what?" Sonntag asked.

"Eddy Walsh is talking to the Machinists. Frank Silva's trying to find Ginger's kinfolk."

"Where's my car?"

"It's getting tires. The city okayed four used Firestones; they said yours were worn. But you get four new inner tubes out of it."

"I'm thrilled and grateful and forever indebted."

"They rebuked the department. They said you shouldn't have been sent out in your own car. It costs the city money. Next time, come to the station and pick up a patrol car."

Sonntag laughed, but laughing made his ribs hurt.

"The Machinists aren't talking, Joe. No one saw anything, it wasn't one of theirs, and maybe some scab shot some other scab and tried to blame the strikers for it. Not even smiley Eddy Walsh can open them up."

"And Ginger?"

"Local address. He's from here. He lived in a rooming house on Mitchell. No phone. Frank Silva's over there, getting permission to go in."

"What do we know from the autopsy?"

"One shot from a forty-five. No other wound. The bullet shattered; no ballistics."

"Have we talked to any of the men coming off-shift with Ginger?"

"No one is saying anything. No one saw it."

"So we don't know whether this was a random hit, or someone was going after Ginger."

Ackerman licked his gummy cigar. "We don't know nothing."

So not much had happened during Sonntag's day in bed. "Are the West Allis cops doing anything?"

"Not if they can help it. Sonntag, here's how it is out there. Two brothers go to work building tractors, and the third brother becomes a cop. Or one brother builds turbines and the other brother runs the union."

"In other words, they'll barely go through the motions."

"You got it, Sonntag. At least your brain isn't as busted as the rest of you."

Ackerman wandered off. He never gave anyone under him a chance to zing one back.

Sonntag opened the wallet with a new badge. It shown back at him. It was only the second one he'd had since joining the force before the war. He stuffed it into his breast pocket.

He had a hunch this case would gradually grow cold. Not unless Ginger turned out to be some millionaire or he was related to the governor.

He wondered which way to go. He could work on Ginger. Who was he, and why was he shot? And was it just a random killing? There were reasons for things. A reason someone aimed a service automatic at Ginger and shot him. Six or seven men had come out of the dark just after Sonntag had put the brass casing in his pocket. Beaten him badly and took the evidence. That suggested a cabal; a bunch of the strikers had been in on it; a bunch were cleaning up all evidence. He needed to find that bunch. Or wait for a break.

He chose to pursue Ginger. Who was he? Maybe that would tell him more about his killers.

Silva was late, which was not like him. But when he showed up he had an explanation. A trolley wire had fallen, shutting down all the streetcars in the line up from Cudahy.

"I didn't expect you to come in," he said.

"I have a bad case of curiosity," Sonntag said. "It keeps getting me into trouble."

"I got permission to get into Ginger's rooms. That's where I'm headed, unless you've got something else for me."

"I'm coming with you."

"Landlord's a wounded vet. He'll let us in when we get there. He has the upper flat." Silva paused. "I think I'm going to carry."

Sonntag didn't know why, but always respected Silva's intuitions.

They ended up with a broken down cruiser that threatened to quit on them. Ginger lived deep in the south side, where English was the second language, and in some areas you were likely not to hear it at all.

Silva parked in front of a brick house, not much better than a tenement, but on a generous lot thick with birch trees that hid the old building from the street.

"This got split into two flats. There's a vestibule."

Silva opened the door. Within was a stair and a door.

"Landlord lives up there. I'll get the key," he said. "Don't climb any more stairs than you need to."

Sonntag waited in the vestibule. He discovered a mail slot in the door of the flat, and hoped there would be some letters inside. Letters might help out.

Silva returned with the landlord, a balding man in a tee shirt.

"This is Anders Gropius," Silva said. "He'll let us in."

"This your place, sir?"

"I cut it up for income. I'm a disabled vet."

Sonntag could see nothing disabled about him, but that was common enough. There were wounds the world never would see.

Gropius unlocked, and pushed the door open. A couple of letters lay on the floor. The air of the flat had a closeness about it that offended nostrils.

They entered, finding a sparsely furnished parlor, kitchenette, and bedroom. The furniture was modern junk: chrome and plastic dining set, ancient horsehide couch, an old Tiffany-style lamp.

"Mr. Gropius, have you known rented to Joseph Ginger for long?"

"That's not his name. He goes by it, but he's from some place like The Soviet Union or Ukraine or Latvia."

"Why isn't that his name? What is his name?"

"I don't know. He came here after the war. Just another refugee. But it sure's not Ginger. That's just what he goes by."

"Did he have relatives?"

"A loner. No one around here."

"We've a tough request, sir. Could we drive you to the morgue to identify him? It won't be easy."

"He's dead, right? Am I gonna have nightmares?"

Sonntag hesitated. "He was shot in the face."

"No ID or anything?"

"Not enough."

"I guess I'm stuck with it, right?"

"It would be helpful, sir. Do you know what Ginger did?"

"He couldn't speak much English, so that slowed him down. He could read it okay; just not talk it."

"But he got jobs?"

"He once told me he was a mechanic in the Red Army. He knows machines."

"So Ginger would have been useful at the tractor plant?"

"They'll hire anyone to bust up a strike, right?"

"You mind of we look at things around here? Like those letters?"

"He's dead, right?"

Sonntag took that for a yes. Silva scooped up the two unopened letters lying below the mail slot. One had foreign stamps; the other was postmarked Milwaukee.

"There's no return address on this foreign one," Silva said. "It's got some Cyrillic text on the cancel, but I can't make out the place. Red army, Soviet maybe?"

"He hated Communists," Gropius said. "He couldn't say much but he said plenty about that. He plain hated Stalin and the whole lot."

"Molotov?"

"That whole batch. I always thought they ruined him and he somehow escaped from there. I'd run too, right?"

"We need to find his next of kin," Sonntag said. "Anyone visit him here?"

"I never saw such a loner."

"Alone or unable to connect with relatives over there?"

"Like, most loose males around here go to the taverns. There's a friendly one, Brodsky's, right on the corner, but he never went there. Like he didn't want to talk to anyone in there."

"Did you ever try to get his real name? His history?"

"Well, it sure wasn't Ginger. Once he got over here, he put all that behind him."

"Why did he come to Milwaukee?" Sonntag asked.

"Plenty of Russians, plenty of work for a mechanic, maybe a relative, right?"

"You didn't mind renting to someone with a fake name, whose business you didn't know?" Silva asked.

"You ever been in war?" Gropius asked.

Somehow that was answer enough.

"Mind if we look around, sir?" Sonntag said.

"You're cops, right?" Gropius said.

Sonntag took that for a yes. He and Silva began a sweep, under Gropius's alert gaze.

"He have a bank account?" Silva asked.

"Don't think so; he paid rent with cash or postal money order. I pay the heat; he paid the electric."

They went through the man's limited wardrobe, finding nothing of consequence. A drawer revealed three of those letters from abroad. One had a stamp featuring Josef Stalin. In another drawer were receipts from the postal money orders, and a small ledger with expenses and income in it. There might be something in that. There were stacks of magazines. Ginger could read English, even if he didn't speak it well. He had picked up copies of Time Magazine off the racks– they were store copies, with no name or address on them. He had a library card stuck in a drawer. That might help.

"Did he ever say why he called himself Ginger?" Sonntag asked.

"Yeah; Ginger's easy to say; not like the tongue-twister he was born with."

"No relatives over here with names like that?"

"I never saw anyone else in this place, right?"

"We'd like to have these letters translated. They're the closest we've come to a relative. That all right with you?"

"He's dead, right?"

"You got an hour? We'd like you to identify the remains."

"I saw a lot of dead in my day," Gropius said. "I'm ready any time you are."

They drove Gropius to the morgue downtown, waited there while an attendant pulled the body out of its cold vault and rolled back the sheet covering the face.

Then they led Gropius to the cold, hospital-green room, and let him look.

"Who do you see?" Sonntag asked.

"Not sure. It doesn't look like Ginger."

"Try looking from over here. Now who?"

"That's not Ginger. That's someone else."

"Are you sure?"

"No, not very. His face is so bad, it's hard to say."

"But you're not willing to make a positive identification?"

Gropius sighed. "I don't know who that is," he said.

Chapter Five

The identity of the strikebreaker was less and less certain, and Sonntag wondered whether this would end up in his cold cases file. But there were the letters. Three of them from the Soviet Union, and a postcard with the image of Lenin on one side, and a bare sentence or two in Cyrillic text on the other.

"Where to? Marquette?" Frank Silva asked.

"Good as any," Sonntag said. "Beats trying to find out in Madison."

The University of Wisconsin would have an expert in Slavic languages who could translate; Marquette might not. The Jesuit-run university was only a few blocks distant, and Sonntag checked out an ancient unmarked Ford, and drove over there. Detectives routinely got the lousiest vehicles on the lot. This one had stains in the seat fabric that looked a lot like some heavy bleeding had stained the upholstery.

It took a while to get steered to the right rooms, a warren of messy academic cubicles in an ancient annex but eventually they did connect with a Russian émigré professor who taught French, Ilich Borovich by name. The thin old man greeted them warily.

"Professor, we've got a dead man we can't identify for sure, and we've got a few letters from the Soviet Union here, and we're hoping you can help us. The man was using the name Joseph L. Ginger, and that's about all we know. Could you read these?"

"Ginger, eh? There must be some meaning in it, eh? I am White Russian, lived in Paris since the revolution, finally got over here where I am a little more employed.. Now, dear sirs, what is this thing about, eh?"

"Just trying to identify a man, sir."

"You devote the resources of the police to that?"

Silva glanced at Sonntag, who nodded.

"He was shot. We need to know who and why. These letters might help. Are you game?"

"Shot, was he? And the letters are from the Soviet?"

"We think so. That's for you to tell us."

"Ah, this is the Communists at work again. They kill people anywhere in the world, anytime they choose, by means of assassins and poisoners and knifers. An ice pick does very nicely, you know. No blood. It's a favorite of the NKVD."

"Soviet security?" Silva asked.

"The web stretches everywhere, sir. Where and how was he shot, eh?"

Sonntag intervened. "Before we talk about that, maybe you can tell us about these," he said. He handed the frayed letters and the card to Borovich.

"Why should I tell you?" Borovich asked.

"We have an unidentified dead man; knowing something about him might lead us to the killers."

That seemed reason enough to the professor, who donned thick, horn-rimmed glasses and perused the envelopes first.

"Moscow. Forty-six, and these two in forty-seven. The last, this postcard, forty-eight. No returns, and that tells you something, eh? Letters that can't be traced back. Someone who doesn't want to be known to the secret police."

He studied each letter closely. There wasn't much to study; no more than half a dozen sentences in each.

"It is as I say; letters that reveal nothing but have a little meaning only to the correspondents. See? No names. Signed with words like Beloved. Your own. Your loving wife. As for the contents, sirs, they won't tell you much. I went to Nevsky Park. There were no apples. A late frost destroyed the blossoms."

He smiled. "There is no meaning here for anyone other than the writer and the recipient."

"Like, code?"

"Oh, more like references. Each sentence refers to something in the memory or experience of the other. That's the only privacy they have. The Soviet postal authorities routinely open and read all foreign mail."

"Would you translate these anyway, sir? And give us a literal translation of everything? And add to that your instincts about what it might mean?"

"I will do that, officers. Yes, it will be a good thing to do."

"Tomorrow? Can you have it tomorrow?"

"Later today if you wish. I wish to be a part of your investigation. I will bring things to it that you know nothing about."

"Such as?" Sonntag asked.

"This man Ginger was assassinated."

"Why do you say that?"

"A Russian. A man who escapes from the Soviet. A bullet for him, yes?"

"You seem to know something we don't know, sir."

"Absolutely. There is a bullet for any Russian the secret police want to shoot. There are agents of Stalin, agents buried underground, agents who will kill the enemies of the revolution one by one, but all of them. Let me ask you this. Was he the man killed in the Allis-Chalmers strike?"

"Yes."

"There, you see? That is a Red union. There are Communists running it. It doesn't matter that the membership isn't Red; it only matters that these men, and this union, are a part of Josef Stalin's underground network."

Silva didn't like that. "Hey, that's bull," he said.

Borovich stared. "Is it? If you poke around in the Machinists Union, it is quite likely you both will die."

"Is that a threat or a prediction, sir?"

"I will have a mass in my Orthodox church said for the repose of your souls, sirs."

"You mind telling me what's what?"

"We investigate a killing of a man who might or might not be Russian. And the Reds are going to kill us?" Sonntag said.

"Was this Ginger shot in the face?"

"What's that got to do with it?"

"It is a favorite technique. Shoot them between the eyes with a hollow core bullet. They like that. There's often no face left. Who can even say who died?"

"How do you know that, sir?"

"You are very innocent, you two Milwaukee police."

"So how do we become less innocent, professor?"

"Consult with me about everything! Everything."

"We can't do that. We can't share our investigation with anyone outside the force," Sonntag said.

"Where shall I send funeral wreaths, then, my good officers of the law?"

"I tell you what. Do you know a Russian when you see one? Like the man we're trying to identify? You want to come to the morgue with us?" Silva asked.

"Let me get my hat," Borovich said.

They loaded the man into the black Nash cruiser and drove over to the anonymous morgue. Sonntag thought this was crazy, but Silva was smiling. Maybe that was the game, Sonntag thought. Let the old Russian spin his conspiracy theories. They were calling it the cold war, threats and conspiracies, spying and state secrets, huge defense budgets. But in this old Russian, it seemed more like paranoia. Enemies everywhere.

It took only a few minutes for the attendant to prepare the deceased. The naked body was covered with a sheet, but now sheet had been pulled back from the ruined face. The brain had been opened from the rear to remove bullet fragments. It was all ghastly, and not easy even for Joe Sonntag to stomach.

They led the professor in, and let him examine that face.

"I thought so. A missing student of mine," the professor said.

That sure was news.

"Dimitri Karl. That's his name. He never would say how he got to this country; what he did in the war. What he was doing now. Now here's the mystery. He was learning Russian from me."

"This man isn't Joseph Ginger; he gets letters written in Russian but is taking your Russian language course?"

"Things are never what they seem," the professor said.

"How do you know that's him? His face—it's ruined."

"It's him. He was a spy for someone. Strikebreaker? He was spying."

All of this was getting far ahead of Sonntag's orderly mind, but he thought just to let Silva keep evoking the professor's comments.

"He was the master spy. I should have known. He runs a major spying operation in the United States."

"Ah, how do you know that, sir?"

"It will be in his letters when I can decode them."

"Say," Silva asked, "did he talk about Russia much?"

"The Dodgers, sir. He was a great fan of the Brooklyn Dodgers."

"He talked about that?"

"That was to prove he was an American. That's how they trip up spies. Ask someone what they think of Stan Musial and just wait and see. If they're American, you'll get a good answer."

"So what do you think of Stan Musial?"

"I am not an American, and not a Soviet spy, and my émigré status is plain to see on my papers. I wouldn't know Stan Musial from Joe DiMaggio."

The swart morgue attendant was getting itchy, so Sonntag hastened thing along. "So, again, you identify this man as Dimitri Karl, a student of yours? Are there records? Does Marquette have a photo of him? Most college applications require a photo."

"We'll find out," the professor said.

Sonntag wasn't happy with any of it, but he nodded to the attendant, who covered the remains and wheeled them back to the vault.

In the morgue office, Sonntag filled out an identity form, saying that the witness had viewed the body, the time and date, and identified the body as Dimitri Karl. The witness was unable to provide information about next of kin.

"If this is suitable, professor, would you sign it and include your home and business addresses?"

Silva had a cryptic smile on his face, one that took practice to discern.

"We're going to be talking to you some more, sir. About what the deceased said, and whatever you can remember about him. Where he was from. Why he was here. Write that down and we'll talk to you again, okay?"

"I love that American word, okay. It's a universal word. It can mean anything. You even made a question of it. There's nothing in Russia like it."

They dropped the Russian at the cramped annex. No sooner was the man out of the car than Silva exploded.

"He's a loon. All those Russians. They're paranoid. They live through long dark winters and it makes them nuts."

Sonntag wasn't so sure. "I'm getting a little suspicious myself. Of everyone we've talked to. How come the landlord, who sees Ginger constantly, couldn't identify him? How come this Russian identifies the man instantly and gives him a name? But can't explain why the man's in a Russian language class?"

"Maybe the class is a cover for a master spy running a whole string; maybe they're all spies. Maybe it's a Communist cell." Suddenly Frank was laughing. "Maybe we're all nuts."

"Or none of the above. You game to rattle the cage over at the Machinists Union?"

"You're going to pick on them, are you?"

"Someone in their crowd late at night shot a strikebreaker."

"Who deserved it, probably."

Frank Silva took sides, and took them harshly sometimes.

"We still got to get it nailed down," Sonntag said.

He steered the old black Nash, which had a violent rattle in one of the wheel wells, from hitting too many Milwaukee potholes. Maybe some day the department would have enough cash to buy a modern fleet.

"Drive past the plant. I want a look-see," Silva said.

So Sonntag headed out Greenfield Avenue, a drab stretch of proletarian life The scene at the gate was fairly quiet for a change. Maybe a hundred strikers in the picket line, snaking back and forth, sometimes crossing into the entryway until the cops drove them back. Things would heat up in a couple of hours at shift time, when the scabs poured out, and when another bunch of scabs poured in.

"Fair wages," one sign said. "Fair pension," said another. Fair hours, fair overtime, fair bargaining rights, union shop. There were six or seven issues on the table this time. The Machinists wanted a big raise, more than equal to the runaway inflation of the postwar years. They wanted job security, a night shift wage differential, a serious pension, earlier retirement, workmen's compensation for injuries, and a seat on the Allis-Chalmers board of directors.

"I hope they get it all," Silva said.

Sonntag parked in front of the storefront union headquarters, which was plastered with signs.

There were about twenty tough-looking machinists in there.

"Lieutenant Sonntag here, Milwaukee police department," Sonntag said. "We'd like to talk to some of the union officers."

"Get your ass out of here, and stay out," one said.

"This is Detective Silva," Sonntag said. "We're here to talk to some of you people about that shooting."

"You heard me, cop," the man said.

"Let's start with you," Sonntag said. "Come on out to the car, and we'll discuss a few things."

For an answer, every machinist in the place bulled in, grabbed Silva and Sonntag by whatever handle they could get a hold of, and propelled them both out the door. One final shove sent them reeling. Silva stumbled and fell, scrambled aside just as a big boot parted his hair. Sonntag's busted ribs were howling.

They got back into the car while machinists swarmed around it and started kicking it.

There was no radio in that ancient Nash.

"We're going to need help," Sonntag said. He started the car, but the machinists blocked it, all the while kicking the fenders and side panels. Then, suddenly, they parted, like the Red Sea, and Sonntag drove through, to the sound of laughter.

Chapter Six

Silva had an odd smile pasted on his face.

"Well?" he asked.

Sonntag steered the old black Nash a few blocks away, and then pulled over and stopped. He knew what Silva was thinking. Disorder had to be met with force. The immediate, proper response was to restore public safety by whatever force was necessary. Not to do so was to tolerate anarchy. Governors had been known to call in the national guard to quell rioting strikers, often with bloody results. The theory was that if you don't immediately respond in force, you invite worse trouble next time. Sonntag's task was to get to a phone and call in the troops.

"We're in West Allis," he said.

"I was thinking the same thing."

"We'd have to call in the West Allis cops. They're the ones with the badges here."

"Yeah, and the Machinists know that."

It was a hard choice to make. His whole instinct was to get to a phone and call in the flying squads. Milwaukee had plenty of tough cops. But the West Allis chief would have to okay it. Red ink. Politics.

"You got any ideas?" Sonntag asked.

"Report it to the West Allis people and let them decide. It's their turf."

That suited Sonntag just fine. Minutes later they were talking with Chief Martin Gruber, of the twelve-man West Allis force.

"So it's your turf, your baby," Sonntag said.

"Lieutenant, thanks for letting us know," the chief said. "We're going to go over there and have a little talk."

The chief drove them over to the union hall in his shiny new black and white, and led them straight into the storefront headquarters. Somehow, it was very different this time. They knew a police chief when they saw one.

"These men are investigating a shooting. You'll cooperate. You'll help them every way you can. Hear me?"

No one was laughing this time.

"This is Milwaukee Investigations Lieutenant Joseph Sonntag, and Detective Frank Silva, and you will answer their questions truthfully, or face the consequences."

They didn't like that, but they were listening at least.

"The killing of a man, any man, is a crime against us all," the chief said.

"Nah, it's stamping out a bug," said one of them.

Chief Gruber stared. "I do not forget a face," he said. "These men will be back to talk to you. Do it or face the National Guard."

The machinists stared back, but the defiance was out of them. Sonntag admired the chief, and his dozen-man force.

"Come along, men," he said. Silva and Sonntag followed him out, amid a tense silence.

"Will that hold when we get back?" Silva asked.

"I guess you'll have to find out yourself," Gruber said.

At the West Allis station, Sonntag reclaimed the Nash and they drove back to the storefront union hall. Or strike headquarters. This time, there were only three men in it; the rest had conveniently vanished. Sonntag peered around at chaos. There were stacks of ruined posters and picket signs, debris from coffeemaking, a pile of stray shirts and caps and even some overalls. The strikers were out in all sorts of weather, and kept dry clothing around just in case. There was only one desk; mostly the place was full of folding chairs.

The place could be vacated overnight. It'd blow away the hour the strike was over, he thought.

The machinists eyed the cops silently. One was a gaunt gray man in wire-rimmed glasses. He wore a brown suit and a tie. The others were in their shirt sleeves and looked like they were fresh out of high school.

"Frank Silva here. I'm a Milwaukee cop. And this is Lieutenant Sonntag," Frank said. "You mind if we ask a few questions?"

"If you're wondering who shot the scab, you're wasting your time. No one knows, and no one cares," the gray one said.

"You are, sir?"

"You can call me the secretary, Machinists local."

"And your name, sir?"

"Stanley. Stanley Argo."

"You run the show?"

"The brothers run the show."

"But you're in charge, right?"

"Wrong."

"And who are these gents?"

One of them, the one with too much Wildroot soaking his hair, volunteered. "Call me Max. Call me the security man. That's Arnold. He's the other security man. We protect the brothers."

"How do you do that, sir?"

"By however we feel like."

"Who threatens the brothers?"

"Mostly little old ladies with blue hair."

Silva laughed. Sonntag smiled.

"I sort of sympathize with you gents," Silva said. "My old man was a socialist alderman from the south side. I joined the Socialist Workers Party and handed out tracts and got beat up by cops. So, we share a thing or two."

"A pinko," said Argo. "Pinkos are pastel Reds. Sort of pale imitations."

"Yeah, I guess so. I always wanted to do it peacefully. Not much of a revolutionary, I guess."

"Yeah, I want to do it with the ballot box, you know?" Silva said.

Sonntag was wondering where all this was heading, but at least Silva had gotten a foot in the door, which was more than what Sonntag expected.

"Ballot box! Cop, you don't know how the world is. The moneymen own the ballot box," Argo said.

"That's the weakness of it," Silva said. "Me, I'd go for the one big strike, like the Wobblies were pushing."

"And get shot up by the nearest army," Argo said. "Now, Pinko, are you done here?"

"Well, I just want to talk politics a little."

"Politics is what comes out of the barrel of a gun," Argo said.

"Sounds like a Stalinist talking."

"Cop, I don't carry the card, get it? I'm not in the party. I'm a union man, and we're going to bring this company to its knees, get it?"

"How you gonna do that, Argo? They've got scabs working. They're making tractors. You're out on the streets, using up strike funds."

Argo smiled. "For the moment. Maybe the scabs won't want to work around here any more."

"Why not? They make good money. They've got a good job. They've got cops protecting them when they come and go. You guys starve, and they pocket the dough."

"They haven't seen any heat yet, cop. They don't even know what heat is."

"So what's heat, Argo? What's legal?"

"Wait and see, cop."

Silva sighed. "Yeah, you're right, Mr. Argo. Maybe you'll win this strike and get your people back to work. They'd like that."

"Sure they'd like it, but it's not going to happen for a while."

Silva turned to the two toughs lounging in the storefront. "Max and Arnold, is it? Big, tough machinists need protection, do they? I'd think they could take care of themselves."

Neither responded.

"I'm just curious what you do, fellas. Hang around here? For what?"

"They protect me," Argo said. "I'm here alone sometimes.

We keep strike cash here. A brother has to come here, picket, to get his strike benefits."

"Yeah, but these guys– you in the protection business, fellas?"

They smiled. It was apparent to Sonntag that these two had been ordered to keep their traps shut.

"Who'd steal from the union? I don't get it," Silva said.

"Scabs," Argo said.

"Nah, scabs wouldn't come a country mile from here. Must be someone else you're worried about."

"You guys done with us? I'd like to get back to my job."

"Yeah, we're done. That scab that got shot; we finally got some ID on him. He's maybe from the Soviet Union, if we got it right. Isn't that something?"

"How'd you find that out?" Argo asked.

"A couple people knew him. He was quite the man."

"What do they say about him?" Argo asked.

Sonntag marveled. The union boss had gone from dismissing the Milwaukee cops to looking for information in a single moment.

"It's unraveling fast," Silva said. "We'll know why he was here and what he was doing here pretty quick now."

"Looks like he was snooping around," Sonntag said.

Argo stared.

"They shot the wrong guy," Silva said. "Boy, is it gonna blow the lid off."

"Yeah, maybe you lost the best friend your union ever had," Sonntag said.

"Now they'll have to start over," Silva said.

"Those trigger-happy guys didn't know what they were doing. Whoever's got that brass casing, he's gonna have Captain Marvel on his case. That brass, it's the key to the whole thing."

The two thugs were staring.

But no one was talking.

"Let's get out of here," Sonntag said.

"Yeah, we'll get the report on the dead man." Frank turned to Argo. "That wasn't his name, you know. He had other names. Those guys really screwed up. Shooting that scab was the dumbest thing they ever did."

"Sin in haste, repent at leisure," Sonntag said. "Now then, if you gents have second thoughts about any of that, give us a call. Sonntag or Silva, downtown station. You got it?"

No one said a word.

"Oh, yes. Concealing a crime could make someone an accessory. When it's murder, the accessory doesn't get off lightly. Got it?"

It was stinking in there. The whole place smelled of sweat. Sonntag was glad to get outside, suck in some hot summer air laced with car exhausts, and head for the Nash.

Silva got in and seemed uncommonly cheerful.

"I think the union bosses are a little nervous now," he said.

"What do you think Ginger did, or was, and why did they shoot him?" Sonntag asked.

"Damned if I know. It might have been a random shot, just to scare some scabs."

"It might. But I don't think so," Sonntag said. He rolled down the window to let some torpid air cool the interior.

"What'll they do now?" Silva asked.

"Two things. Try to find out what we know. And try to cover their tracks."

"I could do something with that. There's nothing like a killer trying to cover his tracks, go back over everything."

"It wasn't a bad visit, at least the second one. Are you hurting from that roughing up?"

"Only where you can't see it," Silva said.

"We could start writing up the charges, and see whose name we'll write in," Sonntag said.

He drove downtown thinking that he should have called in the whole force. He should have rounded up everyone in that storefront, charged the whole lot, hauled them off, locked them up, and kept the heat on until they coughed up the man who shot Ginger. But it was too late for that.

"Want to stop at Marquette?" Silva asked.

Sonntag grunted, and headed toward the old annex where Borovich lurked in his littered office. The windows in the hallways were open, admitting summer breezes to the stuffy warrens of the language department. The professor's door was open, and he was in his shirtsleeves.

"Too hot for a Russian," he said. "It is an excellent thing that you came. I have plumbed the secret."

"Something secret about these letters?" Sonntag asked.

"Absolutely. Every sentence in them is copied out of a grade school primer for Russian children. I have one, and I've verified it. The words and sentences are meaningless. What matters is the hidden meanings. Maybe there's code arranged from the primer. A code known only to the sender and receiver."

"So Ginger got letters with sentences copied from a Russian school textbook?"

"Exactly, and you can be sure there's a world of spying in it, policemen."

"Okay, let me get this straight, professor," Silva said. "This guy Ginger is in your class, as Dimitri Karl, and he's learning Russian, and he's getting letters with Russian sentences from a schoolbook?"

"Exactly, my dear officers. He was as ignorant of Russian as Harry Truman is. But he was a good student, learning vocabulary daily."

"But he's got a Russian name?"

"American, my friends. He had no accent. Standard Midwestern American."

"So we've got an American named Ginger who's learning Russian from you?"

"No, I teach French."

"I thought he was learning Russian from you."

"Oh, he was having me tutor him privately in Russian. A few extra dollars for me, you know? Twice a week, one hour, right here."

"No, I don't know," Sonntag said.

"It doesn't matter. The man was a Soviet spy, and you should report him to the FBI," Borovich said.

"Maybe we should," Sonntag said. "But not yet."

"Watch out for your lives," Borovich said.

"Why?" Silva asked.

"You are treading where no man should go," the professor said.

Chapter Seven

Sonntag was not happy with the way the investigation was turning. Another day, another bunch of stone walls. He corralled Silva just before the detective escaped into the summer heat.

"Need a favor," he said.

"Sure, I'll buy you a beer," Silva said.

"I need to get us both over to the tractor gate after dark."

"You can by me a beer– for a month."

"We've got to work out this shooting better. If it was a random shot by some machinists trying to scare the scabs, that's one thing. If it was an assassination, that's another thing."

"So?"

"That's dim light. I'm not sure there's enough light even to pick out Ginger from the rest of the scabs. And I'm not sure how he could be shot in the face from the pickets on either side of the gate."

"So I've been recruited. And I take a night owl streetcar or two back home."

"I got a better idea, Frank. Stay with us tonight. They are– junior's in the army. My car's got tires; we'll drive over around ten, full dark, and see what we can. That's between shifts. No one but a cop or two around."

"And I'll stink tomorrow."

"You got stuff in your locker?"

"Yeah, I do."

Cop work was hard on clothing. Most officers kept some spare stuff in their lockers. Sonntag was counting on it.

"You come with me? We'll have a good evening. I'll take us out for chop suey so Lizbeth doesn't have to rustle up a meal."

"You mean I get to hold your hand when we cross the Wells Street viaduct?"

"Cut it out."

Silva loaded up some stuff in a ditty bag, and they caught the Wells car, which ground westward toward the trestle over the Menomonee River valley. Sonntag sweated. This time he would have to show that smartass detective that he was good as gold crossing over that thing. But when the orange car crawled into space, and the world dropped away, Sonntag's hands were white-knuckling the wicker seat in front of him. And Silva was having himself a very good time. Sonntag was ready to punch him if he opened his mouth, and knock his block off if he smart-alecked. But Silva was content with a smirk and that's how it went until the earth rushed up and the car rode on solid earth.

They got off at 56th, and headed for the dead-end on 57th, and Silva kept his mouth zipped tighter than a fly at a convention of Evangelicals. Lizbeth greeted them with a flash of worry, that swiftly dissolved into curiosity, a shy peck on Sonntag's cheek, and a fast appraisal of Frank Silva, all in the same moment.

"It's like this, sweetheart. We've got a little business at the tractor gate after it gets dark, so I've asked Frank over. Stay in one of the boys' rooms."

"Oh," she said, "why, you're just in time for dinner. I've meatloaf just starting to warm, and I'll boil some potatoes." She eyed the kitchen, and the dining table in the alcove, and seemed satisfied with it.

"Nope, put that all away, love. We're going for Chop Suey on North Avenue."

"But Joe, there's enough, and I've got it started..."

"Chinese," Silva said. "It's a night for noodles."

"I should have called, but there wasn't time," Sonntag said, guiltily.

"It's going to be Chinese, Lizbeth. You are going to resolve a mystery that's been hanging over me for years," Silva said, his white pearlies shining between brown lips.

A what?"

"A mystery. This time, I get to look at your fortune cookie. I've a big bet with your husband. I bet that Lizbeth's cookies always have good news."

"Oh, oh, I wouldn't know. It's all silly, you know."

"Will it be good news, Lizbeth? Will I win my bet?"

She smiled suddenly and undid her apron.

They jammed into the old coupe, with Lizbeth in the middle because she didn't mind if the gearshift lever played games with her knees.

"Good tires," Silva said, upon hearing them go wah-wah-wah-wah.

"Yeah, the city fixed me up," Sonntag said. "Four baldies."

The tires wah-wah-wahed all the way to the Chop Suey palace on 71st and North. Sonntag knew exactly why the tires wah-wahed; they'd been pulled off a car that needed its wheels aligned.

"That's Milwaukee socialism for you," he said.

"That has nothing to do with socialism," Frank said, his voice climbing.

They settled in a booth, and soon were sharing egg rolls, chop suey, wonton soup, and chicken chow mein.

"So what's at the tractor gate?" Lizbeth asked.

"A flood of scabs, moving as fast as they can to stay out of trouble, and a shot that kills one man in the face. A mysterious man. Is it random, or deliberate? Was Ginger, if that was his name, an accidental victim?" Silva asked.

"How can you tell?"

"Light. Was there enough light to do an assassination?"

"Also, the shot in the face. The union picketers were on both sides of the gate, not out in front."

"I got jumped when I found some brass on one side," Sonntag said.

"The answer will be in my fortune cookie," she said.

Silva stared.

"I just know some things," she said.

"So someone in a noodle factory stuffed this fortune into the cookie you're going to open up in a few minutes, and this is going to tell us what happened?"

Lizbeth was enjoying herself. "I'm just a dumb broad, Frank."

"Like hell you are," he said.

"So where's the fortune cookies?"

"We're hardly into the chop suey."

Frank waved at the elderly Chinaman who had served them.

"Fortune cookies now, chop chop," he said.

"Frank, don't offend him."

"Chop chop your head," the waiter said, but nonetheless he laid three fortune cookies on the table.

They waited for Lizbeth to pick one, but she dabbled with her chow mein, ignoring them.

"Hey, there's the solution, sitting right there, Lizbeth," Frank said.

She dabbed her lips and continued to spoon chow mein into her. "I'm not much for chop sticks," she said.

"Frank, why don't you hand out the cookies?" Sonntag said.

The cookies sat there, wrapped in cellophane.

"I'm a slow eater. Don't let me slow you down," she said. "Do want some dessert?"

"Withholding material information from an official investigation could be a criminal offense," Silva said.

"I didn't know that, guys. Tell me how that works," she said.

"You could be the accessory after the fact," Silva said.

She sighed, set down her spoon, and twirled the three fortune cookies, finally selecting one of them and tearing it out of its cellophane. She toyed with it, trying to free the fortune, but it wouldn't release, so she sighed and smiled. Even Joe was glowering.

She broke the cookie and extracted the fortune. "The sideways glance is filled with sorrows," she read.

"That's it!" Silva said. "He turned sideways and took a bullet in the teeth.."

Sonntag grinned. He wasn't going to say one word.

"You've given us the key," Silva said.

"To a wild goose chase," she said.

"It was a random shot. Some union guy was scaring the scabs and fired low."

"Maybe," Sonntag said.

"It doesn't matter who Ginger was. All the conspiracy stuff. Communists killing White Russians, or whatever. That's all crappola."

"Let's go see," Sonntag said.

He waited to see if Silva would pluck up the check, flushed with victory.

"I'll get this. We've got it half solved," Silva said.

Sonntag smiled.

They squeezed Lizbeth between them, too much intimacy in the old coupe, and drove her to the bungalow. It was dark enough now, so they dropped her there and drove out to the plant to see what they could see.

This time, Sonntag parked well away from the gate. He was aware that the last time he poked around in the dark, he got jumped, beaten, and his tires were wrecked. This time he had Silva, but neither of them was armed.

"Frank, I got jumped last time."

"Yeah, I'm thinking the same thing."

But this time it was different. Maybe a hundred machinists were clustered on both sides of the gate, waiting quietly for something. Sonntag spotted two West Allis cops, but nothing else by way of law enforcement. Argo, the union secretary, was standing on the far side, in a trench coat. That seemed odd on a hot damp night.

Sonntag headed straight toward the uniforms.

"Sonntag, Milwaukee PD. Detective Silva here. What's this?"

"We don't know. Something's up."

"This picketers aren't picketing. I don't even see a sign."

"Beats me," said the cop.

"That's the secretary of the union in the trench coat. Why's he in a coat?"

"Concealing something," the cop said.

It was hard to make out faces in that dim light. The union guys weren't talking, just waiting. It was midway between shift changes, which added to the puzzle.

"Anyone in there, coming out you know of?"

"No one tells us anything," the cop said. "But there's supposed to be some buses in there."

"Allis-Chalmers buses?"

"Beats me."

"We're working on that shooting, and we'll be wandering around here."

"The scab? I guess you do what you gotta do."

Sonntag headed for the gate, which was closed. Silva headed to one side and waited in the dim light while Sonntag traced the exit of the scabs. The union guys watched silently.

Sonntag headed over to Silva.

"You see me well enough to identify me?"

"Nah, not even close. You were just some guy walking out from the gate. A lot of moving shadows."

"There would have been a bunch of scabs with him. He was in the middle. You think anyone with a gun could pick him off deliberately?"

"Like the cop says, beats me, Joe. It's too damned dark."

"Okay, I'm gonna walk out again. This time, you get out to the street, straight out from the gate. This time, see if you can see my face straight on, like you were someone waiting out there for me, and me alone."

"Doesn't fit the facts, Joe. You found the brass over there, where the machinists are."

"Do it anyway. And remember, a scope on a rifle gathers light."

Sonntag headed for the gate again. Deep inside, two headlights were slowly boring through the darkness toward the gate. There were other headlights behind. He turned at the gate, worked his way toward Silva, who stood out at the street. Behind him, the headlights were throwing light ahead, silhouetting him in Silva's eyes. This test wasn't going to work.

The union brothers seemed to go even quieter as the vehicle crept toward the gate.

Sonntag saw the headlights crawling slowly toward the gate, and abandoned his testing. Instead he trotted straight toward Stanley Argo, who seemed to be in charge of the machinists.

"Sonntag, Milwaukee police. What's going on here, Argo."

"Stay and watch, copper."

"You are about to give me an answer," Sonntag said.

Argo smiled.

Sonntag saw Silva running up.

"Mr. Argo has decided to join us for the night," he said.

Sonntag grabbed one arm, and Silva the other, and oddly, Argo didn't fight. Neither did the machinists do anything but stare.

They half-dragged, half-wrestled, Argo away from the machinists, and got him over to the West Allis cops. The buses had reached the tractor gate, and the gatekeeper was opening up for them.

"Argo, you're going to let those buses through," Sonntag said. "You say so, loud, right now."

"So take me in," Argo said. "Three buses of scabs, coppers. Three buses. We've got 'em bottled up. They're stuck. I can't tell the brothers no. They won't obey me. Get it? There's nothing I can do."

The buses full of strikebreakers were crawling out of the plant now. The machinists waited, poised for action, until all three had crawled outside of the plant, and the gateman was swinging the gates. Then they rushed the lead bus, a hundred howling brothers, smacking into it with amazing force, tilting the bus under their force, and lifting its wheels up. Another bunch rammed into the bus with their shoulders. Others lifted. With the second push, the bus teetered, hesitated, and then tipped sideways, crashing on its side, while the scabs tumbled like exploding popcorn.

Argo was laughing. "Some strike, eh?" he said.

The machinists were regrouping, ready to knock over the second bus.

The West Allis cops had retreated to their black and whites, and were radioing for help.

Sonntag realized he and Silva weren't on duty, didn't have any way to secure Argo, and the scabs trapped in the overturned bus were screaming. Diesel fuel was running freely on the pavement. He roughly patted down Argo, found a chest-holstered Army officer's automatic, and yanked it.

"Hold the bastard," he told Silva.

He fired high, sending the slug into the brick wall of the plant. That single shot caught their attention, fast.

"Back off," he yelled. "This is the police."

It took a moment, but they did, and many of them slid into the night.

The scabs started crawling out of the windows. The scent of fuel was thick in the darkness. Maybe no one would die.

Chapter Eight

Captain Ackerman was not happy. The forty-five automatic rested on his desk. A dead yellow cigar rested on it also, bitten clear through in a toothy spasm.

"Let me get this straight. You discharged a firearm in the village of West Allis?"

Sonntag nodded.

"And you and Silva were there off-duty?"

Sonntag agreed.

"And this weapon is not yours?"

Sonntag nodded.

"And it belonged to a man who was standing quietly, not agitating, not disturbing the peace?'

"That's debatable."

"And the shot hit the brick wall of Allis Chalmers?"

"That's where I aimed, yes."

"And this was after the Machinists had tipped the bus and were about to land on anyone climbing out? And when they heard the shot they ran?"

"That's it, sir."

"I'm going to have to write all this up, and I hate writing. How do you spell Allis?'

"A-L-I-C-E, sir."

"Smartass."

Actually, the whole episode had ended without fatality, and only a few bad bruises. The bus had teetered on an angle so long that the scabs had slid to the bottom. Given the circumstances, it could hardly have ended better. The West Allis cops took Stanley Argo off, but didn't charge him.

"What are you going to do today, in addition to repent?"

"I'll spend it repenting, sir."

"Where will this heart-rending take place?"

"I'm taking Silva with me to talk to Ginger's landlord. We've a few things to straighten out."

"Such as?"

"The landlord, Gropius, says Ginger was a war refugee, could barely speak English, talked Russian but didn't visit any local taverns where that was the tongue, had been in the Red Army–but Gropius couldn't identify the body. Borovich, the Marquette language professor, said the man's name was Dimitri Karl, identified him as his student, identified the body, said he spoke English but was learning Russian privately, and thinks the man was a Soviet agent. So, it's time to find out why none of this works."

"We should atom bomb Moscow and be done with it," Ackerman said.

"Silva's sending a wire to the Personnel Records Office at the Pentagon. We want whatever they have on Joseph L. Ginger, Dimitri Karl, Illich Borovich, Anders Gropius, and for good measure, Stanley Argo."

"It'll take a while. Three million men in service. A lot of files. A lot of duplicates if you don't have dog tag numbers."

"We don't, but we think it'll give us something."

"Just one other thing, Sonntag. Try the same names on the casualty lists. Killed in action. Maybe we have a living dead man."

There were times when Sonntag admired the captain, and this was one of them.

"We'll do that."

"Not very many men get to die twice," the captain said. "Milwaukee's the home of the second coming."

"We've got a murder that's getting colder by the day," Sonntag said.

He found Silva waiting at the door.

"They'll get back to us. Take a day or two. Lot of records to go through. A pocket file on each serviceman."

"I wouldn't want to be a records clerk," Sonntag said.

They headed south, into those corners of Milwaukee where Silva was most comfortable, where the English was accented, and whole neighborhoods spoke in a tongue the next neighborhood couldn't decipher. They found a For Rent sign in front of Gropius's place.

"That was fast," Sonntag said.

They hiked up the interior stairs and rang. Gropius, in an army khaki tee shirt, responded, looking grumpy.

"Sonntag, sir, Milwaukee Police. And Silva. You have a little time for us?"

"I thought you were done with all that."

"You got the place cleaned out fast."

"There wasn't much. Gave it all to Goodwill, just junk."

"You find anything in there that might have helped us identify Mr. Ginger?"

"You looked it over yourself, so you can answer that."

Sonntag thought there was a little edge in that. "Hey, can we buy you a cup of java somewhere? Maybe talk about Ginger a little? We've got a lot of stuff that doesn't match up, and we're trying to figure it out."

"There's no coffee shop around here. This is mostly Croat around here. Unless you want slivovitz."

"We can't drink on the job, but I'll buy one for you, sir."

"I can't be gone long. Who knows who'll show up and rent?"

But he steered them out the door and down the block a way. The place was actually a restaurant and bar, with gaudy orange neon striping the walls and a big flashing Wurlitzer juke box. There were photos of draft horses lining the walls.

"Hey, we can get some tea," Silva said. "Ten cents, it says."

Sonntag bought three teas, which a dowdy, dimpled dame brought to them.

"It must be tough, making a living, come home wounded, and what do you do?" Sonntag said, waiting for the hot tea to cool.

"I was wounded in forty-three," Gropius said. "They gave me a little cash out the door in forty-five, enough to get a start."

"Where was that?" Silva asked.

"Sicily, the Italian campaign. I got hit in the head and don't remember anything after that. It's all a blank. I wasn't good for anything."

"What outfit?"

"I've got it written somewhere. Man, when something hits your head, there's not much you know after that."

"Army, right?"

"I guess so. Artillery."

"So, how'd you meet Ginger?"

"I got this place fixed up. I knew I'd rent it. Housing was scarce; nothing built during the war. Ten minutes after I put up a sign, this guy rings my bell. It's Ginger. He's got an accent, like Ginger isn't his name, and he mostly uses a pencil and pad to say he wants this flat, and I say sixty, and he says okay, and peels off the bills. Simple as that."

"Now that's where we're puzzled, Mr. Gropius. What language did he speak?"

"I never bothered to ask."

"You must have been curious about him. He's going to be a tenant, after all," Silva said. "You mentioned he was a Russian, in the Red Army, a mechanic I guess, and a refugee who got over here, right?"

"My head wound still bothers me," Gropius said. "Sometimes I hear things, you know. Sometimes I think maybe I'm a little crazy."

"You're saying it isn't so? Ginger wasn't all that?"

"I get real confused, and tell people what they want," Gropius said. "Otherwise I'd have a job and make a living. That's what the war deals you, right?"

Joe Sonntag itched to tell the man to cut out the crap, but didn't. You never knew. And a guy with shrapnel in his head, or whatever, might be that messed up. On the other hand, Gropius seemed a lot more lucid when he was telling the cops about the

Russian named Ginger, a Red Army mechanic who found his way to America.

Silva wasn't buying it either. "We've been able to find someone who identified the remains," Silva said. 'What do you think of that?"

"I'm blind in one eye, almost."

"This other witness gave us another name."

"Who is this man?"

Sonntag intervened. "We don't do that," he said. "Which eye is almost blind?"

"Well, neither is much good, as far as that goes."

"Do you have a eye-glass prescription for them?"

"Hey, this was just gonna be about Ginger. Why are you picking on me?"

"Just trying to get the stories straight. Now this other witness says that the deceased talked standard upper-Midwest English, without an accent. So we sure are curious."

"Those letters," Silva said. "The ones from the Soviet. Did your tenant talk about them?"

"Sure, those were his family. He escaped from the Red Army, so they made contact somehow."

"He told you that?" Sonntag asked.

"Nah, I figured it out. I sort of wondered if he was really a Red, you know, spying on us. Milwaukee's a big industrial city, with a lot of technology. That's what I thought he was after. When he went to work as a strikebreaker, he could maybe look over every part of every tractor, you know? And get all the details how an assembly line works. Stuff like that."

"But you didn't take your worries to the government?"

"They wouldn't pay attention to some old wounded vet."

The conversation came to an odd impasse. Sonntag didn't know where the hell to go with it. Silva was staring into his brown tea.

"Hey, man, who do you think Joseph L. Ginger was?" Silva asked.

"I think he was some guy planted by the Machinists Union to spy on the scabs. And when he switched sides, they wiped him out."

"Why do you think that?"

"Hey, officers, it's pretty obvious."

"Yeah, Mr. Gropius, thanks for your time. We've got to get a move on," Sonntag said.

"Hey, is Gropius your real name?" Silva asked.

"That's the name they gave me after I went blank."

What's Gropius? Norwegian?"

"No, German."

"Not the name you grew up with?"

Gropius shrugged.

"You know, sir, the army's not going to give you a new name."

"I gotta go back and wait for renters."

That's how it went.

Sonntag fired up the Nash and started rolling.

"Now where did that get us?" he asked.

"We'll know more when we see some military records," Silva said.

"We haven't done anything with Ginger's Social Security card. We can get date of birth from it, and maybe time and place of issue."

"You know what, Joe? Let's bury the guy. Release him to the county. We've got better things to do."

"A killing's a killing. I don't have to like the victim."

"That's not what I'm saying. Let's work the union. Someone'll talk if we keep pushing on it. Someone shot that man. It was supposed to be a scare tactic, but it went bad."

"How do you know that?"

"Because it was too dark for a deliberate shot, like they were gunning for him. We looked it over. There was no way, in that light, anyone could pick him out from the rest. A couple of dim lights, lots of shadow. Why do it there? Witnesses everywhere. You can't hit a target in the middle of a crowd in that. He wasn't shot from the street. You found the brass off to the right. So this thing wasn't a deliberate killing, or anything like that. The union wanted to scare hell out of the scabs."

Sonntag couldn't say why he wasn't buying it. Maybe it was just that he liked to close all his cases. He hated the ones that sat in a file, unresolved. "Let's see what the military records do for us," he said.

There had been sporadic violence at the plant for days. The most common was simply brawls. Some Machinists would bull through the police lines, pound the hell out of the scabs, and before it was over a few would be in the West Allis lockup, including some temporaries, and a few more would be in the hospital getting patched up. There was no end to it. Neither management nor the union had budged, and now they were moving farther apart, their lines hardening. The management had the best of it, so long as it could keep tractors and generators and turbines and transformers rolling off the assembly lines, with temporary labor. No wonder the Machinist Union was getting desperate and violent.

But so far, only one death.

"He was shot in the face. That's what gets to me," Sonntag said. "Not enough left of the bullet to help us."

"You always say you're gonna quit the department and sell vacuum cleaners," Silva said. "But it won't happen."

They returned the car to the lot, and confronted the heat of sun-soaked asphalt. He was glad to escape the Nash, which was rank with the smell of burned oil. The car needed new crankshaft bearings, not to mention a set of piston rings.

The bullpen was empty. The air was close and oppressive, and no one hung around in there if he could help it. Silva headed for the teletype, hoping for some word from the Pentagon, while Sonntag sat down to write some notes on the Gropius interview. He wondered what to say on paper: he and Silva had wasted an hour on a bewildered, brain-injured vet whose story shifted with every sip of tea.

That's when he spotted the message, handwritten by someone, lying in his wire basket.

"A Mrs. Ginger called long distance from Watertown," it read. "She wants you to call her about her son." There was a number.

Chapter Nine

Sonntag stared at the message. Call Elsie Ginger, Watertown. He dialed operator, put in a person-to-person call, and soon heard the phone ringing.

"This is the Ginger residence," a woman said.

"This is Lieutenant Sonntag, Milwaukee Police. I'm returning a call from Elsie Ginger."

"Oh, that's me, sir. I thought I'd better call you. I've had such a disturbing thing happen that I can hardly think about it."

"I'll help any way I can, ma'am."

"The paper runs death notices, you know. It ran one for my son, Joseph L. Ginger. I didn't see it, but a friend called me. Now, maybe it's just a coincidence, but it sent a shock straight through me."

"Coincidence, ma'am?"

She paused, searching for words. "You see? He's missing in action. Ever since nineteen forty-three. Not dead, not alive, just missing. I have the letter from the Air Force."

"Was he... in combat, Mrs. Ginger?"

"Well, not in that way. He was a pilot in the Lend-Lease program, ferrying planes to the Soviet Union. We sent thousands and thousands of planes over there, you know. The pilots flew out of

Alaska, and avoided Japan, and landed them in Siberia for the Red Air Force."

"So your son flew those planes?"

"He vanished, sir. He vanished over Soviet air space, and was never heard from again. We never knew..."

"Joseph Ginger vanished over Siberia?"

"That's guesswork, sir. The Air Force doesn't know, and things have gotten so bad that they can't pursue it with Soviet authorities."

"I'm sorry, Mrs. Ginger. That's the hardest blow of all, not knowing year after year."

"He could be alive, you know."

Sonntag seized the moment: "He might be. We can settle that. The remains are here, at the morgue."

"You want me..."

"It would be very hard, I'm sure. He was injured in the face."

"No, sir, it wouldn't be so hard. His father's gone now, and there's just me. But I never imagined he might still be alive. So, you see?"

"I do. It would settle things for you."

"Yes, it could."

"Have you photos of him? We would like to have them. We, ah, can do some comparing. Also, any school records? Height? Weight? School photos?"

"They're in a little, oh dear, a little shrine in his bedroom, sir."

"Oh, and another thing. Did he have a job before the war? Did he have a Social Security card? And number?"

"Oh, yes, sir, he spent a summer in an appliance store, delivering stoves and refrigerators, and he got a number."

"Do you have that number?"

"No, sir."

"Could you bring us what you have, ma'am?"

"It's a long way to Milwaukee, sir."

"Do you have a car or driver?"

"I had to learn to drive after my husband passed away. But mostly it's just around Watertown. Downtown Milwaukee, that really scares me."

"Let me see about sending a driver, Mrs. Ginger."

"No, a person had to face hard things, and driving in traffic is one of them. You don't grow unless you face things. I'll put together what you want, and start in. I should be there in an hour or more."

"I'm Lieutenant Sonntag, ma'am. Ask for me. I'll help you any way I can."

Sonntag hung up, and stared into space. Russia again.

Ginger went down in Siberia, as far as anyone knew. A White Russian language professor was trying to teach Russian to someone with a Russian name, Dimitri Karl. A war-wounded landlord was spouting conspiracy theories about Soviet spies. And then there was the Left-dominated Machinists Union, militant against reactionaries and capitalists. And none of it made sense–yet.

Elsie Ginger was as good as her word. She sailed in on time, wearing a straw picture hat and a white suit with a string of pearls. She had soft red hair and green eyes and a direct gaze that took in Sonntag with one glance.

"You even look like a detective," she said.

"And what do you do, ma'am?"

"I teach Sunday School, and I'm a candy-stripe lady at the hospital. I go around cheering up patients and emptying bedpans."

"And this is the first time you've driven in?"

"There now, that wasn't so bad. I've gained ground today. I can drive downtown and drive home without fear," she said. "Here."

She pressed a folder into his hands. Only then did something very soft fill her eyes.

"Let's have a look," he said.

He slipped a high school graduation photo out of the folder. It was a black and white five by seven that had been tinted.

"Your son's a redhead?"

"Flaming red, sir. Carrot doesn't describe him. He's redder than the Kremlin. My husband was black-haired, but the two go hand in hand."

"This is good. Are you ready to go over there? If not, we can wait."

"I've seen a lot of dead in my day, sir. Let's get it over with."

He remembered to bring the picture, and escorted the lady to a seedy Ford the department was about to discard. It smelled of unnamed troubles but she entered gamely, and he soon was escorting her into the cramped antechamber.

"You'll need to wait here a moment, ma'am."

A few minutes and a few forms later, he was ready. "Do you wish to go in alone, or would you prefer that I go with you, Mrs. Ginger?"

"I think, sir, I'd like you with me, and I would like you to be at my elbow."

The sheet had been drawn back as far as the shoulders. She hesitated, and then stepped forward and studied the remains.

"This is not my son. Not any way, shape or form.," she said. "Not even if I can't make out the face. This man has brown hair."

"Joseph had bright red?"

She nodded.

"This man is older," she said. "Quite a bit older."

"You remembered a youth, ma'am."

"I saw him in forty-three, on furlough, in uniform, early twenties. This man, forty?"

That seemed right.

"This man is shorter. Joseph was five feet ten."

"I'll ask an odd question, Mrs. Ginger. Does the name Dimitri Karl come to mind?"

"That's a complete blank, sir."

"Good. That is probably who this is, but how your son's name cropped up we don't know. There was a social security card in his wallet with your son's name."

"I've seen enough," she said, and headed toward the anteroom.

He nodded to the attendant, who restored the sheet and rolled the body back to the vault.

"This has been valuable to me," she said. "I've always known Joseph is gone, but this, well, buries him. Now, as long as I'm downtown, I'll head for Gimbels."

"Before you do, I'd like you to sign some forms, and give us permission to keep the photos for a few days, ma'am."

"Bureaucracy never ends, doesn't it?"

"Do you know whether your son was carrying identification, like a driver's license, or military dog tags, when he vanished in the

Soviet Union?"

"He could drive. He had a license. He could fly. He carried all of that."

"That's helpful, Mrs. Ginger."

"I'm going to have a funeral, Mr. Sonntag. All these years of waiting, you know, missing, maybe caught over there. Never a proper burial. Now I'm going to have at least a memorial service. He was a strong, able boy. He would have been a commercial pilot, now, and I'd be a grandmother."

"I'd like to come, ma'am."

She smiled. "I always thought police never had a sentimental bone in them."

"We all have a sentiment bone, ma'am. Mine's the size of a dime."

He dropped her off at Gimbels.

For all of her bravura, he was sure she was on the ragged edge of tears.

Back at the station house, Sonntag found a teletype from the Pentagon's Personnel Records office lying in his basket. There was nothing on Dimitri Karl, nothing on Anders Gropius, nothing on Ilich Borovich, a record on Stanley Arpo, and one on Joseph J. Ginger. He studied that one first. It handsomely confirmed everything he had just learned from Elsie Ginger only minutes before. The ferry pilot had gone missing in 1943, in the Soviet Union, and his whereabouts were unknown. There was a lot more: training, promotions, commendations, transfers, and the commands to which he was attached.

The Union secretary, Stanley Arpo, had served in the infantry, remained a private because of disciplinary problems, saw no combat, and was discharged without honor in 1945. But what intrigued Sonntag more was the total absence of any record for Anders Gropius, the head-wounded vet who was Ginger's landlord. Was that his name? Would it all come out with another name? And how could one check that out, given the man's strange conduct and belief?

He didn't expect anything on Borovich and Karl.

He stared at the teletypes. Somehow, this all was sucking him into a world of international intrigue, far removed from the routine crime he was used to investigating. Here were the maneuvers of shadowy men, serving causes Sonntag barely understood.

He found little assurance in the reality of the bullpen, the phones on desks, the faint odor of cigars and urine, the grimy windows looking out on a gray city.

"What have you got?" Captain Ackerman asked. "Why are you wasting time?"

Ackerman had spotted him gazing into space, which he always interpreted as goldbricking. That and coffee breaks offended the man. He sometimes even called local coffee shops to see what uniforms were in there.

"I've got a ferry pilot who vanished in Russia, and someone's using his name and papers, and that someone got killed in front of the Allis-Chalmers gate. I've got a landlord who says he got a brain injury in combat, lost memory, and spends his time now looking for Red conspiracies. Except there's no record in Military Personnel. I've got a White Russian who identified the strikebreaker as an English-speaking Russian named Dimitri Karl, who wanted to learn Russian privately, if you can buy that. And I've got a union full of people who at least play footsie with the Communist Party."

"Drag 'em all in and pound on them alittle," Ackerman said. "Commies, the whole lot of them."

"You know something, captain? I'm a city cop., and nothing else."

"We got to stop the red tide," he said. "You got to stick your finger in the dike." He winked, and stank his way through the room.

Frank Silva asked the right question: "So who's in the morgue?"

"The only person who seems to know is the professor."

"So, let's go talk."

"Let's go talk to Marquette admissions first."

"A guy gets shot during a strike, and the next thing we know, we're in the middle of the cold war," Silva said. "Does this make you a little sweaty under the armpits?"

"More like drowning," Sonntag said. "I'd like it to be an ordinary murder, with ordinary Milwaukee people, committed for ordinary reasons."

"But it ain't. It's murder out of ideology. Someone's stamping on somebody's ideals, and someone gets killed for it. I sometimes think I could kill a few scabs myself."

"Frank, Stanley Argo stayed buck private his entire time in the infantry. He got busted for various stuff. He wasn't honorably discharged, and he wasn't dishonorably discharged. He was just kicked out, after the Army didn't need him. He's worth a second look."

"Maybe. I'd like to see how many Argos there are in the world, soldiers who hated the army, dodged it, fought it, but who didn't quite make the stockade. Just got busted over and over and thrown out. Turned out he had some talent after all. He's commanding his own army now, and they've got a big company halfway bottled up."

"So, how do we get the slippery capo to spill a few secrets? Like who shot the man?"

"You know what? This case is driving me nuts," Frank said. "When we talk to people, we're talking to crazies. Maybe we should stick to facts, if we can find anything worth calling a fact. What I'm thinking is, Marquette has an admissions office, and maybe whoever's the current Joseph Ginger might have applied there."

They drove over to the Marquette, found their way to the cluttered office, lorded over by a crucifix that occupied most of a wall, and corralled a skinny clerk.

"Milwaukee police, sir, Detective Silva here, and I'm Lieutenant Sonntag. I'm hoping you can help us. We're trying to track down a person named Joseph L. Ginger, and another named Dimitri Karl, who may have applied for admission last semester."

"I don't know that I can share that, sir."

"They might be secret Communists."

"Oh, in that case, I'll be glad to help out. Ginger and Karl? I'll look right in here."

The clerk headed into a file room, while Sonntag stared innocently at the wall, whistling Yankee Doodle, and Silva glared at him.

The clerk returned carrying a manila folder. "Nothing on Ginger, sir. I checked our master list, and he's not there. But Karl, you can see he applied, wanting to major in languages for a bachelor degree program. He decided the tuition was too steep, even with the GI Bill, and said he'd try the University of Wisconsin."

"He got an address or anything?"

"Right here on the form, sir."

The address was that of Anders Gropius.

Chapter Ten

The strike crawled into its sixth week. Both sides were dug in, and weren't even meeting. The Machinists were rapidly consuming their strike fund, while the plant was running at a quarter of its capacity. The violence of the early weeks had largely slipped into sullen resignation. There were fewer picketers, they were less vocal, and more inclined to stand quietly instead of snaking militantly around for the benefit of Pathe News camera crews or reporters.

But that didn't make it any more peaceful. If anything, the anger brimmed explosively at the margins of riot. No one did much to clean up the picketing area, which was littered with strike posters and trash. The strikebreakers ducked in and out with less fear, and few of them were hit by rocks or spit.

Sonntag and Silva drove to the storefront one morning, after deciding to push the investigation from that end rather than try to identify the shadowy victim. Even the headquarters seemed worn out. The strike signs in the window were sun-faded. They found Stanley Argo alone, which was a good omen.

"You again," the secretary said.

"Us again, Mr. Argo. We're after something; the roster of your members. The people in your local."

"Forget that. It's none of your business and our membership is private."

"You can resist, in which case we'll subpoena the roster. Every man in your union is a suspect. We've a killing of a temporary, and the shot came from your crowd, and we'd have no trouble getting a court order, if that's how you want to play it. We can also get an employee list from the company. I'm hoping to save you the trouble. If you want your members to stay under a cloud, do nothing. If you want to help us sort it out, you'll do your members a favor."

"Some favor," Argo said.

"Somebody shot that man. Do you want to help or not?" Silva said.

"No, we're brothers; we're solidarity. You don't pick on one brother. We're in it together. If you think one of us is a suspect, then we'll all be suspects. So screw you."

"That doesn't work, Mr. Argo. Just try telling your members they're all suspects. Go ahead."

"Hey, cops, you don't get it. We're brothers, get it? Brothers."

"Well, all right. Here's a subpoena for you. There'll be a coroner's inquest. See you at ten tomorrow morning."

"Like hell I will. You'll have to find me and drag me."

"You got yourself in trouble in the army, did you?"

"Why don't you cops leave a man alone?"

"Because a man's been killed. We think you have some knowledge of it, and maybe the public will learn something when you testify under oath."

"If I help you, will you delay that or call it off?"

"We can ask the county attorney to postpone it."

"And if you catch the man, what then?"

"That would be up to the county attorneys."

Argo rummaged in a file and pulled out a mimeographed roster. "It's up to date, give or take one or two."

"Anyone missing, please add him in longhand," Sonntag said.

Argo scanned the list and crossed off three names. "They're out, gone, quit."

"Why'd they quit?"

"We always lose some in a strike. Some brothers, they think maybe they'll move to Florida or some place."

"All right, you mind taking a little trip with us?" Sonntag asked.

"Sure I mind. I'm tending the store. I'm running the strike."

"Won't take long. We'd like to take you to the morgue and have you identify the dead man."

"Me?"

"You, and under oath. We'll have some people there who can swear you and record your statements."

"Me? I don't know who he is. There's no point in doing that stuff."

"You want to come along, or do I have to pull the papers out of my pocket and hand them to you?"

"What papers?"

"The ones that will compel your presence at the morgue."

"How can you get away with that? You can't drag me there."

"Well, maybe you're a material witness, okay?"

"What's that?"

"Let's say a witness who knows some stuff about the crime. We can arrest material witnesses. We can arrest accessories. You come in with us, and tell us what you know, and maybe we won't have to arrest you."

Stanley Argo peered from one cop to the other cop, looking trapped. "Okay, if I come over there and have a look, and tell you I don't know nothing, then what?"

"Guess you'll have to find out, Mr. Argo."

"I hear rumors. That's all I know, just rumors. I hate to give out rumors because they're not reliable, you know? Might get an innocent man in trouble."

"Well, if you come voluntarily, and tell us what you know, maybe we won't put the cuffs on your wrists, okay?"

"Jeez, you cops."

Argo locked up the storefront, slid the key under the doormat, and allowed Silva to frisk him and seat him in the rear of the black Ford, which was segregated from the front seat with a wire screen. He glanced around desperately, looking for some brothers to rescue him, but at the moment there were none.

Argo did not make the trip silently. "You're barking up the wrong tree. The scabs, they're trying to kill us. You should frisk them before they go in and out of there. You'd see more concealed weapons than there are scabs. We got men so badly beaten when the cops weren't looking that we had to excuse them. You know, stay home. Don't picket. Family men, they got the crap beaten out of them by the scabs. But you cops don't do anything about it."

"You got some guys we could talk to who'd tell us about it?" Silva asked.

"I can find a few. Just give me a day."

"They're armed? With what?"

"Like big toad-stickers. My brothers get stabbed all the time."

"We'll talk to them. Look at the wounds," Silva said.

"How come they didn't go to the hospital?" Sonntag asked.

"I'll ask them when I get back."

"So, have you scared off many scabs?"

"Yeah, some don't come back. We're working on it."

"You'd like to scare them all off, right?"

"They're taking money out of our pockets."

"How do you scare them off, Stanley?"

"Oh, man, you got to hand it to the brothers. Here's one way. We just follow them. They come out, run our picket lines, and they think that's it, they're out, they can go home– it ain't home, they don't have homes. Some get on the streetcars, and we can't do nothing, but some walk, and man, they'd better walk in bunches because a few blocks from the plant, they're gonna meet some brothers. Oh, boy! Oh, man! So they learn fast, and don't come back, and the company has to hire more scabs."

"Company's still shipping tractors," Silva said.

"We're working on it," Argo said.

Sonntag pulled up at the anonymous concrete block morgue, enameled gray, and parked.

"Never been in one of these joints before," Argo said. "How does it work? You run out some bodies and I get to choose?"

"Nah, Argo, we lie you down in the middle of some bodies, so you get to see what it's like," Silva said.

"How are they kept? I mean, don't they start to stink?"

"Thirty-three degrees," Silva said.

"Gotcha," Argo said.

They had the union secretary wait in the small anteroom while the attendant rolled out the remains that had started as Ginger and had been identified as Dimitri Karl.

"All right, Mr. Argo, we'll take you back in there. It's cold, but that's necessary," Sonntag said.

The body had been rolled under a bright lamp and the sheet rolled back from the face.

"Man, this'll be a story to tell the brothers," Argo said. "I bet there's not one ever been in a morgue before. I sure haven't."

He reached the remains, stared at them for a while.

"Man, right up the nostril. That sure improved his breathing," Argo said.

Sonntag and Silva said nothing.

"Was it a dumdum? Man, it messed him up. I hardly ever seen someone messed up that much. He got hit with a howitzer. That poor sucker never knew what hit him."

Sonntag stared off at the shadows.

"Wait until I tell the brothers! They'll buy an extra Schlitz tonight. This guy was public enemy number one."

That brought Sonntag's attention back to the body.

"You know who this turkey is?" Argo asked.

Sonntag shook his head.

"He's the number one strikebreaker in the world."

"Yeah? Who says?" Silva asked.

"I say. If there's anyone need to be lying there with a dumdum up his snout, it's this turkey. Management, they got troubles with a union, they bring in this turkey. All over the country. He's the Wyatt Earp of strikebreakers."

"So, how come he just goes in and out like the rest of the strikebreakers?"

"That's so he's not noticed. He just gets into dungarees and goes in and out with the scabs."

"But he doesn't work in there? He's not on the assembly line?"

"Hell no. He's like the field marshal. He's the one came up with those buses in and out. He's the one that'd send hit squads to kill a brother. He's got an army of goons. They're dresses like scabs going to work, but they're goons, and they got blackjacks in their pockets, and maybe a few snub-nose guns."

"I don't get it," Silva said. "Why would management hire a torpedo?"

"They ain't out to win the strike; they want to bust up the union."

"But why? How can they bust up a union?"

"You're so dumb, coppers. This is mob. You want to line your pockets? You take over a union and collect dues. You knock heads, you get rid of people like me, I'm for the brothers, and you pound on people like me until we go or get carried out, and you take over the brotherhood, and you make a sweetheart deal with management, and you collect the dues, and everyone's happy."

Sonntag scented something here. "Okay, Argo, let's go through that again."

"This joker here, he's trying to muscle into the brotherhood."

"But why pose as a strikebreaker?"

"Because he is one. And he's got his mob with him. It's not just scabs going in and out."

"So, Stanley, how do they do this?"

"There's no one way, coppers. But here's how it happens. The strike starts to die, see? The strike funds are gone, management's not budging, the scabs go in and make stuff. So about then, the thugs move in. They tell the brothers the headquarters, the international union, send them to run the union. They take over. Anyone objects, they get the crap beaten out of them. Or their families get hurt. Want to make a brother keep his yap shut? Bust the bones of his kid. So they move in, boot me out, like I'm public enemy number one. If I don't leave alive, I leave dead, get it? It's all mob muscle, and when they've got the union, and got the brothers scared, they cut a sweetheart deal with the company, and get themselves a Cadillac."

"They threaten you yet?"

"They don't have to say anything. They don't have to see you. Yeah, they got me in the crosshairs." He pointed at the remains. "But sometimes it goes the other way, right? This one here, he's cold meat. He's one. Maybe there'll be more."

"More mobsters killed, Stanley?"

"Hey, cop. You used to call me Mr. Argo, and now you're calling me Stanley."

Sonntag smiled. "This is valuable stuff, sir. You're helpful."

"I don't mean to be. The cops are usually in bed with management."

"So, Stanley, you know something about this dead man, right?"

"I do. I got my sources. He's the biggest cheese of all. Whoever put him out of his misery did the brothers a favor. Maybe even scared off the mob. The brothers are tough, you know. They don't take any crap. Sometimes, a mobster tries to muscle in, and gets himself a nice shiny coffin for his efforts."

"What mob, who?"

"Not Milwaukee. From maybe Chicago."

"How do you know that?"

"This stiff has a reputation. This stiff, he's known. He shows up at a strike, and man, word gets out fast."

"Yes, but where does he come from? How do you know? Are here photos? He shows up at a strike, and who tells you this is a mobster?"

"You know who slips us the word? The company."

"The company? How do they know?"

"Don't be so dumb, coppers."

"Okay, Stanley, can you put a name to this stiff?"

Argo nodded. "The name of this turkey is Anders Gropius."

Chapter Eleven

Stanley Argo blubbered all the way back to West Allis, plainly glad he was not searching for a bail bondsman. But the more Argo yammered, the more Joe Sonntag liked it. Argo had supplied more good stuff in an hour than the investigation had nailed down since the shooting.

Argo was out of the black Ford the instant Sonntag pulled up in front of the storefront. The place was full of machinists, so someone had opened it up. Sonntag watched pensively as Argo fled inside, and soon was caught in heated discussion in there. Sonntag was in no hurry to move, and soon saw Argo gesturing toward the police cruiser, while burly machinists stared.

"You going back?" Silva asked.

Sonntag shifted into gear, eased out the clutch, and the car slid away.

"Sort of self-incriminating, right? Nothing like a motive or two," Silva said.

"Yeah, but who got shot?" Sonntag said, steering into Greenfield Road traffic.

"Argo's positive; he wasn't letting a hole in the face slow him down," Sonntag said.

"So now it's Gropius? Who's the Gropius we talk to who says he's a wounded war vet but isn't?"

"Beats me," Sonntag said. "But someone who knew Ginger was missing in action."

"We're on the south side. Want to go bug Gropius for a while?"

"So maybe he's Dimitri Karl, who's maybe not dead, whose person is now inhabited by whoever's inside the current resident?"

Silva laughed. "This is getting entertaining," he said.

"Do you believe Argo?"

"I never believe anyone entirely, not until we get the case nailed down. But I'll say this; I believe him more than anyone else we've talked to and that includes that Marquette professor."

As they penetrated the south side, a thunderhead was building to the northeast, over the lake. Then a few drops of rain splattered the dust on the windshield, turning it to mud. Sonntag turned on the vacuum windshield wipers, which sometimes worked. As he drove past Irv the Workingman's Friend, where he bought his suits off the pipe racks, the rain hit hard, and he spotted Irv wheeling sidewalk pipe racks to safety under the awning. Irv like to stick his suits right into the face of browsers. They always fit Sonntag fine when he bought them, but they usually got baggy. But hey, where else could you get suits for nineteen dollars?

"So what is it, Frank? A cold war conspiracy? A mob deal to take over a union? An accident? A management scheme to have themselves a sweetheart union?"

"I think it's men from Mars," Frank said.

Sonntag pulled into the crowded street, and immediately some boys playing street baseball dissolved to let him crawl past.

"It's the cops," yelled one.

"How do we do this? Tell Gropius he's just been identified at the morgue?"

Silva started laughing. "Who don't you tell him that you're Anders Gropius, and who's he?"

"Or maybe I'll tell him my name is Karl."

When they reached Gropius's sawed up residence, they found some construction. A guy was up on a ladder working on rain gutters. Another was on a stepladder scraping chipped paint from downstairs window frames. Some work had been done on the walkway to the front door. Two segments of concrete had been poured, and these were guarded with a couple of sawhorses.

Sonntag and Silva entered the small foyer, and found the lower apartment door open, and the place cleaned out and shining. They headed upstairs, and found that door open– and the place empty. It, too, was shining. One quick glance confirmed that it was ready for new tenants.

"Gone. Gropius flew," Silva said.

"Or whoever it was," Sonntag said.

They headed downstairs and out, only to run into a stranger. The man wore sunglasses and had a broad scar across his forehead. He was twice as wide at the shoulders as at the waist, and it wasn't shoulder pads doing it.

"You looking for something?" he asked.

"Yeah, Anders Gropius. We're police. We want to ask him a few questions."

"Never heard of him," the man said.

"He own this place?" Silva asked.

"I own it."

"Who are you?"

"What's it to you?"

"Sir, we're trying to find the owner, whose name was Anders Gropius, as far as we can tell."

"Wrong place, fellas."

"You know where he went?" Silva asked.

"What am I, nuts? I tell you I don't know him, and you ask me where he went."

"You have a name, sir? A name on a deed, or a mortgage, for instance."

"Yeah, sure, Parvenu."

"That's your name?"

"Yeah, my friends call me Fats."

"The name doesn't fit, sir."

"Yeah, it's not my waist, it's what I eat. Gimme a steak and I leave the meat and eat the fat."

"Your deed registered at the courthouse?"

"You betcha."

"What's with the remodel?"

"I'm moving in."

"You rented this before now?"

"Deadbeats."

"What were their names?"

"Man, I wish I could remember."

"You can't remember the name of your tenants?"

"They come and go. I got tenants to hell and back, fifty places, rents coming in or not coming in, and this guy, he's maybe tenant two hundred forty-seven, so how should I know?"

"You own this yourself, or is it a company?" Sonntag asked.

"Look, pal, it's in the records. Now you mind if I get back to work?"

"Go ahead, sir," Sonntag said.

Something was on his mind, tickling it, but not until they were a few blocks away did he connect.

"I know that name," he said. "Tony 'Fats' Parvenu. A minor-league player in the Chicago punch-card racket."

"So who is Gropius?" Silva asked.

"A fantasy," Sonntag said. "I think we need to keep an eye on Fats."

"Maybe that's Fats, in the morgue."

Silva was laughing his ass off.

Back downtown, Sonntag hiked over to the county courthouse, found the registrar of deeds, supplied an address, and waited while the male clerk began digging through enormous gray ledgers.

It took fifteen minutes, but eventually the clerk returned, ledger in hand. "That property belongs to Anders Gropius. There's no mortgage on it. The taxes are paid up. Its assessed value is six thousand four hundred."

"How long did Gropius own it?"

"Oh, let's see. Yes, since nineteen forty-six. Not long, then."

"Is there any lien against it? Mechanic's lien?"

"I'll need to look elsewhere, sir."

The clerk vanished again, and returned shaking his head. "Nothing against it, sir. No second mortgage. Bought on March eleven, nineteen forty-six. We have no record of any arrangements the buyer might have made."

"Gropius. Was there an address? The buyer's address?"

"Yes, sir. Buyer was Anders Gropius, twelve-seventy, Room Two, National Avenue."

"That's helpful, sir. Thanks. Oh, one last question. He may have deeded his property to someone else within the last day or so. Do you have any documents that haven't yet gone into your ledgers?"

The clerk swiftly went through the day's intake, and returned shaking his head.

"Fraid not, officer."

Sonntag drove alone down to National Avenue, located twelve-seventy, which was a furniture store with a second floor, reached with a street stairwell. Cheap gray horsehair sofas and chairs filled the windows, along with an easy-credit sign. Sonntag climbed the long, dank, narrow stair and found himself in a rooming area, six doors and a common bathroom at the rear. It wasn't exactly the most pleasant place to exist.

Room two was the second on the left, so he knocked. He waited and knocked again. He heard nothing. He tried Room One, in the street corner, and was immediately rewarded. A scruffy male, unshaven, and smelling of cheap booze, eyed him.

"I'm looking for Anders Gropius, next door. You know anything about him?' Sonntag asked.

"I used to see him now and then in the bathroom. Big guy, right?"

"Well, not so big. Average."

"The guy in there, he was a big guy."

"You mind giving me a description? I really need to find him."

The man scratched his gut. "Always in dark glasses, like he didn't want no one to see him as he was looking at you. And a big old scar, yeah, a scar on his forehead. He'd been in something bad once, a wreck or something."

"That's Gropius for sure? He live here long?"

"I don't know that, pal. Me, I've been here since I got out of the army, forty-six. I'm studying welding on the GI Bill."

"How long you been studying, friend?"

"Two years now." He grinned, revealing holes where teeth once lived.

"When you're gonna finish up?"

"When they decide I've had enough welding."

"So this guy Gropius, was he around here much?"

"Nah. Mostly he wasn't here. The walls are thin, you know? I never heard nothing next door. Just a lot of nothing. A scream once. I thought Gropius had a parrot, but he didn't. They don't allow pets in here."

"So Gropius, with the scar, he's not around?"

"Not hardly. I don't think he lived there. I think he just kept the place for when he missed the train."

"Train?"

"Yeah, he came from Chicago. Once I saw him get into a car, below, with Illinois plates. Cook county."

"I heard he runs unions. Like the Machinists."

"How come you're asking?"

"Oh, I've got what I need to know, thanks."

"You FBI?"

"No, sir."

"Well, you're something. I can smell the police a mile away, buddy."

"Hey, if Gropius shows up here, call me, okay?" He handed the man a card.

"Lieutenant, are you? Jaysas."

"And who are you, my friend?"

"If I'm gonna be a stoolpigeon, I want to be paid."

"Keep the card, pal. Let me know what's what."

Sonntag left, while the man studied the card.

Sonntag climbed into his car, ticked off. There were two or three bodies tied to each name, or maybe the reverse. As long as he was on the South Side, he thought he'd see what Stanley Argo knew about Fats. He drove past the West Allis plant just as the afternoon shift change was occurring, and saw the usual picketing, a violent, snaking conga line of picketers, weaving in and out, brandishing their strike posters, shouting at the scabs, who had learned to move in and out in flying wedges, trotting through the gate with their biggest and strongest guys on the outside. The whole thing had become ritual, and the West Allis cops rarely bothered to intervene. Usually, there were a few missiles landing, or a fist or two, but in larger scheme of things, nothing changed.

Argo was over in his roost at the storefront, his feet up on the desk, enjoying the company of a few machinists. But when he saw Sonntag standing in the door, he rose at once and herded the lieutenant outside, a few yards from anyone else.

"Didn't expect you, sir."

"Okay, Stanley, give me a straight answer. Do you know anyone named Tony 'Fats' Parvenu?"

The union secretary went green. Sonntag swore to it. The guy's flesh went green. "Jaysas," he said. "I'm dead."

"What do you mean. Stanley?"

"Fats Parvenu's got a new hobby, collecting unions. He's the president, or secretary, or treasurer, of about eight unions. And you want to know something? When he gets himself a new toy to play with, the old officers show up missing."

"The old elected guys?"

"Listen, I'll be cast in concrete and dumped in Lake Michigan if I don't cave. He always makes an offer."

"Which is?"

"Get out right now and maybe live."

"And has he been in touch?"

"I ain't gonna wait to find out. He's here, right?"

"He seems to own the house where Ginger, or Gropius, or Dimitri Karl, whoever it was, lived."

"I just quit. Goodbye, cops. I'm not telling you where I'm going. But it's not around here, that's for sure."

"You want protection?"

"Not from you, I don't."

"Hey, come with me and we'll go talk this over with the chief."

"Listen, Lieutenant, you're death. If Parvenu sees me talking to you, or hears about it, I'm six feet under. You think I'm joking? You think I'm making it up? You got a lot to learn."

"Okay, what do we look for?" Sonntag said.

"Black leather bomber jackets. Like war surplus. Summer, winter, any time."

"Okay, Stanley."

Sonntag watched the Machinists secretary collect a jacket and leave the storefront, without looking back. The union guys were still sitting in there on folding chairs. The summer sun still cooked the pavement. Nothing changed, and yet everything had changed.

Chapter Twelve

Blouk Neumeyer, professor of labor relations at University of Wisconsin, Milwaukee lakeside campus, did not sit easily. In fact he seemed so wound up that Lieutenant Sonntag wondered whether he'd cooperate. He welcomed Sonntag and Silva dourly, not wanting to be bothered by some Milwaukee cops.

This was Silva's idea, so Sonntag let the detective take the lead.

"Professor, it's kind of you to see us," Silva said. "You're the expert. We're a couple of flatfoots. We're hoping you can help us."

"If it doesn't eat up my time," Neumeyer said.

"We just need a few minutes. You can help us. What do you know about the mob and labor?"

"Absolutely nothing."

"We think maybe there's a man in town who's sort of leaning on locals. He's got a few, and looking for more. Like the Machinists local at Allis-Chalmers."

"You expect me to know something about that? I'm in labor relations."

"Yeah, well, we're sort of in the dark here. A strikebreaker was shot a few days ago, and we don't even have his name. But he maybe lived in a house owned by a Chicago mobster who's got a few ambitions."

"What does that have to do with my field?"

"Well, you know something about strikes, I guess."

"Every strike's different. It's too complex a topic to open here."

"Okay, what's unique about this one?"

"Radical leadership. Mostly fellow travelers, you know, or sympathizers with the Socialist Labor Party."

"Does that help in the negotiating?"

"Make it much worse. The union leaders have to prove they can get more."

"So the strike goes on?"

"It's a long strike, and they're running out of strike funds. And the International Headquarters in Pittsburgh can't help them. Once the strike pay runs out, there'll be real pressure on the leaders."

"So, what happens?"

"They're already looking for money. Big money. You can't get that kind of money from banks. You've got to go somewhere else for it."

"Like?"

"Ah, I see what you're driving at. Yes, the mob can be a source, if the brotherhoods want to take that step. But it's simplistic to think that's the only way they get money. It's not all black and white, you know. Arrangements can be far more complex than, ah, police usually deal with."

"So, give us an example."

"An example? But that would require simplifying things. Each case has its own nuances, and none are alike. I couldn't possibly give you an example that would contain more than a modicum of truth. You know, you can't just barge into a subject that takes expertise."

Sonntag thought the man was a genius at getting rid of unwanted guests, but Frank Silva wasn't done: "Okay, I'll give you an example. A union, let's say the Machinists local, is in the middle of a long strike. Both sides are standing firm. The local is running through the last of its strike funds, and can't get any more. The company's got enough temporaries to keep the shop open. It's making tractors, but not enough to make much money. So, arbitration has failed. The workers are restless. Strike funds barely buy the groceries. And now those are nearly gone, and the rank and file know it. So, along comes Mr. Mobster, who likes owning unions, and pockets a little of each man's dues. How does he do it?"

"There are so many ways, officer, that I couldn't begin to tell you. Each case proceeds on its own vector."

Silva stared out the window. Off to the east lay the shimmering blue of Lake Michigan.

Professor Neumeyer, in turn, seemed to study the bookshelves on one side of his small office, shelves that brimmed importantly with transcripts, journals, hearings, case law, and statutes. Then he made a slight concession.

"It's simplistic to suppose that a mobster simply takes over a union. What does he want? Does he want actual control, with his hand-picked surrogates in office, bossing the union? Maybe, maybe not. Maybe all he wants is to lend the union some juice, and get it back fast and double or triple. Maybe he arranges a loan, but requires that the local's officers resign, and his own be appointed. So it's far more complex and variable than you've considered."

"Sort of over the head of cops, eh?" Silva said.

"Well, with proper background, I'm sure you could fathom it all."

"Yeah, well, suppose a mobster's around here, but he's on the other side, hanging out with the scabs, renting to scabs. How would you explain that?"

"Well, that's more complicated than you may realize," the professor said. "Consider the temporaries levers. You want to own a union? Keep the temporaries working. Protect them. Keep the company going. If a temporary gets hurt, blame the union. That's how to bust a union. And by the way, don't call them scabs. That's union parlance. It's important to adapt a policy of strict neutrality. They shouldn't be called scabs or strikebreakers, which carry connotations. Objectivity is primary in labor relations."

"They look sort of scabby," Silva said. "You know, they got stuff growing on them."

"Well, that's the unrefined mind at work, and you'll want to avoid that."

"Okay, but under every scab there's some pus," Silva said.

Blouk Neumeyer looked pained. "The very first thing to master in labor relations is the overcoming of stereotypes. A temporary may or may not be a perfectly decent person. A striking union man may or may not also be a fine person. And ethnicity has nothing to do with mobsters. I must say, to paraphrase, that anyone can be a mobster, without regard to race, creed, color, or previous condition of servitude. I'm joking, of course."

"Yeah, that's funny."

"But underneath my levity is an important point, which is that in labor relations there is not good or bad, but just relations."

Sonntag intervened. "Professor, could you talk a bit about intimidation? How does a mobster operate if he wants to control a union and there's opposition? Brothers who resist him?"

"Oh, that's a very complex subject, too long to get into here. Labor racketeering is a hot topic in Washington, and in the next year or two there's to be hearings on the issue. I understand Senator Kefauver's interested. There's some worry that labor racketeering is interfering with interstate commerce, which therefore makes it a federal issue."

"Well, thank you, but how do they do it? How do they strongarm their way into a local, and run it, sir?"

"That's a complex issue, and beyond the scope of this little interview, but I am preparing a lecture on that very topic, which I will offer in a couple of months."

"Is there physical intimidation?"

"Oh, that's an option, lieutenant."

"Are there threats? Do mobsters threaten the elected officers of a union?"

"Yes, and their families, too."

"Is union balloting secret?"

"Most members would like it to be, sir."

"But is it secret?"

"Oh, I'd have to answer that on a case by case basis."

"If balloting isn't secret, does that pose a threat to anyone who votes against the mob?"

Neumeyer looked pained. "Some things, officer, ought to be obvious, to anyone who ponders them."

"Does the mob go for all the offices, or just, say, the treasurer?"

"That depends on circumstances, officer. It's going to depend on the union charter, and what duties attach to what offices."

"Okay, who's the boss? Who's the guy who runs the local?"

Neumeyer looked at his Bulova. "My good friends, I'm due in class in twenty minutes, and I haven't yet washed up."

"One last question. Do mobsters use thugs to keep members in line?"

"Well, that depends– it's rather difficult to say, sir."

Sonntag sighed. "Thanks for the time, sir."

"I wish I could have been more helpful. If the questions had been more specific, you know."

Sonntag and Silva retreated, both of them feeling like whipped dogs. They stepped into the summer sun, noting the cool lake breeze that make the campus one of the most pleasant corners of Milwaukee.

"Are you simplistic, Frank?" Sonntag asked.

"Only on weekdays," Silva replied.

When they parked the newly-washed gray Nash and headed into the station house, Sonntag felt an odd pleasure. A station house is a sad place, where criminals are booked, and unending tragedy plays out, and one is never far from rage or tears or fear or bitterness. But this time, its grimy confines seemed like home to him, his little bit of turf. His friends were there; his own brotherhood of blue. He had worn the blue for years, before he became a detective, and the blue was home to him too.

At the university he felt that he was treading forbidden hallways, where people who were a lot smarter and better schooled than he had exclusive claim to those precincts. He had his high school degree; he had some specialized training. He was neither smart nor dumb. And he was immediately comfortable there.

At least until Captain Ackerman landed at his desk.

"Well? You get anything out of Neumeyer?" Ackerman asked.

"A little. He mostly talks at levels I don't get."

"That's the trouble with professors. We're in the fact business. All we need is facts. Cases are simple. Crimes are simple. Usually, a simple line of inquiry, some simple questions, leads us to a simple solution. Put a professor in search of a criminal, or have him try to figure out the crime, and he'd be looking for Mickey Mouse at Walt Disney Studios."

Sonntag smiled. Professor Neumeyer was telling him he was too simplistic all afternoon; his boss, Captain Ackerman, was telling him he was too wedded to theory and all that counted was fact.

Maybe they both were right.

"Well, this case is growing cold. You're not getting anywhere, and I wish you'd get cracking," Ackerman said. "Quit interviewing professors."

"I'll have you do that next time," Sonntag said.

Ackerman beamed, and waggled his gummy cigar. "I'd show them who's smart," he said. "You know what, Sonntag? You're missing the biggest clue of all. Why's that guy Fats Parvenu fixing up that house down there? Why's he scraping paint and pouring concrete? It's camouflage. It hides whatever's going on down there. He doesn't give a crap about the building. What does he care if a rain gutter's leaking? Tell me that, eh? And scraping window frames. Why's he fixing the walkway? If you were all cop, instead of half professor, you'd have this case figured out."

Sonntag laughed. There was nothing like the station house to lift his spirits.

It was quitting time. He collected his black lunch bucket, which had held a peanut butter and jelly sandwich this day, and hiked down to Wells Street. He was ahead of the rush hour, but there were plenty of women who'd been downtown, shopping at Gimbels and the Boston Store, waiting for the orange car to grind to a halt.

After the door flapped open, he let the weary ladies board, and settle their shopping bags in their laps. He boarded, and was soon followed by four young males, all of them in black leather bomber jackets, the detritus of war. The scattered themselves through the car, one behind him, two forward near the door, and one across. What was it that Argo had said about young toughs in black leather jackets?

They were the mob army; they were the troops, doing the tough and dirty when it came to shaking a union local by its teeth. He eyed them warily, but they didn't seem to know one another. Coincidence, maybe, or maybe they'd transfer to the West Allis car at the junction up ahead. He furtively studied them. Clean-shaven, soft gazes that dodged his when he stared directly. He thought to memorize their faces, but that wasn't easy as the car lurched forward, ozone lingering in the air.

This would be a sweaty ride, too many bodies and too much heat. The car saw a lot of traffic in and out its door, and the motorman was handing out a lot of transfers. It was the end of another shopping day.

Sonntag braced for the viaduct, his nemesis every ride he took between his home and the downtown station. The car crawled out on its spindly trestle over the Menomonee River Valley, grinding slowly over thin air, tarred roofs below, warehouses, brewery buildings. He clutched the wicker seat ahead of him, and hung on until it was over and the land rushed up, and the car was on solid earth again. His armpits had sweated, darkening his white shirt, which clung to him beneath his gray suit. The uniform his detectives all wore.

The black leather boys didn't transfer to the West Allis car at the junction. The car was half empty now, heading ever westward toward the village of Wauwatosa. Fifty-sixth, his stop, approached. He rang, and headed for the door, only to discover all four of the leather brigade were rising from their seats as well. He wondered about it, but stepped out of the car after the door flapped open.

The route home took him along Wells another block, to Fifty-Seventh, which was a dead-end south of Wells. The black leather gents serenely followed, several paces back. He debated whether to turn onto his home street; whether by doing so he might put Lizbeth in peril. He debated whether to keep on walking on Wells, a well-traveled street. He thought maybe he was imagining things, but the foursome hung back and continued exactly at his own pace. He was not armed, save for a lunch bucket he well knew how to use effectively, and maybe that was a good thing. At Fifty-Seventh he simply stopped and waited.

The foursome slowed, smiled, and continued west on Wells Street. He watched them amble toward Hawley Road, and didn't turn toward home until they were well away.

It had not been an accidental encounter. And he got the message.

Chapter Thirteen

Wolf Yablonski lived in a white shiplap cottage with rambling yellow roses crawling up trellises, and a small bathtub Virgin in a bower. Sonntag had heard about bathtub shrines, but had not seen one before. The upended white bathtub was planted a couple feet into the ground, and a blue-clad porcelain Virgin occupied it.

Wolf was the president of the Machinists Union local. And also a national leader in the Socialist Labor Party. He called himself a Polish Catholic Socialist atheist, and a brother to all working brothers anywhere.

He answered instantly.

"Mister Yablonski, Milwaukee police. May we have a word with you?" Sonntag asked.

"Hell yes. I'm glad to see you. Cut around behind, and we'll sit in my back yard."

Somehow, that wasn't what Sonntag expected.

"A machinist with gardens," Silva said, as they cut across side lawn and discovered Yablonski putting pillows into wooden lawn chairs.

"I was kinda hoping you'd come around," Yablonski said. "You like my garden?"

Everywhere, a well curried garden bloomed. The flowers were traditional. Hollyhocks, petunias, nasturtiums, and whole carpets of roses in array.

"It's a fine garden, and makes me feel at peace," Sonntag said.

"Gardens are the salvation of the world," Yablonski said. "We build ugly factories, we tear the earth apart when we quarry for stone and oil and metals. We cut out our own hearts when we ruin the world in our mad quest for money. But gardens are our salvation. A poor man with a garden is rich. A rich man without flowers is starving."

"You do all this yourself?"

"I tried wives, and they don't bloom," he said. "Then I tried socialist poetry, and I still wrestle with it, but it doesn't catch the heart the way a fine scarlet rose does. I'll read some if you'd like."

Sonntag detected a wicked humor in the man, and shook his head.

"This is about the strike, right?"

"No, sir. We're concerned about your safety," Silva said.

"Oh, you've been listening to Stanley Argo," Yablonski said.

"Maybe you'd like to tell us what's cooking," Sonntag said.

"The strike, or the scabs, or the commies, or the mob?"

"All of it."

"First, what's your stake in it?"

"We try to protect lives, sir. Including yours."

"Oh, Stanley's been talking. He scares. He runs. He's probably hiding in the Bahamas."

"Do you want to tell us about this?" Sonntag asked.

"If I lose mine, sirs, I have asked to have my ashes spread here, in my gardens, so that a bit of me will bloom for the next generation, the people who come after me and inhabit this world we are desolating. We have to take a stand. My local is filled with fathers, skilled, hard-working men who aren't earning a fair wage. This postwar inflation never ceases; today's dime is tomorrow's nickel, and time is robbing us. We, the officers elected by these men, have been authorized by an open vote of the brothers to strike for a better wage, for a better pension when our bodies burden us, and as long as I feel the pulse of their will and commitment, sirs, I will hold fast; and so will our negotiators at the bargaining table, who carry within them the same passion. I am not expressing my will; I'm expressing a thousand-strong will, rooted in the blood and bones and brains of a thousand men and their families."

"But there are dangers," Silva said.

"You already know how. The way to break a strike, and a union, is to support the strikebreakers, and then take over the union when it runs out of funds."

"You call them strikebreakers; your brothers call them scabs."

"They are working-class men, like us, with families. They are the poor and lonely and desperate. They are my brothers too."

Joe Sonntag marveled.

"Okay, there's some worms in the apple, sir," Silva said.

"Fats Parvenu, perhaps?"

"What's he gonna do?"

"What he always does. Rally the strikebreakers, keep the factory humming, wait until the union's broke and the strikers are starving, offer a loan at mob juice rates, with his own men running the local. After that, cave in, settle for whatever the company wants, and fatten on union dues."

"And where is he now?"

"Nowhere."

"He's scared away your secretary," Sonntag said.

"Argo scared himself away."

"You answered your door when we rang without checking on us," Silva said.

"I'm sorry; it must be the poet in me."

"If it's not confidential, sir, where are you with the strike funds?"

"They're gone. We've gotten some voluntary donations from other union brothers, passing the hat."

"That's where Fats Parvenu wants you, right?"

"If it's Fats. There are other shadows falling across our path."

"Such as?"

"Management."

"Trying to break the union?" Silva asked.

"How do you break a union, officer? No, there are armies moving in the night."

"Perhaps you could explain that, Mr. Yablonski," Sonntag said.

"How do you explain phantasmagorias, officer?"

"I need something real, sir."

"I return over and over to the life and fate of Leon Trotsky, officer. He wanted worldwide revolution; Stalin wanted revolution in one country, the Soviet Union. An attempt was made on Trotsky's life in Mexico. It failed. Then a Spaniard, Ramon Mercador, calling himself Frank Jackson, found a welcome in Trotsky's inner circle and beat him to death with an alpenstock."

Sonntag pondered that. "Has any Frank Jackson come visiting you, Mister Yablonski?"

"Men with assumed names, you mean? Several. A man called Joseph Ginger paid me a visit. So did a man named Anders Gropius."

"Not the same man?"

"Totally different."

"Could you identify them if we showed you some photos?"

"Probably, sir."

Silva returned to the president's strange topic: "Are you a Trotskyite?"

"The Socialist Workers Party believes in One Big Strike, nationwide, to bring capital to its knees. That makes us the Trotskyites of Organized Labor."

"I am fascinated, sir. Your union is straying away from the CIO?"

"Not at all. Some of the unions have Red leaders; others don't. Walter Reuther is not a Red at all. We're mostly socialists. But there's some Reds around."

"But there's a struggle? The Communists against the socialists?" Silva asked.

"Always that, sir."

"And you sense there's a jurisdictional contest here?"

Wolf Yablonski yawned. It was almost as if he had lost interest. Or grew tired of explaining the rivalries and ambitions of various labor organizations.

"So who shot the scab?" Silva asked, suddenly.

"The name given in the papers was Joseph L. Ginger. Fat chance, eh?"

"Where do we start looking, Mr. Yablonski?"

"See this beautiful garden? A sea of roses, and a carpet of blooms. But under the blooms there are bugs that suck juices, worms, leaf-eating insects, parasites that use these blooms as hosts. Beetles and slugs and worms and caterpillars. Start there."

"Who are the guys in leather jackets?" Sonntag asked.

"They are called stewards."

"Your guys?"

"The brotherhood is striking. There is a need for discipline. Our people can get out of hand. The ones in the jackets are young members, performing a service."

"Pretty warm for leather," Silva said.

"Not in the evenings, officer."

"Are these guys entirely from your brotherhood?" Sonntag asked.

"I understand they roughed you up," Yablonski said.

"Who are they?"

"I don't know, entirely. There's a thousand of us."

"I'll want their names, Mr. Yablonski. You'll supply them?"

"I see this little visit is no longer friendly," he said.

"That's entirely up to you," Sonntag said.

Silva was getting restless. He was perched on the edge of his lawn chair, ready to land on something or other.

"Let's get back to the Trotsky thing. Someone wants this local. Or at least wants you Socialists out of the way. So who's pushing?"

"Fats Parvenu's girlfriend."

"Who's she?"

"A Molly Maguire."

Silva was grinning, but Sonntag couldn't imagine why.

"Nice made-up name. It fits. What's her real name?" Silva asked.

"I don't know. Her name is Anastasia. I know the name of her weapon. A thirty-two caliber Smith and Wesson. She's offered to protect me. She says I need someone around."

"Protect from?"

"I think when she gets the word, she'll shoot me. She says she's Fats' girlfriend, but she's not. She's one of those female radicals floating around organized labor."

Sonntag sighed. "Frank, fill me in. I'm over my head."

"Molly Maguires were radical coal miners in the last century."

"I'm still lost."

"We're all lost, officer. A Molly Maguire would just as soon point her gun at me as she'd point it at management."

"Could you call us when she's around? We'd like to learn a little about her."

"I once knew an Anastasia," Frank said softly.

Yablonski rose suddenly. He was a burly man, with great biceps, an Atlas dwarfing his back yard. "No, sir. That's our fight, not yours. You may, if you choose, see about the mob, but the rest isn't your business. See my garden? There's red roses and pink roses. They're all the same to me, making a beautiful new world, if not today, then tomorrow. If red and pink struggle, it's none of your business. The mob, on the other hand, might be your business. Fats Parvenu might well interest you. It's been a fine afternoon, and much was accomplished."

He plucked a pocket knife from his cavernous pants, sliced a bright red rosebud from its prickly stem, and handed it to Frank Silva.

"A token of solidarity," he said, and then slowly crowded them around the side of his cottage, toward their Nash Rambler.

"What does she look like?" Frank said.

"She's the most ravishing woman ever to walk the good earth," Wolf Yablonski replied. "You should see her red fingernails coiled around the grip of a revolver."

"We'll stop back with some photos," Sonntag said.

"I'm not sure I could identify anyone at all," Yablonski said.

Sonntag climbed in, and Silva joined him.

"I think that's the first time since I became a cop that I've been herded like a cow," he said.

"And confined to a few squares on the chess board," Silva said. "There are no enemies on the left; rivals, differing visions, but not an enemy off your left shoulder."

"But he told us the story of Trotsky, killed by Soviet agents. And he thought his Socialist Workers Party was the Trotsky of labor."

"Joe, I'm a socialist. There are disputes but no enemies on the left. There are competing visions, but solidarity is the thing. Get it? A united front. The Commies spend fortunes cobbling united fronts."

"Well, damn," Sonntag said. "His new girlfriend has a revolver. And revolvers point in any direction."

"Joe, take my word for it."

But Joe didn't. The struggles of various leftwing groups was as murderous as any other struggles. That was Frank, for you, he thought.

They headed east, slid into Milwaukee, and into a world that made more sense to Joe Sonntag. He never had any particular passion working on him, and couldn't fathom people who seemed the slaves of their ideologies.

"What do you think?" he asked.

"I think Wolf Yablonski can take care of himself."

"Okay, who wants him out?"

"Management, the mob, maybe the Communists."

"And how do we untangle it?"

"We don't," Silva said. "It will untangle itself."

Sonntag felt oddly helpless. There are times when the police watch things unfold, knowing that trouble is looming and yet without power to prevent trouble. Mostly, cops don't enter the picture until after a crime is committed, or is about to be. He liked Yablonski, but felt a certain foreboding. Something bad would happen to the Machinists local president. That was his gut talking, and he hoped he was wrong. Maybe Yablonski would lose office; maybe worse was in store.

"Were we talking to a dead man, Frank?" he asked.

"It's the other way around, Joe. He's our prime suspect right now."

"How do you figure?"

"He owns the leather jackets. He owns the ones who jumped you when you found a bullet casing. They took that casing out of your pocket. He owns the ones who gave you a warning on and off your streetcar. He's the only one who doesn't want cops looking closely at what's coming down the pike. And the names we're wrestling with were familiar to him."

"Aw, Frank, no man who raises red and gold and yellow and pink roses like that, and gardens like that, could be guilty of anything more than misplaced idealism."

"Try that out on the great and sensitive artist, Adolph Hitler," Frank said.

Chapter Fourteen

The county buried the dead man. The police had photographs and a fine artistic rendering of the man as he would have looked before his face was destroyed. Who he was remained a mystery. The only thing Sonntag was sure of was that he wasn't Joseph L. Ginger, who was still missing in action. The case was growing cold.

For some odd reason, Sonntag thought to attend the burial. He had no reason other than that he saw the dead man as a person, alive with dreams and hopes; a person who had parents and grandparents, maybe a spouse and children too. He thought he must be weak in the head to ride out to that plot in the county cemetery and pay his respects.

"I'm going to the burial," he told Captain Ackerman.

"Then work overtime to make it up," Ackerman said. "Sometimes I don't know about you."

He caught the 27th Street car south to the Woodlawn cemetery, and found the place. Potter's fields were invariably in the rearmost corners. Two cemetery gravediggers were filling in the dirt when he arrived. The morgue attendants had already come and gone. It was an indifferent day, with cirrus clouds ribbing the sky and a dry breeze curling through the tree-patched burial ground. There would be no headstone; only a small concrete marker with the date of death and Unknown scraped into it.

He wasn't alone. A striking woman stood in the shade of a crabapple tree, a bouquet of yellow roses in her hand. He hadn't noticed her at first. She had stood quietly, fifty yards off, watching the gravediggers finish the burial. But there she was.

Sonntag could barely keep himself from trotting over there and grilling her. He wrestled with himself for a while, and finally compelled himself to wait and see, to discover whether she was connected to this grave and this unknown man, and above all, not to scare her off or drive her into silence.

His mind raced through the possibilities. She knew the dead. She knew his name. She was a relative. She was a wife. She was just a morbid woman wandering around among the dead. He had seen a few of those, people who embraced cemeteries communing with the lost, people who lived among the dead.

Still, he eyed her furtively. She wore a wide-brimmed straw hat, and had rich brunette hair, and was dressed in a summer suit, an open white blouse, and a simple necklace of some sort. She was eyeing him, but not overtly, just as he was eyeing her. She was a handsome woman; he was too far distant to learn anything else about her.

So he watched the gravediggers push brown clay over the pine box, thought about the mysterious life that had ended a few yards outside of the factory gate, and finally, when the diggers were done, except for putting sod down later, he pulled off his old fedora. He didn't have any words for the unknown. He just stood there, offering a moment of respect, and a moment of notice. Let the man's spirit know that someone in the lonely universe cared. That's all he could offer.

The diggers loaded up their wheelbarrow and walked away. They would be back with sod sometime. Sonntag thought that the woman would make her move soon, so he simply stepped back and waited.

And she waited.

He walked over to her. She was lovely, a wry smile on her face.

"If you want to decorate the grave, don't let me stop you," he said.

"If you want to leave, I won't stop you," she retorted.

"I didn't expect anyone to come here, for this," he said.

"The police would be watching, wouldn't they?"

He wasn't wearing a uniform. People always glanced at him and knew.

"Not watching. I came on an impulse. Someone's son died and is being buried."

"Maybe someone's husband, too?"

"Yours?"

"No, not mine."

"Maybe someone's brother," he said.

She pondered that. "In a way, yes, a brother."

"No man is an island," he said.

"John Donne," she replied. "No man is an island entire of itself; every man

"is a piece of the continent, a part of the main;

"if a clod be washed away by the sea, Europe

"is the less, as well as if a promontory were, as

"well as a manor of thy friends or of thine

"own were; any man's death diminishes me,

"because I am involved in mankind.

"And therefore never send to know for whom

"the bell tolls; it tolls for thee."

She finished with that wry smile and a gaze so direct it intrigued him.

"There," he said, "a brother."

"I will leave my roses and go now," she said.

He was uncertain whether they were Wolf Yabonski's roses, but he thought that was a distinct possibility.

She hastened to the grave, laid the roses tenderly on the naked clay at the head, stood for a few moments, and stepped back.

She started away, and turned to him. "No, I won't give you my name. No, this was not a person whose name I know. But you know something? You don't need to know a name to know a person. You need to know a life. This life here, cut short a few days ago, was a life devoted to the brothers and sisters who want a better world. So forget the name. He probably had several. Look to his works; look to the legacy he left for us."

"What is his legacy, ma'am?"

The wry smile appeared again. "I like cops," she said. "Don't change that."

He watched her walk away, walk under tree-shaded rows of tombs, past headstones, through shadows and sunlight. She never looked back. Never sought to know whether he was tailing her.

He didn't. He was halfway in love.

In a distant parking lot he saw a light colored car crawl away.

Did Wolf Yablonski say the woman was Fats Parvenu's friend? Fats didn't deserve her. She didn't deserve Fats.

The roses were fresh and bright on the grave. In a while they would wilt but the memory of them would always be bright in his mind.

It was a long ride in two orange streetcars back to the station house. He would put in some spare time on Saturday, even though he and Lizbeth had planned a country drive to the cheese factories west of Milwaukee, one of their favorite summer adventures.

Who was she? He sensed that she was the key; if he knew what she knew, he could cut this Gordian knot. He sensed that she didn't know the name of the buried man, but he had been valuable to her cause, so valuable that she came to pay her respects to the stranger.

When he returned to the station house, he described the whole episode to Frank Silva.

"There's a female breed I'll call Red Molly" Frank said, "and I think she's one. Believe me, I know. She's a True Believer; she'll fight the good fight every way she can— mind, heart and any other asset she may have."

"So does that insight help us solve a crime and lock a murderer?"

Silva grinned. "Maybe it's time to put this into cold storage. We're sitting on about fifty other cases."

"This one gets to me," Sonntag said. "I'm wasting my tax-paid time."

"Yeah, you could say that. I'm the one who should be obsessed. I'm the boy radical."

"Why aren't you?"

"No enemy on the left," he said.

"Nothing makes any sense to me," Sonntag said, "but there are two people I want to talk to; Parvenu and his girlfriend. And maybe some more with Wolf Yablonski."

"You mind if I assign myself to some other case, or two?"

That took Sonntag aback. Frank Silva was the Rottweiler of the detectives. It didn't matter whether he liked or disliked the victim, or who the suspects were; if there was a case to be solved, he sunk his teeth into it and didn't let go. Until now.

"You got a good reason?"

"No, no good reason."

Silva stared, waiting, his gaze unwavering.

Sonntag wrestled with it, and finally surrendered. "Yeah, you can see who stole the hubcaps."

"I was thinking of quitting the force."

Sonntag could hardly believe he had heard it from his top man.

"Before you pull out, would you mind briefing me? I don't have a handle on any of this. You're the closest I've got to an expert. So, try a theory out on me."

"I don't have any."

Sonntag stared. "Sure, you can work on other stuff, Frank. But there's one thing you gotta do first. You come out to my place this evening for beer and bratwurst and some potato salad in my back yard. Okay?"

"It's a weekday."

"I'll drive you over to the Cudahy streetcar after."

Silva stared, and then nodded. He sure as hell was solemn.

"I'll call Lizbeth," Sonntag said.

He dialed, but Lizbeth wasn't in. He tried a half hour later, without results. One of her Mending Club days maybe. He knew a deli on State Street where he could get all the stuff. He looked up the number, left an order to pick up at four.

Just at quitting time he got through to Lizbeth, told her what was brewing, asked her to get some beer and he'd bring the rest.

"Joe, he's a sweetie. Bring him over and we'll stuff him," she said.

He found Silva staring out a grimy window. "You want to come with me?" he asked.

"No, I can't stand to see you wet your pants going over the viaduct. I'll come along after a couple of cars."

That suited Sonntag. He couldn't stand to see himself white-knuckle it over that trestle.

An hour later he arrived at the 57th Street bungalow, loaded with their supper.

"So what inspired this?" Lizbeth asked.

"Silva's thinking of quitting the force."

"Why?"

"I hope to find out."

"The Allis Chalmers strike."

"More like an ex-girlfriend or gal he knows is the prime suspect in that homicide."

"That shouldn't slow someone like Silva down."

"There's stuff in his head, Lizbeth. Maybe a couple of beers'll shake it loose."

"It just doesn't sound like him, unless it's the love of his life he's thinking pulled the trigger."

"It could be, and for reasons he agrees with entirely, babe."

"Life's a crock, right?"

It was only then that he kissed her. "Thanks for doing this on short notice," he said.

"All I did was clean the toilet bowl."

She had taken the stuff in hand, inspected it severely, being a stickler for good food. She tasted the potato salad, grimaced, and set to work doctoring it with boiled eggs and chives and stuff. But she was smiley, and he knew this evening would make her day.

He got the charcoal ignited, and settled back to wait for Silva, who waited two cars and got the third, which put him a half hour behind. But he did show up, as solemn and duty-bound as he had been down at the station house.

"Oh, Frank, I'm so happy you came!" Lizbeth said, and planted a kiss on Silva's cheek.

The young detective seemed embarrassed, almost as if this were an ordeal to get past, and not a happy social occasion. Joe opened a can of Schlitz for Frank, built a Manhattan for Lizbeth, and poured his usual bourbon, all the while watching Frank settle in melancholy silence out in the back yard.

It was odd how silently the evening progressed, with Sonntag quietly grilling the meat and sipping his bourbon. Lizbeth tried to rev up some sort of conversation, switching from gossip to politics to movies, and finally gave up.

"Hey, Frank, you ready for another brat?" she asked.

He nodded, and she forked a sizzling sausage into a lightly braised bun, added some sliced onion, and handed it to him on a paper plate. He smiled, sipped his third bottle of Schlitz, and seemed to sink even lower into his lawn chair.

"Pretty soon there'll be so much light around here we won't see the stars anymore," she said desperately.

"Factories are dragons that eat up the natural world," Frank said.

It was virtually the first thing he had said of consequence.

"They eat up our world of people, too," she said. "Nothing's the same. I grew up in a different time, and I'm not even old."

Joe Sonntag watched Frank nibble on the bratwurst, which he plainly didn't want, and thought the evening was a bust.

"I'm bad company tonight. I'm sorry," Silva said.

"You're always good company, Frank. You don't need to say a word. We're just glad to have you here. We don't see enough of you," Lizbeth said.

"I think I was engaged to the woman who shot Ginger, or whatever his name was," Silva said.

That stopped everything.

"Her name was Anastasia Ryan, and I'm pretty sure she's the same woman whose a friend of Wolf Yablonski, and the same woman you saw in the cemetery," Silva said.

"How do you know that?" Sonntag asked.

"She's a radical, and it's a long story," Silva said. "John Dunne was her favorite poet."

Chapter Fifteen

Frank Silva leaked sadness. He stared at his Schlitz, stared into the hollow heavens, and finally focused on Joe and Lizbeth.

"You know, before the war, I was an activist. Hell, a firebrand. In my teens. I was going to heal the world. Everything was wrong, and it was the whole economic system that was wrecking us. The Depression. Wrecking the lives of working people, the poor and humble, the sick and wounded and desperate. Just wrecking it. You know most of that. My father, the socialist alderman. I stood on street corners and handed out tracts. Socialist Labor Party. Change the world. One Big Strike."

He sipped some beer, almost as if he wanted it to loosen his tongue, lubricate the words so they could slide out of him.

"She's older, you know. I wasn't even out of school when she found me. She's about ten years older, and probably a Communist now. I'm not sure of it. We sense these things. She wasn't when I knew her, but she was what do they call it? A fellow traveler. She was a lady who wanted to change the world, and was willing to pitch her life into the task, no matter what."

"Anastasia Ryan?" Joe asked.

"Anastasia. But she may have a different last name now. "

"I guess she inspired you," Lizbeth said.

Frank smiled. "She, ah, taught me about life."

"I think I'm getting it," Lizbeth said.

"She found me, saw that I was material for her causes, and sort of took me in. She lived on the north side. I don't know how she supported herself. So we went there and her flat was full of books and literature and petitions. I, well, sort of fell for her, and she let me. I was too young and heated up too much to know I was being recruited."

"Recruited?"

"She thought I'd be valuable to the party. That was all she talked about. Changing the world. Revolution, not reform. Throw out everything. She told me she'd started as a reformer, and saw that it didn't work; you couldn't fight the money and the power that way. You couldn't be a socialist. You couldn't be a liberal. You couldn't be a Labor Union leader to get it done. You had to start something big, like taking over a whole country. That's what she told me."

"A firebrand," Joe said.

"An idealist. A dreamer. She loved all of mankind. That's why she loved the John Dunne poem. She wanted every living soul to be part of the whole."

"Even if it meant killing people– like the Bolsheviks?"

"She never let it slow her down."

"So, what happened? What broke you two apart?" Lizbeth asked.

"I might have been a kid, but I didn't believe in that. And I knew I was being recruited; that the times we, ah, when she was teaching me, as she put it, she wasn't really interested in the boy, Frank Silva. She wanted to throw my father, the alderman, to the dogs. Also, there were other, older men. She had several. I figured that out. Sometimes she flatly told me to get lost. I saw her a few times with older men."

"By older, you mean her age, Frank?"

"When you're a boy, any adult male is older. Yeah, her age. She was thirty or so."

"And she's still around Milwaukee?"

"I hear of her now and then. In socialist meetings. She's around. And what she's doing with Wolf Yablonski, who is, like he says, a Trotsky type, is bad."

"You know why she showed up at the grave? If that's her?"

"Okay, you won't believe me, but I'll say it. To pay respects to the man she killed."

Neither Lizbeth nor Joe Sonntag could think of a thing to say.

"Okay, now I'd like to go home, and thanks for the evening," Silva said.

"Frank– is this just a hunch?"

"Just forget I said it."

"But why would she kill someone?"

"You don't know people like this. You live out here in a quiet, pleasant neighborhood. There's not many people around here that work on a factory floor. You don't get into politics. You don't know about hot-tempered people. You don't know about people who sit in a café and talk, or go to regular meetings to hear lectures, or get organizers in, or hand out sheets on corners, or spend evenings planning to change the whole planet. You don't know about women who wear their hair long, or guys in beards, or guys who won't shave with one brand of razor, or gals who boycott some brands. You don't know what it's like to plan to burn down a church or a warehouse. Or rob a bank to get money, and teach the crooked bankers a thing or two. You just live here, and don't see any of it."

"I guess I don't," Sonntag said.

"Who would she kill?" Lizbeth asked. "Why kill a scab walking out of a plant?"

"Is she even trained?" Sonntag asked.

"I don't know," Silva said. "I don't know anything. But if there's someone who's betraying one of her causes, or who's ready to blab, talk to authorities, switch to some other side, yes, she would. Anastasia Ryan, whatever her name is now, would do it. And do it over and over. There's a type driven by ideals, and for them the means justifies the end. Kill someone to protect the revolution."

"But a friend of Wolf Yablonski's?"

"A friend of Trotsky killed Trotsky."

"Where would we find her?"

"Yablonski said she's a friend of Fats Parvenu."

"That's a twist. Why a mobster?"

"A friend of Trotsky killed Trotsky. A friend of a mobster might kill the mobster. Then again, mobsters are useful. A woman like Anastasia might have all sorts of reasons to snuggle up with a man whose little army can pull triggers."

"Frank, are you just playing with ideas, with theories?"

"It's in my bones, Joe."

"Why would she mess with a union president? Or a mobster?"

"Ask her."

"How do you feel about her?" Lizbeth asked.

Silva smiled. "I never got over her. I'm the same as I was when I was a boy, and she took me home, and the next thing I knew, I was in a different world, and nothing I grew up with made sense to me, and everything I learned in high school was no good, the dead past, and all my virtues were vices, and she was so beautiful, so wise, so bright, that she was like a rising sun. If you could hear her voice, if you could listen to her even for one minute, you'd know."

Then a silence thickened.

"Frank, I'll put you on another case," Joe said. "I don't want you tearing yourself to pieces."

"I need to go now. I'll catch a car."

"Owl car, once an hour. No, I don't want you standing at the stop for most of an hour. I'm driving you," Joe said.

"I need to be alone."

"I'm driving, and I won't ask you one question. You'll be as alone as I can make it."

Silva nodded, and sagged. Joe thought he'd never seen a man so lonely among friends.

He cranked the starter over, and fired up the Hudson coupe. The three could squeeze in, but Lizbeth elected to stay home. Frank climbed in, some sort of wall around him, and stared into the city as Joe drove along State Street, through pale-lit hinterlands where nothing was built and no one lived. It wasn't terribly late; after eleven. The city thickened and aged as Sonntag shifted gears from one stoplight to the next. It was a quiet city, where hard-working men and women fell into their beds after another day's labor. Milwaukee didn't have much night life; it did have some good restaurants, like Mader's or the John Ernst Café. He cut south, crossed Wisconsin Avenue, and found an orange car waiting. Frank wouldn't have to stand in the darkness.

"Joe? I ended up a cop. I almost ended up throwing Molotov cocktails. She did that to me. And you know what else? This is going to be the longest and loneliest thirty-block streetcar ride I ever was on."

"Frank, I'm half in love with her just from meeting her at the cemetery."

Frank clapped a hand to Joe's shoulder, and eased out of the coupe.

Joe watched him enter the bright-lit car and find a seat. Then he eased the coupe into gear, and drove back through the deepening night. Not much ever happened late at night in Milwaukee–except the murder of a strikebreaker.

He sensed that Silva would be back on the case soon. And his insights into Anastasia Ryan would be the most valuable asset the police had.

Lizbeth was waiting for him, curled up in a living room chair. "What did he say?" she asked.

"You mean, confession in the Hudson as we drove down State Street?"

"He opened up, I know he did."

"All he said was that he almost ended up throwing Molotov cocktails because of her."

"That's how cops are," she said.

"Some of us. Not me."

"He still loves her, a dozen years later."

"Not love. He was a boy; she took him into another world. A boy's in a prison at a certain age. He's full of needs and yearnings, and he's half crazy, and most of us manage to keep the lid on for a while, anyway. But Frank met a woman, she lit all the fuses."

"I hate that woman. Don't tell me you didn't fall for her in the cemetery."

"Do you know what a cop is thinking? Why is she there? Who is she? Did she blow that guy away? Did she know the victim? That's what I was thinking."

"Bullshit, Joe."

He stared at her, amazed.

"There was an attraction," he said, finally.

That was all she needed; a confession.

"Throw away the key," she said.

She rose, switched off the light, and headed for bed, and this time it was Sonntag who was sitting in the dark, wondering why his quarry was a woman, and wondering what had set off Lizbeth.

But when he finally did crawl between the sheets, in the dark, she was wide awake.

"That kind of woman," she said, out of the blue, "doesn't shoot people. She entices others to do it. She works on men; gets them to do her bidding."

"Lizbeth, we're ahead of ourselves. There is no evidence at all connecting this woman to any killing."

"But she caused it. I know she did."

"I won't argue with you. All I know is that she showed up with some roses. She did know who was being buried and when."

"That's all you need! That's it. It was someone she cared about and had to shoot because the party ordered it."

"What party?"

"You know how they are, the Reds. She's one. She'd shoot her own mother if they asked her. Look at Frank. He barely escaped."

"Lizbeth..."

"Don't Lizbeth me. She's a killer on the loose, and it doesn't matter whether she pulled the trigger or had someone else do it, and it doesn't matter if her motives are lofty and she wants to reform the world."

"I don't quite get it."

"Here's what you need to do. You need to track her down. She's active in all sorts of those fronts. She doesn't live in the shadows. Lots of people know her, including that president of the local. She has a history, and you need to find out about it, right down to the last pamphlet. I just know if you unlock her, you unlock this case. You figure her out, and you'll figure who killed that strikebreaker and why."

"Wow," he said, and tried to go to sleep.

She subsided, and soon enough he heard the soft breath of her oblivion.

It was an odd thing, this nibbling at the heels of a woman who probably had nothing to do with any shooting anywhere. If he were to set priorities, he'd put the woman on the bottom of his list. At the top, just then, would be some talking with the temporaries who knew Ginger, or whatever name he used, people who knew what he talked about, who he was seen with, things like that. But now there was this mysterious woman, lurking there, this woman with a Russian and Irish name. If that was her name.

By the time he awakened, the need raged in him. He would make her top priority. It didn't make sense. Anastasia Ryan was a chimera, and he knew it. But sometimes an investigator had to let his instincts rule him. If she was local, he'd track her from grade school up. Everyone had a history, and sometimes a history could reveal the future. But he wished he weren't so damned obsessed with her.

Chapter Sixteen

But she didn't exist. Sonntag tried the phone company, the electric company, the city directory, the school system, the drivers license bureau, and the banks. He called Wolf Yablonski and ran into a wall:

"No, I won't give you the name. You'll track her down, but not through me."

"She's not a suspect, Mr. Yablonski. We think she knows a lot about politics, and we want her help," he said.

"Look, cop, she's my friend. Leave her alone."

"You said once she was Fats Parvenu's girlfriend."

"I did? I must be crazy. I wouldn't let Fats Parvenu's girlfriend into my garden."

"Why did you say it, then?"

"I like monkeying with cops," he replied.

"Well, you're right. We're going to find her, and we're going to talk with her. I want to know why she visited the grave of the strikebreaker. You're right about that."

"You're looking in the wrong places," Yablonski said. "She's like a saint. You want to know who she is? Think Dorothy Day."

Yablonski hung up suddenly.

That last intrigued Sonntag. It was as if he was offering a clue, and also wanted Sonntag to look at her in a different way. There was something about Wolf Yablonski that caught Sonntag's interest. The man had a rose garden.

Sonntag sat at his grubby desk, oppressed by the odors of the station. Nearby, a couple of burglars were being booked. They stank, and not just of fear. The atmosphere smelled of cigars and fear in that station house. He thought maybe it all traced back to Captain Ackerman. Move Ackerman to some other station, and there'd be fresh air in downtown Milwaukee.

Sonntag spotted Frank Silva at his desk, doing paperwork.

"Who's Dorothy Day?" he asked.

"Go to the library and find out," Silva said.

Frank Silva was sure not cooperating. Sonntag was ticked. "Maybe I will," he said.

But Silva softened. "Catholic radical. Founded workers communes. Member of Industrial Workers of the World, Wobblies to you. Marxist and anarchist, but also a believer in Catholic morals, social ethics, all that. Like maybe Anastasia Ryan?"

"Like Wolf Yablonski. He's the one with the bathtub Virgin."

Silva was grinning. "Embezzlement's less messy," he said. "I've got a bookkeeper who's lifted eleven thousand dollars to buy porcelain dolls. You try the Catholic schools?"

Sonntag stared. He had only consulted with public schools.

"Thanks, Frank," he said.

An hour later he connected. Holy Angels Academy, on the near south side, had a student named Anastasia Ryan in 1923, 1924, and 1925, when she was kicked out for reasons not on the record.

Anastasia Ryan was the daughter of a boilermaker named Michael Ryan, and his wife, Natasha Lubitch. She left at the end of her junior year.

The white pages listed an M. Ryan in the fifteen hundred block of West Holt.

A woman answered the phone. "Allo, allo," she said.

"Is this Mrs. Ryan. Mrs. Michael Ryan?"

"What do you want, eh?"

"I'm looking for your daughter Anastasia."

"You don't say that name, not around me."

"Ma'am, I'm detective Sonntag, Milwaukee Police, and I'd like to come talk with you about your daughter."

"She is no more welcome."

"Ah, you mean passed away?"

"I would not know. You got it?"

"Mrs. Ryan, I'm very glad I found you. I'm wondering if I could stop by, or if we could meet in a park somewhere, or a tea shop."

"What is this?"

"Well, I'd like to find out what she knows about unions in Milwaukee. Labor, thing like that. I think she could be very helpful to us."

She remained silent for so long he feared he'd lost her.

"I make some tea," she said.

"Twenty minutes, half hour," he said.

He checked out the oldest cruiser in the lot, A Nash Ambassador, the decals painted over. It started hard. He knew a bakery on south Sixth, and headed that way, bought some strawberry tarts from a blue-eyed Slovak blonde, and ground south through the sweaty south side, where humble bungalows jostled with gilded churches, and every other corner had its own tavern, the parlor of each neighborhood.

The place on Holt was sandwiched between a carpet store and a coal and ice dealer, and set well back from the rotting sidewalk. He parked in front of two boys with a Kool Aid stand.

"Hey, cop, want some?"

"Here's a dime; keep it and give the drink to the dogs."

"Smartass cop," the kid said. "Leftovers go to our parakeet."

Mrs. Ryan opened at once, admired the tarts, and led him into a dark room, shades drawn tight against the heat. He knew he'd soon be sweating. She was in her eighties, but bright-eyed and a little wary.

The tea was very good, spiced in some fashion, and the tarts were perfect. There was a tea ritual to go through before he could ask anything of her, but he sensed she was rapidly relaxing, and would soon be open to anything.

"I got your name from the school records over at Holy Angels," he said.

"Long time ago," she replied. "She was sweet then, but full of ideas. The sisters, they didn't like her ideas and punished her, sometimes real hard, yardstick across the hands, like that. How come you want to talk about her?"

"It's about the strike at Allis-Chalmers," he said. "She would know all about that, we think."

"What is there to know?"

"The politics. There's the Machinists Union, there's management, there's the hired temporary people, there's some efforts by a mobster to meddle."

"She wouldn't know nothing about any of that. She's far away—her mind, it's not here."

"She's not sane?"

"Just far away, sir. Just over in the darkness."

Sonntag eyed the old lady, who nibbled on a strawberry tart, and waited patiently. The room was stuffy, with light and air barricaded at the windows. The furnishings appeared to have been there forever.

"You live alone?" he asked.

"I am widow."

"You came from abroad?"

"Ukraine, but my name confuses people. There are names that fit the people, and names that don't."

"Anastasia is your daughter?"

"Was."

"You married Mr. Ryan here?"

"I didn't want to, but he made me."

"I'm curious, I guess. How could he do that?"

"He get me pregnant and then say, ha! Got you."

"But it worked out?"

"I can see you know nothing about women."

"But you raised your daughter?"

"He raised her. Me, I'm Orthodox, him, he's a heretic, and he put her in a convent school and now look at her."

"Well, yes, what's she like now?"

"I don't want to know. Every bad thought got stuck in her head and didn't come out."

"Bad thoughts?"

"You don't know a thing about my people."

"I hear she left Holy Angels before her senior year."

"Left! You mean pushed out, door slams, she's laughing at the sisters. Frankly, so am I."

"She was wild?"

"Wild? Nah, that's not it. She was real quiet, studious, peaceful. She was something else: she was full of ideas. The sisters would say, you must believe in God, and she'd say there is none. The sisters would say, you got to be moral, and she'd say, there isn't any. The sisters would say, communism is bad, and she'd say, that's what makes it interesting. The sisters would say, you'll be punished in hell, and she'd say, when I'm dead I'm dead, and there isn't any."

"So they refused to teach her?"

"Oh, they tried. Say a hundred Our Fathers, stay an hour after school, change your mind or fail, you know, stuff."

"What did she do?"

"She started meeting boys secretly. Any boy would do. She became very worldly. She knew all about everything before any girl in her class knew anything. The sisters caught her teaching other girls about stuff, you know, stuff like that."

"You see her now, Mrs. Ryan?"

"Nah, I told her to go away, never come back. She's a Communist. My family, my family's in Siberian camps, my family's been murdered, and she's a Communist. It's like she's come out of hell to torment me, and enjoy seeing her uncles and aunts and grandparents sent away and never heard from again. So, I will not see her."

"Do you think she's rebelling against you?"

The old woman sat quietly, pondering it. "Nah, she's like her father. If there's a law or a rule or a barrier, she wants to beat it. No rules! He was like that."

"You think she's still in Milwaukee?"

"I think so."

"We'd like to talk to her. Have you any ideas?"

"Lock her up. She's no good."

"Ah, have you any photos of her we might borrow?"

"Borrow! I'll give you it and count my blessings."

She set down her teacup and headed for a room at the rear of the flat. But then she turned and gestured. "Cop, come back here, I'll show you her room."

Sonntag followed her down a dim hallway. In the rearmost corner was a small bedroom, heavily shaded, so dimly lit he could hardly make out what was there. A twin bed dominated it, and a small dresser.

"This is where she turn herself from good daughter to madwoman."

She plucked a formal portrait of a girl from the dresser. It was a black and white school photo, the young woman in a Holy Angels dark jumper and white blouse, a small crucifix at her neck. He studied it, trying to find some semblance to the woman he encountered at the cemetery.

"She was about fifteen?"

"Yes, and you can already see it, the evil eye."

She looked simply like a teen-aged girl to Sonntag.

Two stuffed dolls rested on the bed, one a Raggedy Andy, the other a Raggedy Annie.

"She laughed at them. She laughed at girls who played with dolls. She called this one Immaculata, and that one Pope Pius."

Sonntag smiled. That did sound like a young rebel.

He left the Holt Avenue flat no closer to locating Anastasia Ryan than before, and yet he knew more about her, maybe some things that would be helpful along the way. She might have been a wild teen, in full-bore rebellion against the sisters and the church, but now she was probably a disciplined member of a conspiratorial party. She would have to do as she was bidden by the party bosses, and toe the party line. He wondered about that; the leap from rebel to virtual slave.

But he also wondered if Anastasia Ryan was the same person who saw Wolf Yablonski; the same woman who said her goodbye to a scab at the cemetery. He sure couldn't tell from the teenage photo.

As long as he was on the south side, he thought maybe to find Fats Parvenu, or whoever it was at the sawed up house that was owned by Anders Gropius, or maybe it was Dimitri Karl. He worked west a few blocks, in comfortable old neighborhoods where everyone knew everyone.

The house had been spruced up. Sonntag parked across the street, noting the new window trim, concrete walkways, and rain gutters. The steps leading up to the front porch had been enameled. Somehow, the place oozed importance in that dowdy neighborhood. He was in no hurry, so he settled back and watched the somnolent house as it baked in afternoon sunlight.

And then he was rewarded. A woman emerged, carrying a purse. She headed toward the street, while he watched, and then she turned east, walking briskly. She wore a straw hat that shadowed her face, but he could see this was an older woman, her hair streaked with gray, her figure thicker than the woman at the cemetery. Her clothing was almost Old Worldly, the hem of her skirts well down on her calf. Sonntag called it a practical dress, not the fashionable one worn by the woman at the cemetery. He couldn't see her features. He couldn't compare her to the portrait lying in the seat beside him.

He ignited the engine, managed a u-turn, and crawled past her as she walked east. There would be a streetcar stop two blocks ahead, and on impulse he headed for it, and parked just a few yards from it in the deep shade of an elm tree. He settled deep in the seat, and waited for her to trot by, which she did soon enough. She was somewhere in her middle years, dark haired, possibly old enough to be Fats Parvenu's mother. She wore decidedly unattractive white stockings, which rose out of very practical lace-up shoes. Definitely not the cemetery woman. She didn't notice him or pay any heed to the nondescript black car.

She didn't have long to wait. A northbound orange streetcar squealed to a stop, the door flapped open, and she stepped in. He watched her settle into a seat midway back as the car whined its way north, carrying a woman known by mobster Fats Parvenu.

Chapter Seventeen

Sonntag wanted to talk to the temporaries on the shift with the dead Joseph Ginger, as he was known to them. But that proved to be more difficult than it seemed at first. The company didn't want production slowed down by pulling men off the line for questioning. Catching them before or after the shift wouldn't gain him anything. All they wanted was to get into the plant or go home.

The best bet was their half-hour lunch break, at eight at night. He told Lizbeth not to wait up, and drove over to the Allis-Chalmers tractor gate, where the gateman let him through, past the usual sullen Machinist Union picketers. The strike had run almost two months and sinking into a bitter impasse. The mood of the strikers was different; less fevered, but more dangerous.

A watchman took him into the plant floor about the time a bell clanged, signaling the break. The temporaries were mostly silent; they didn't know one another well, and didn't congregate into knots of men enjoying a little lunch company. Most of them sat in solitary silence, digging into their buckets for something to sustain them.

Sonntag singled out a few he knew had been near Ginger on the line, bolting transmissions onto engines.

"Hey, Milwaukee PD. We're looking into the shooting of a temporary a while ago," he said to one. "Mind if we talk a bit?"

"I didn't see it, don't know anything about it. I wasn't even working then."

"Okay, could you point to someone who did see it or knew him?"

It proved to be a futile quest, for the most part. These guys hardly talked to one another; what was the use? At any hour they might be discharged and scatter. Sonntag used up most of the lunch break before he finally found someone who had something to say, a skinny guy with a bobbing adam's apple.

"Oh, Ginger, yeah, he was always asking questions. Not about how the tractors got put together, but where were we from, and what did we think of the strike, and why were we scabbing, and how much were we being paid. Stuff like that. There sure was something different about him. He wasn't like the rest of the guys."

"In what way, sir?"

"He wasn't there to earn money. He was maybe looking at us."

"Looking at you?"

"Yeah, and wandering down the line a lot, seeing how tractors got assembled. Asking questions, like you. But he wasn't a cop, like you. He had his own purposes."

"Was he different in any other way?"

"You bet. He got picked up every night after work. Some gal in a car was always waiting for him."

"You see the gal?"

"Too dark, but nice-looking, light-colored car. I paid some attention. Not every temporary gets picked up by a gal in a car."

"And she drove him away, night after night?"

"It takes a real woman to show up well after midnight for her guy, I'll tell ya."

"Did he ever talk about her?"

"He joked once, called her a pope's daughter. Like, here comes the pope's daughter; gotta go."

"But no name?"

"Names don't meaning anything here, except like Swede or Tennessee. People here are where they come from."

"Did Ginger ever say what he believed in?"

"He was pretty quiet. But he hated the managers. They bawled him out for lying once. He hired on as a machinist, but he didn't know diddly squat about machines or tools or stuff like that, that any apprentice knows."

"Nothing about machines at all?"

"Yeah, the supervisor chewed his ass, but kept him because of the strike."

"What did Ginger know about?"

"Communists. He was always talking about how the party was taking over labor unions, and how it had to be stopped, and that's why he was working."

"What else did he talk about?"

"Politics. He wanted to know who was left and right around there."

"Why?"

"Beats me. We got all sorts of guys on the line."

"Did he talk about the mob much? There's mobsters want to get ahold of unions and get the dues."

"He got real silent. That come up at lunches like this, but he got real silent."

The gong clanged, and that was as much as Sonntag was going to get that night, but there were a few things in there that might lead somewhere. The guy stuffed half a sandwich into his lunch bucket and snapped it shut. His name, Grubb, was stenciled across it. Even as Sonntag hiked down the long line, the sound of metal clattering against metal rose behind him. The barn of a building had windowed cupolas, but was dim and dreary at night. He'd rather sell vacuum cleaners if he got tired of being a cop.

So the guy who called himself Ginger was no mechanic, asked a lot of questions, got heated up about the Reds, and got picked up by a lady in a light-colored car. Pretty vague stuff, he thought, heading into the night, and through the gate. A surge of strikers barreled down on him.

"Police," he said. They crowded around him, but didn't mess with him. Half a dozen burly machinists, muscular men by trade, crowded close in the dull light. "And while you're here, tell me about the shooting the other night."

"What shooting?" a wiseacre asked.

"Yours," Sonntag said. "Whoever picked off the temporary could have his crosshairs on you."

"Crosshairs, that's a laugh," the wise guy said.

Sonntag reacted to that in a strange way. He suddenly perceived of the crime as one involving a scope and crosshairs and a rifle, not a handgun.

"You hear the shot? Where'd it come from?"

The wiseacre pointed out toward the street. "It came from there. A pop, from out there."

"Rest of you agree?"

They all chimed in, with nods.

"How do I know you're not just blowing smoke?"

"Because we ran," the wiseacre said. "Like you said, the next one could have been for me."

"Who'd shoot from out there?" Sonntag asked.

"Someone in the rear seat of that car."

"What color was the car?"

"Not dark, too dull to say, but sort of gray."

"You think you saw that?"

"No, none of us saw it. We heard the shot, ran, and while we hit the dirt or ran, the car got away."

"So, not a Machinist Union guy?"

"Far as we can tell, copper."

Sonntag liked that answer.

"What were you in there for?" the guy asked.

"Talking to workers who knew the dead man."

"What did they say?"

"Ginger was the only man who had a car waiting, with a gal driving."

"Yeah, and it ticked us off. We go home on the streetcars, but the scab gets a lift."

"Who was in the car?"

"Some bitch; some female scab."

"Pretty woman?"

"Hey, it was dark."

"Did she shoot Ginger?"

"Beats me," the guy said.

"Rear window was dark and open, usually," said another Machinist.

"How do you know that?"

"Scab gets picked up middle of the night by a dame, we see it."

"If you see that gal or that call again, would you call me immediately?"

That met with silence.

"I want to talk to her."

"Maybe she did us a favor."

"I don't think the man that got shot was a scab."

"You cops, you're something else. The man was building tractors, right?"

"He wasn't familiar with machinery."

"So what was he doing in there?"

"Good question. He talked politics."

"Like whose?"

"Maybe like yours."

That got Sonntag only silence. It drove those machinists into their private reveries, and that was as much as he could get from them. It was late. He cranked up the gray Nash, which he had to return to the station in the morning. Tomorrow, for once, he'd avoid the hair-raising streetcar ride over the Wells Street Viaduct.

He prowled through the dark streets of West Allis, turned north, and reached his bungalow ten minutes later. The lights were burning. That was Lizbeth for you. She feasted on his cases, and wanted every nuance she could worm out of him.

She was there, white cotton robe, looking so seductive he thought he was walking into a boudoir. But that's how she got him talking, with that electricity radiating from her.

"So who was Ginger?"

He just shook his head.

"So who's the lady in the car?"

"Anastasia Ryan, maybe."

"And what was her relationship to Ginger?"

"Boss."

"And what was Ginger doing?"

"Defying his boss."

"And who shot Ginger?"

"She did, or someone in the seat behind her."

"Why?"

"Treason."

"Cloak and dagger," she said.

"Lipstick and bullet," he said.

"How are you going to find her?"

"Radical politics. That's flypaper, and she's the fly."

"How do you know these things?"

"I don't. But sometimes the outlines of something emerge. I see the shape of it, without knowing much else. I think she either shot Ginger or someone in her car did, though I can only guess at the reasons."

"No surprises?"

He smiled. "I never get it right. I never nail it down."

"You never get me right, either," she said.

That surprised him.

"But you always see my shape," she said, "and that's what counts."

She was smiling to hell and back. He liked being seduced. She always put a twist on it.

This was one of those cases that heated her up. Sometimes, he worked on cases that stirred nothing inside of her, and then she was off with her gal friends, doing mending and gossip. But there were other cases that fired up something in her and these made a sleuth out of her, and drew him into her arms. There were cases that made pillow talk; cases that seemed to stir her nature. Like this. He didn't anticipate that. This was a machinist union strike, labor warfare, but here she was, her cotton robe half loose, along with her lips.

The next dawn, feeling his age, he creaked out of bed and dressed for work without stirring her. He got to drive the gray utility Nash downtown, and he liked that. Maybe some day he could afford to drive to work, pay parking, and drive home each day.

He found Eddy Walsh hunched over some paperwork, and took the opportunity.

Eddy was an urbane old detective, cynical, gravelly, tough and gentle. But he had an asset that Sonntag lacked. Eddy Walsh was a genius with women. He understood them, flirted with them, talked them into spilling secrets, sympathized with them, kidded them, and somehow became the Milwaukee police department's liaison with the city's women.

"Eddy, I'm putting you on the Ginger killing," Sonntag said. "It may have been a woman. It may have been a radical woman who turned a teenage boy named Frank Silva into a man, and a man of the left."

"Anastasia Ryan," Eddy said.

Sonntag nodded.

"So Silva's off the case. I'll find the babe. You think she pulled the trigger?"

"Don't know why, Eddy."

"Don't need to know," Eddy said. "Some people don't have to have reasons."

"Okay, here's what I've found out. I met her once, just because I had the impulse to go pay my respects to Ginger, or whoever it was. She was there. She liked an early English poet."

"Hey, don't torment a working flatfoot with that stuff."

"It helps explain her."

"Women don't need explaining. She pulled the trigger? I'll find her."

"It might have been a killing out of ideology. She's probably a Communist."

"More likely she was stood up by the guy."

"No, not Anastasia Ryan. Who may have another name. Not ever her mother knows her name now. But there's a clue, Eddy. She had two raggedy dolls when she was a girl, one named Immaculata, the other Pope Pius."

Eddy grinned. "So I look for a babe named Conception, right?"

"That's all I've got to offer you, except for a lot of talk."

"Let's hear the talk, Joe."

"She could also be a mobster's moll. Wolf Yablonski said she was the girlfriend of Fats Parvenu. I'm going to work on Fats; you work on this babe. She'd be in her forties now, if Frank was right. He was about fifteen when she latched onto him, and he says she was maybe ten years older than he was. That's a boy talking. Frank's still smitten by her. He's torn up by this case."

"I don't like female radicals," Eddy said. "They never wash"

"The woman I saw at the cemetery not only washed, she was well groomed, well dressed, and appeared to be privileged."

Eddy stared. "That helps. She'll be easy to find," he said. "All you gotta do is prove she did it."

Eddy sure knew the weakness of the case.

Chapter Eighteen

The machinists were losing. The union, its strike funds exhausted and its members desperate, caved in. The company, in a fit of generosity, agreed to a three cent an hour wage boost, but resisted a pension or job security or new overtime rules. All this Joe Sonntag absorbed while reading the morning *Sentinel*, the town's Hearst paper. "Union Whipped," was the headline. That paper knew its readership.

The paper reported that the union negotiators had agreed to Allis-Chalmers terms, and the new two-year contract would be ratified or rejected by the membership in an immediate vote. It quoted the president, Wolf Yablonski, as saying it was a bad deal. Stay out a little bit longer and they'd get much better terms. The wage increase, he said, did not even cover the cost of inflation, much less add anything to the well-being of union members. He blamed the presence of temporary workers, which empowered the company to outlast the union, for the bad deal. But he was in the minority. Most of the members were sick of striking, sick of starving, and ready to work. But not all. There was fierce opposition, coalescing around Yablonski.

It was a bitter hour for the machinists union, and by the time the afternoon *Journal* appeared, disgruntled members were demanding the resignation of all the local's officers, including Yablonski, while other factions, a clear majority, were howling for acceptance of the deal. Resisting the contract would be a tough row to hoe; the union did not offer its members a secret ballot.

Sonntag absorbed it all. So maybe Fats Parvenu had won. The old cadre of Reds would be replaced by the new cadre of mobsters, and the working members of the union would find their dues money going into Fats' pockets rather than into rebuilding the strike fund.

In short, it was a disaster.

But Yablonski refused to resign. He would stay on for the duration of his term. He made public his worries that the union would fall into hands that cared nothing at all about workingmen, hands that would cooperate with management, hands that would make it difficult for union members to control their own union. In short, Yablonski was openly telling the members what would happen if they caved in to the thugs who wanted the union in their back pocket.

The next day Wolf Yablonski was shot to death in his garden, the bullet ruining his mouth. And again Joe Sonntag found himself in the neighboring suburb, trying to crack open a homicide that had all the earmarks of premeditated murder. By the time he was on it, Yablonski's remains had been examined at the county morgue. Same story. Shot through the mouth with a large caliber weapon, an exit wound that may have been slightly lower than the entry; no sign of the bullet in spite of a major hunt for it.

Sonntag felt very bad. Yablonski was a helluva fine man. Now there would be no one to tend to the gardens.

Sonntag stood there, surrounded by late-blooming roses, staring at the bit of turf where Yablonski fell. And then he noticed that the bathtub Virgin was nicked. The ceramic halo had been shot off. The slug had flattened against the bathtub and was lying behind the Virgin. Yablonski had been sitting, not standing, when he was shot. A sitting man probably knew and welcomed the visitor. The lawn furniture had been dragged aside by West Allis police to examine the body. Sonntag studied the furniture, and finally decided to have a lab look at the canvas cushions. Maybe there's be fragments of lead in one; blood in another. Who could say? Nothing visible suggested anything.

He had the feeling that Yablonski knew the killer; that Ginger knew his killer; that something almost intimate connected these dead men to their killer. He also was pretty sure that killer was the same person, and not just because both had been shot in the teeth.

The neighbors saw and heard nothing. The body was discovered a neighbor, Mrs. Cressida, whose dog kept pushing through the hedge between the properties and yelping. Mrs. Cressida was a young widow who lived alone. She described Yablonski as very friendly, but he kept strange hours and was always talking to someone in his back yard. The initial autopsy indicated that Yablonski had been killed between seven and nine the previous evening, and had lain in the yard for an hour or so before Mrs. Cressida's fox terrier stirred her to act. A search of the whole area revealed no evidence; nothing dropped, nothing left behind, nothing at the curb or in the house or its porch.

Yablonski had been at the union hall all day, taking heat for the bad contract, urging the brothers not to ratify it. He had obviously returned home exhausted and sat down to a bullet.

Sonntag hardly knew where to start. The union guys, especially the ones who were enraged by the settlement, would be a good place to begin. The killer seemed to have a habit, a bullet through the teeth. That looked like mob turf. And always the woman, the one who picked up Ginger, the one who was a friend of Yablonski, the one who went to burials, maybe of men she had killed.

That reminded him: he would have plain clothes men at Yablonski's funeral; also at the burial. Maybe, maybe, Frank Silva would come back in, at least for that. He would hate it, but there was in him the sort of sadness that made him the best detective in Milwaukee. Detectives lived with their sadness.

There wasn't much more to do in West Allis, so he drove back to the station house. He had a large caliber bullet flattened by a bathtub, and some outdoor cushions. They weren't going to tell him much.

Eddy Walsh had nothing for him. Eddy had been tracking down Red front groups, looking for females, and they were hard to find. Few women around Milwaukee had plunged into radical politics, and Milwaukee was not Greenwich Village or some bohemian place like that.

But there was Frank Silva, quietly listening in. Sonntag didn't say anything. Silva was free to hunt down hubcap thieves or crooked bank bookkeepers this time. But there he was, listening quietly while Joe described the murder of Wolf Yablonski.

"I'll attend the funeral and ID anyone I know," he said quietly. "And I know them all."

That was a major contribution. Silva, the young Socialist, could connect names to faces almost anywhere on the left.

"You sure?" Sonntag said.

"Homicide," is all he said.

So Frank Silva was back in, maybe against his first and most important lover, the woman who shaped his life and the views that still permeated him.

The *Journal's* Matt Dugan came steaming in, spotted the detectives, and headed that way.

"Hey, lieutenant, what's the story?" the reporter asked.

"Haven't got one."

"You got any leads?"

"We always have leads."

"Okay, tell me this. The first victim's a scab. The second's the top dawg of the local? You tell me what's cooking, okay?"

"Beats me," Sonntag said.

"Someone's stirring the pot. I hear we've got Fats Parvenu in town. He collects unions like some gals collect diamonds."

"He's in town."

"In town, hell, he profits from strikes. Maybe he wants this to continue?"

"You've offered us an interesting theory, Matt. You just speculating or do you know something we don't know?"

"Well, my motto is, never let the truth get in the way of a good story," Matt said. He was grinning.

Actually, Mat Dugan was an ace reporter, and his crime stories were always more grounded than the Hearst *Sentinel's.*

"Okay, you think these killings are connected?"

"Yes, we do. There's a pattern we're observing."

"You mind telling me what?"

"Can't tell you that, Matt. But I'll say there's a pattern, and the killings are connected, but we don't know how or why."

"Readers hate stories like that. Why don't you tell me you're closing in?"

"Hey, Matt, you want to print the truth, the whole truth, and nothing but the truth?"

"So who's the Molly McGuire, and what's she got to do with it?"

Sonntag watched Silva climb inside of himself.

"Who's that?" Sonntag said.

"Gotcha, lieutenant. That's your game when I'm getting warm."

"This Molly is a mobster's girlfriend," Silva said.

"Naw," said Dugan. "Now I've heard everything. That's like putting Ex-Lax in my candy bar. So what else can you tell the eager public?"

"Someone's stirring the pot. Labor unrest, violence, trouble. And we have no indication it's management."

"How do you know that, lieutenant?"

"They won. This homicide came after."

"Will it change the way members vote for the contract?"

"Ask them. We're cops."

"Yeah, I guess I will. Care to spill any more beans?"

"Nope, Dugan. Now do me a favor and tell me who shot these persons and why."

"Lieutenant, you're a card."

"That's what my wife tells me."

They watched Dugan tuck his notepad back in his pocket, scrutinize the culprits being booked at various corners, and retreat a couple of blocks to the newspaper building.

"Yeah, how do you know it's not management?" Silva asked.

"Maybe all cops are pro-management and against labor and Commies."

"Joe, I want to help."

"You're back in, then. Give the hubcaps to Willis."

"I have a hunch. About her."

"Is this a new hunch or a hunch you've been sitting on for days?" Sonntag asked. He was suddenly ticked off.

"Let it go, Joe," Eddy said.

Frank Silva looked strange. He looked as if he were about to turn in his badge and walk out. He looked as if he was ready to jump into Lake Michigan and keep swimming until he couldn't. But most of all, he seemed uncertain, as if two sets of ideals were fighting for his soul, and he wasn't sure whether to heed one or the other. Joe Sonntag thought he saw a dozen feelings take hold of the young detective.

"Do you know Mrs. Herbert Case?" he asked, almost in a whisper.

"Society," Eddy Walsh said.

"Top of the heap," Sonntag said. Even he knew who Mrs. Case was. He didn't even read the society pages in the papers, but he knew who she was."

"She looks familiar," Frank Silva said. "Older, different hair... but maybe the same woman."

"Same as who?"

"Anastasia Ryan. I see her photo in the paper now and then. She's in there, both papers, often enough. A couple of times I got the itch to find out. Then I'd say nah, she's not the same. She's rich. She lives with her rich husband in the biggest lakeshore mansion around here. The one with the third floor ballroom, where debutantes are introduced, where you can practically see across the lake."

"A Commie?" Walsh said.

"All right, dammit, you've got my hunch," Silva said, on the brink of stalking away.

"Could you connect the dots?" Joe asked, gently.

"There aren't any. I look at those grainy black and white photos in the papers and they remind me of her, and I just laugh at myself. But then it comes back; she could be anyone, anything; she could be still devoted to the cause, or maybe she abandoned it. She could be rich as all creation and still be a Communist. She could devote herself to charities, and still try to bust unions."

"You're talking about an agent, a spy, a double life?"

"I'm not talking about anything," Frank said, and slid away.

Joe and Eddy stared at the young man, who was giving them his back. Joe felt a lot of sympathy: it had taken a lot of moral courage for a Socialist cop to point a finger at someone who might be trying to make the whole world socialist.

Eddy simply whistled. Eddy never whistled.

"Okay, Eddy," Joe said.

"Mrs. Case ain't Anastasia Ryan. She gives whole cathedrals to the Episcopal Church. She and her husband go to banker conventions. If she met a real live Communist she'd call the cops."

"Maybe you're right, Eddy. But that young man saw something, and it's eating at him."

"Coincidence. We're all young just once. There's a memorable woman in his life; now he sees her ghosts in the shadows; sees her image on news pages, and can't reconcile the woman who changed him with the woman who lives in that red stone mansion on the lakeshore."

"They aren't all conservative, Eddy. Look at Marshall Field."

"Yeah, piles of dough and liberal, left causes and papers. Only Anastasia Ryan wasn't liberal or left; she's a Bolshevik."

Sonntag remembered the well-dressed, quietly elegant woman at the burial of Ginger, or whoever it was, the woman who could recite John Dunne, and who eyed Sonntag with such a pleasant gaze. And who drove away in a light colored roadster.

"Eddy, find out if the Cases have any light-colored cars, especially tan or light brown or somewhere in there."

That took only a few minutes with the state automobile registry, and then the answer was wired back:

It was yes, a tan Milwaukee-made Nash.

Chapter Nineteen

No one had ever seen a funeral like Wolf Yablonski's. A bitterness lay over Milwaukee. Every petal of every flower that burdened his coffin was a tear. His parents were gone, but there was a half-brother, a grandmother, and some Chicago relatives. But the real family was the brotherhood, several thousand strong, all of them wearing black armbands as they walked their measured way from the West Allis school gymnasium to the lonely grave a mile away.

The papers scolded. The radio whined. The governor and aldermen and politicians lamented. Management and labor fulminated. But it didn't matter. Wolf Yablonski, a great labor leader, lay in his plain oak coffin, murdered, and the horror of it was staining the city and darkening its spirits.

This was a West Allis affair. The industrial suburb was draped in crepe. The Allis-Chalmers management sent a lavish bouquet and its polite condolences. The new contract, about to be signed and sealed, lay in tatters. The strikebreakers, given twenty-four hour notice, were being summoned to continue. But none of that lay at the heart of it, where the grieving machinists stood vigil over their fallen leader, a man who understood steel and roses.

There were no sermons, no fulminations, no accusations from any pulpit. Instead, there were simply expressions of loss and esteem. The brotherhood knew not to politicize a funeral, so Wolf Yablonski was eulogized and buried in deep and troubled silence.

An overcast heaven turned into a drizzle at the cemetery, but none of the thousands in the brotherhood sought cover; not even an umbrella. Joe Sonntag watched quietly, his own fedora in hand, letting the rain splatter against his suit. Through the crowd, his plain-clothes detectives were studying people, looking for a certain woman, whose image they knew only from society page photos. They didn't see her. They didn't see anyone else they were interested in, such as Fats Parvenu. The grieving machinists were burying their leader in peace. Whatever separated some of them from Yablonski, such as anger at the poor outcome of the strike, had vanished in the afternoon drizzle, and now they stood silently. There was no prayer for a man who believed in no god; there was a simple eulogy of a man who cared about other men, and fought for them.

Then it was over. The family was escorted to its black Cadillac and driven away. The dampened machinists dissipated under a gloomy sky, and Wolf Yablonski was returned to the earth. Sonntag saw no beautiful woman standing apart in the trees. He only saw a few thousand bitter machinists walking away in deep quiet.

"You done?" Frank Silva asked.

"Not quite. Yablonski's house."

"That's family."

"That's why," Joe said.

He drove slowly west, found the neighborhood, cruised past the house, noted black-clad people crowding it, and looked for a parking place.

"There," Silva said.

He was pointing at a tan Nash sedan.

Sonntag drew up in front of it, wrote the license number on his notepad, and then parked a block away. As they walked toward Yablonski's home, they both peered inside the Nash, which hadn't so much as a scrap of paper inside of it on the brown seats.

A family affair. And Frank and Joe would be spotted at once. There was no hiding a cop, not even in a black funeral suit. But Joe knew that one word would explain it: security.

There were a lot more than Yablonskis there. She was standing in the back yard, next to the yellow roses, elegantly coiffed, dressed in maybe Chanel or Dior. Joe was guessing. What the hell did he know? A gray suit, anyway, high heels, small patent leather handbag. Joe had the odd sense that it was about the right size for a pistol.

She was much the best dressed.

"That her?" Joe asked Frank.

"Frank just glowered. He was itchy. "Maybe," he finally muttered.

"I'll start the ball rolling," Joe said. "Mrs. Herbert Case wouldn't know me."

The Yablonskis were mostly inside. Just who these people in the garden-girt yard were, he couldn't say. And why Milwaukee's foremost *grande dame* was on hand, was beyond explaining–unless she once had a different name and view.

Actually, she broke the ice: "I do believe you're officers," she said. "How very good of you people. This is so deeply wrenching to us all."

"Yes, ma'am, Joe Sonntag, and we're here to help out. That's my colleague, Frank Silva over there."

She gazed benignly toward Silva, swallowed him in a glance, and met Sonntag's gaze.

"He looks familiar," she said.

"You're close to the Yablonskis?"

"I'm close to liberal causes, and there's no one I've grieved more than Wolf," she said. "He was the rare sort who was changing the world. When I read in the papers..." she hesitated. "Oh, dear, when I read it, I couldn't grasp it, and I thought the whole world was tumbling down."

"No man is an island," Sonntag said.

She didn't respond at all. In fact, she was smiling at someone else who wandered in. And that was Fats Parvenu. Fats had stood before a few police cameras, and Sonntag had studied the results.

Fats was dressed as inexpensively as a cop. Maybe Irv the Workingman's Friend had sold Fats his black gabardine suit, that was already sagging off the shoulders. Fats spotted Sonntag, registered the cop, and drifted elsewhere.

"Friend of yours?" he asked Mrs. Case..

"I'd rather not be seen with that man," she said. "He's not savory."

"How do you know that?"

"Oh, heavens, how do I know anything?" She flashed an electric smile. Everything about her, from teeth to fingernails, was manicured.

"You're in the papers now and then," Sonntag said.

"Oh, you must mean my causes. I have so many I can't keep them straight. It makes me more public than I want to be, but that's the price we pay, isn't it?"

"Pay for what, ma'am."

"For our ideals. Everything has its price. There's a movement in England that's dear to my heart. Breathtaking. It's to abolish the monarchy. Imagine it! We're all democrats now. I've sent them fifty dollars. I wish I could afford more. The monarchy is such a burden on the working men and women of England, you know."

That wasn't where Sonntag was hoping the conversation would go. "Yeah, well, I'll introduce you to my colleague here. Bright young detective, Frank Silva."

"I'm sure he's bright, sir, but I need to circulate. Wolf, well, I was his social secretary, you might say. And that's what I'm doing now. Mrs. Yablonski, the grandmother, is in a wheelchair, and the rest, well, I'm sort of family."

She edged away, but Frank pounced. "Detective Silva, ma'am."

There was the smallest flash of something. Sonntag smiled. "Well, now you've met. Frank, Mrs. Case is a great advocate of causes that interest you."

"Me, I'm solid pinko," Silva said, faintly mocking. "No enemies on the left."

"Well, if you'll excuse me. Thanks for coming," she said, artfully sliding away.

They watched her retreat into the Yablonski house.

"That her?"

"It's been a lot of years, Joe. I was fifteen."

"That her?"

Frank looked like he was swallowing cod liver oil. "Anastasia Ryan," he said. "But run through a Maytag and hung out to dry."

"Why do we see her here? Why did I see her at the cemetery where a man of no acquaintance to her was buried?"

Frank Silva seemed to curl deep into himself, almost as if he didn't want to face whatever was slipping through his mind.

"I guess we'll have to find out," he said.

The tone of voice was different from anything Joe Sonntag had ever heard in Frank.

"I need to do this. I need to know," Silva added.

"Want to talk about it?"

Silva sighed, and stared at the knots of people in Jablonski's gardens. This was a post-funeral family gathering, family and friends, and the two cops seemed as alien as outer space.

"Let's go," Silva said. "I've work to do."

They slipped through the side yard and away, the unwelcomed.

"Drop me off at the *Sentinel,*" Frank said. "I need to know how long ago she became high society."

"And why?"

"I already know why. Proving it's the tough one."

"What?" Sonntag asked.

"I'm not ready to say it."

"We're cops, conducting a homicide investigation."

"When I'm ready, I'll tell you," Silva said, and slid back into himself.

Sonntag dropped him at the Hearst newspaper. Silva would head for the morgue, as the archives were known to newsmen. Also talk to the paper's society doyenne, Dorothea Blue, who had ruled Milwaukee's social life for years.

Sonntag didn't even have time to sort through messages at his desk before Captain Ackerman descended, wreathed in yellow gases from his dogturd cigar.

"So who shot Yablonski?" he asked.

"We're like dogs pissing on an electric fence," Sonntag said.

For once Ackerman beamed. "Now you're talking," he said.

"The killer wasn't around. The person or persons who put it in motion were around. I'm thinking. I don't know."

"Around what?"

"Around Yablonski's place after the funeral. Family and friends. Including Fats Parvenu and some high society."

"Mrs. Case. Did Silva put the finger on her?"

"He's pretty certain. She's all gussied up now, Paris fashions, but he thinks underneath all that gloss is Anastasia Ryan, the radical, the card-carrying member of the CP."

"Jaysas," said Ackerman. "Once a commie, always a commie. She's just a rich commie now, that's all."

"That's debatable. Wealth does lots of things. It moderates. It can turn Reds into Pinks. Turn a fire-eating babe into a progressive, or a liberal."

"Oh, bull, Sonntag. Once they're bitten, man, they're bit. They got a whole world to overthrow. She's likely to overthrow her rich husband when the day comes."

"So I'm more interested in Fats Parvenu, family friend, union collector, present and smiling, shaking the hand of old Mrs. Yablonski, in her wheelchair."

"This is fun, Sonntag. I like this one."

"Al Capone used to send funeral bouquets," Sonntag said. "Kill 'em and console the widow. But that's not what he was there for. He's a pal of Anastasia Case."

"Hey, Sonntag, you've even got me confused. I never get confused. High society's a pal of the mobster?"

"They were rubbing elbows."

"That's nothing new."

"Captain, suppose a Red wants to rub out someone/"

Ackerman chewed on his slimy cigar, and smiled. "High society," he said. "Getting entertaining around here. Okay, professor, what's your deal?"

"I think it's the other way around. Fats wants the union. Now he's got it. He's bumped off the only serious obstacle, a strong union president. Nothing could be more useful to him than a rich gal full of progressive politics, a rich gal who makes friends with union bosses. A rich gal who's maybe cuddling up with mobsters, too. So

Fats is going to get his union. Everything's stirred up again. The strike was over, but not it's not over, and that's how Fats wants it. He'll get his own slate in there, and they'll take over the union."

"You think Fats is pulling the strings?"

"You got any better idea?"

"Yeah: who shot Yablonski?"

"And who shot Ginger?"

"Somebody's itchy little finger pulled the trigger, Sonntag. And we're going to find out who, and find out before the whole city lands on us."

Sonntag watched his superior vanish into his cubicle. You had to be a captain to get a private office. That was just as well; Ackerman's cigars were coating the whole station with brown stink.

There were notes on his desk. Dugan of the *Journal* wanted to see him. Eddy Walsh left a note saying that Anastasia Ryan went to England in 1936 to study socialism, and stayed there.

Frank Silva returned with a manila envelope.

"I've got both papers digging," he said. "There's so much stuff about Anastasia Case that it's going to take them a day or so to dig it up and photocopy it for us. Meanwhile, I got this."

He pulled a couple of black pages with white print on them from the envelope. They were a wedding story, from 1938. It was about the marriage of Anastasia Ryan to Herbert Case.

Sonntag read the blurry columns, and studied the blurry picture, which had lost its halftones but still revealed a gorgeous bride and groom.

The wedding had occurred on the terrace of the red granite Case lakefront home, with the blue of the lake behind the wedding party. Miss Ryan, vaguely described as the daughter of Michael and Natasha Ryan, Milwaukee, was wed to Mr. Case, scion of a prominent Milwaukee shoe and leather family. He was a graduate of Princeton, with further study at the London School of Economics. The pair had met abroad, where Miss Ryan was doing graduate work on the poetry of John Dunne.

Chapter Twenty

Frank Silva looked blue.

"You'll figure it out," Sonntag said.

It was a lousy ending of a lousy day.

"I'm not sure it's her. This woman's different, Joe, even though she gives me the willies. This woman...godalmighty. Anastasia Case isn't the Molotov cocktail thrower who found a boy called Frank. But, but, but, oh well. I'll get over it."

"What doesn't work?"

"Almost everything. Anastasia had big warm eyes that would gaze on a socialist teenager with joy; this woman... I don't know. Anastasia, she was passionate– I mean, about leftwing causes. I mean, she could talk endlessly, she could pick out her enemies, she could dream of a better world, and you know, she'd join any man at the barricades if there was a revolution. Hell, she'd knit sweaters and cheer while the guillotine cuts off heads. This woman, maybe liberal but cold as a grave."

"She thought she recognized you for a moment there."

"Yeah, and I recognized her. But now I just don't know."

"You saw her in the mid-thirties?"

"Yeah, the Depression, just when the Reds were dreaming of taking over the world. They were the Future! And getting rid of rivals, like the Socialist Labor Party. Like Trotsky. That's when Anastasia was a human torch, scouring each headline, going to rallies and meetings– but not this woman."

"Did Anastasia Ryan ever talk about her family?"

"All she talked was Socialist stuff. Bomb Congress. Bomb governors. Throw out the old world."

"Weren't you curious? About her? Her past?"

"She was teaching me other things, Joe."

He said it in a way that made everything bright. A boy, an older woman, a mesmerizing communion.

"Okay, maybe changed to something you hardly know. But there's still one thing I don't get. Why did she show up at the burial of the scab, Ginger? Why did she watch them bury him? This rich liberal lady? Why did she pick him up after his night shift, at the factory, as far from the lakeshore mansions as you can get?"

"Bed, Joe. This woman had lovers. That scab, who probably wasn't a scab; Wolf, and Fats. Who knows how many more?"

"I'm dumb," Sonntag said. "I'm the last person on the force to figure that stuff out."

"No, Joe, there's no one on the force who puts things together like you."

Sonntag felt uncomfortable with the compliment.

"So who does Anastasia Case kill next?" Frank asked.

"Jesus, Frank."

"Fats would be about right."

This was one of the strangest moments in a strange life, he thought. "Want to go rattle Fats?"

"Tomorrow?"

"First thing."

Joe Sonntag grabbed his black lunch bucket and headed for the Wells Street car stop. It was a soft summer afternoon, the kind when no one should be working. No one should be striking. Labor leaders shouldn't be lying in new coffins. Milwaukee wasn't a violent place; it was mostly filled with humble people who wanted a good job and were willing to work hard and enjoy a few hours of respite on weekends. Afternoon streetcars were filled with weary people, crowded in seats and aisles, hanging onto the straps, glad to be done for the day. The orange car crawled westward, and at 35th it lost a dozen, and Sonntag got a seat. He preferred riding the Wells Street viaduct seated. When he stood, that shifted the center of gravity upward, and made the trip over the trestle more perilous. He itched to make everyone sit on the floor of the car when it was on the trestle. Or at least hunker down below the level of the seat backs. Ideally, everyone should lie flat on the floor until the car reached safe ground. Of course no car had ever fallen off the viaduct, but that didn't mean anything. This trip, or tomorrow, or six weeks from now the viaduct might collapse and carry him to his doom.

But next he knew, he was on the west side of the valley, and preparing to leave the car a few stops ahead. He couldn't explain to himself how he had come to buy the bungalow when it was on such a perilous route to work.

Lizbeth took one look at him and started to mix drinks. Sometimes he arrived home in viaduct-shock, and this was one of those moments. He let her. All he wanted was to hug the good earth, or at least sink into a chair which stood on a floor, which rested on a foundation, which was dug into the solid ground of Milwaukee.

"So who's Anastasia Case, besides a woman who's in the society pages?" she asked.

"She's a friend of Fats Parvenu, a friend of whoever was shot a few weeks ago, a friend of a late union president, and a very vocal voice for leftwing stuff."

"Okay, copper, how do you explain it?"

"Lovers."

"A scab, a mobster, and a labor leader?"

Sonntag felt uncomfortable. "There's no explaining it," he muttered. The bourbon was very welcome on a summer's eve. Maybe they should move to the bluegrass country. Beer had always tasted like cat piss.

"I shouldn't say lovers," she said. "This woman wouldn't know a lover if she saw one."

"She knows how to turn men into her robots," she said.

"Yeah, there's always those."

"No, I mean, Frank Silva at age fifteen was being recruited. Do you what an older woman can do to a fifteen-year-old boy?"

"But that was Anastasia Ryan."

Lizbeth smiled suddenly. "Yes, and Anastasia Ryan Case was the lover of Joseph Ginger, and Wolf Yablonski, and now Fats Parvenu. That's her way."

"Anastasia Case?"

"She's not a rich liberal. She didn't go to England to study John Dunne. When she returned from Europe she was a disciplined agent, maybe not a spy, but agent with tasks assigned to her."

"You have an imagination that runs without brakes."

"An agent does what she's assigned. She'll sleep with a scab for whatever reason; she'll sleep with a mobster. She'll influence a powerful labor leader, or see him killed it it plunges a union into chaos, and a strike explodes to life just at the moment it was being settled."

"A provocateur?"

"A saboteur. Maybe a Stalinist."

There was something tempting about Lizbeth's notion, but finally Joe set it aside. "I'll keep it in mind," he said.

Lizbeth looked crestfallen. "It explains everything."

"Except that Ryan and Case are different women."

"Yes! The one Frank knew was lost forever; the new one was born somewhere in Europe, maybe after six months of intensive training. Maybe in Moscow. Maybe in a safe house. Maybe in some neutral place, far from prying eyes. Anastasia Ryan didn't hesitate to use her body or give her intellect to her masters. They found her, or she found them, and sometime before the war she was transformed. Now she's a liberal society lady– and an agent of a foreign power."

It was tempting to Joe Sonntag to think along such bizarre lines, and he resisted it. She seemed almost fevered with her idea, and he thought it best to humor her.

"It's worth looking into," he said, intending to dismiss this whole line of thinking.

"That's a no," she said, and grinned suddenly. "Here's my last shot, Mr. Detective. You're thinking about thugs and robbers and hit men when you should be thinking about people driven by obsession.

These are political crimes. Ginger died because of something political he did or didn't do. Yablonski died because he was upsetting the plans of somebody. Joe, people kill each other because of beliefs; religion; obsessions. Revolutionaries kill, all for what they think is a noble cause. You need to look for one thing: the time when Anastasia Ryan vanished from Milwaukee. Just look for that. For a month and a year. When her socialist friends didn't see her any more. And then find out when Anastasia Case showed up in the society pages. Somebody owns her now, and I'm not talking about rich old Case himself."

He thought that seemed worth doing. Maybe Frank would remember the names of some of the activists, or the groups, or the pamphleteers.

It was odd the way she kept eyeing him, through meatloaf and mashed potatoes and Borden's vanilla ice cream. He both enjoyed it and wanted to dismiss her whole elaborate notion. This was Milwaukee. It didn't attract spies. The politically obsessed, they congregated in Greenwich Village or Boston or Washington. But then he thought of his own friend and colleague, Frank Silva; and the socialist mayors of Milwaukee. And the machinists union, brimming with self-described Trotskyites. Maybe murderous political struggles had arrived in sedate Milwaukee.

She didn't say any more. They listened to Fibber McGee and Molly, and Little Lulu, and that was the day.

The next day, as soon as Frank Silva arrived, he tried out Lizbeth's ideas on him.

It was odd. Silva wouldn't accept or reject them. He listened carefully, and finally said. "She's not the woman I knew."

"That's Lizbeth's point, in a way. Could you at least find out when Anastasia Ryan seemed to vanish around here?"

Frank nodded. This was tender turf again.

Ackerman steamed out of his cubicle. "There's a machinists union meeting in the high school gym out there. They'll vote the contract up or down. There's a new president, supposedly someone Fats Parvenu put in. He's wanting the contract accepted, the union back to work, and the scabs gone."

"What's his name?"

"William Bagatelle. They call him Billy Bags. He supposedly is out of the International Headquarters of the Machinists. Actually, he's a Parvenu bagman being promoted."

"And the local accepted him?"

"I heard there were guys with leather jackets and bulges in their pockets. It was also not a secret ballot."

"What if it's closed and they don't want us?"

"Show your badge, but don't push it."

"Where you hear this?"

"Sonntag, I got more stool pigeons in my desk drawer than you got in Milwaukee."

That was Captain Ackerman for you.

"Where's management?"

"They say they've put the contract on the table; it was agreed to; they're waiting for the strike to end. The plant could be humming by tomorrow if the strike ends."

"Who's opposing it?"

"Not a soul, Sonntag."

"Who's likely to fight it?"

"This is gonna be smooth as goose grease."

"What do we know about Billy Bags?"

"He moves money around. He's a mob courier."

"Like union dues."

"And payoffs from management. Mob unions are patsies."

"All right," Joe said.

They checked out an unmarked black Chevy, and drove once again out to West Allis, parking at the high school gym. It was going to be boiling in there, in spite of big ceiling blowers. Even a half hour before the ten A.M. meeting, a lot of union guys were knotted outside, most of them pretty quiet. The strike had worn hard on them, and they were not far from being dead broke. Joe wondered how far ahead they would be from the strike; he thought it would take the better part of a year to make up what had been lost in wages, even with strike fund money sustaining the members. Part of it was simply hope, simply dreams. A good wage seemed like a bright spot in their lives.

"Let's go on in," he said.

He and Frank headed for the gymnasium door.

"Where's your card, fella?" asked a steward at the door.

"We're police," Sonntag said.

"You show a card or you don't go in."

"We're here for security."

"You heard me, copper. This is a union deal. No cops, no press, no radio, no nothing but guys in this local. You get it now?"

"Where do we talk to the union management?" Silva asked. "We'd like to ask for permission."

"They ain't talking to you. No cops, do you get it?"

"We'll wait," Sonntag said. "We'll be right here."

The steward at the double door glared.

"This is a strike vote, right?" Silva asked. "I thought you already had a strike vote."

"That was before the trouble." the steward said.

"Why do you need another vote?"

"The negotiators that signed the agreement, they're no longer with us."

"They got axed?"

"They're gone."

"Who didn't like it?"

"I told you, copper, you're not welcome here. This is a private meeting, and you need a card to get in."

Sonntag shrugged.

They watched he machinists file in as the hour approached, and at ten the steward cranked the metal doors closed. Whatever might happen in there was beyond the reach of the public.

They drifted out to the street, wondering whether to hang around. Frank nudged Sonntag and pointed. There, down the block a little, was a tan Nash, with a woman and a man inside. Anastasia Case and the mobster.

Chapter Twenty-One

It sure was tempting.

"Do you want to have a little conversation?" Silva asked.

"They don't even have to roll down the window. Let's see what happens."

"Or who happens."

There were a couple of West Allis cops outside the gymnasium, and a few stray people, including a reporter or two. Sonntag thought he recognized a *Sentinel* guy. He and Silva headed to the unmarked car and settled in, as the morning heat built up.

"Dull hour," Silva said.

"Usually doesn't pay off," Sonntag said. "He'd spent a lot of dull hours, night and day, watching the other people. He usually got faster results by shaking someone until his teeth clattered.

Nothing was happening at the tan Nash, either. Sonntag eyed the couple, a society lady and a gangster. They were waiting; he and Silva were waiting. And the reporters were waiting. Only the two West Allis cops weren't waiting for much, except the end of the closed meeting.

"That your girlfriend over there?" Sonntag asked.

Silva finally smiled. "It might be the same body, and same brain, but it's a different person. No, I take that back. It's all her, new phase."

Time ticked along. No messengers emerged with news for the mobster. That's what Sonntag was hoping for. A look at some couriers. But then the double metal doors exploded open, and two guys manhandled a third outside, and delivered a few kidney punches and a couple of kicks that knocked the victim flat on the concrete. Then the two enforcers retreated, the doors banged shut, and a man was sitting on the concrete, hurt.

The West Allis cops ignored him. The press rushed in. The guy stood, shook his head, and tried to get away, but the reporters were hounding him, demanding answers to shouted questions.

Sonntag and Silva burst from their car, and headed for the clamorous crowd collecting around the downed man. It had all happened so fast that no one had figured it out.

"Cops here," Sonntag said, running in. "You hurt?"

"I don't need cops," the man said.

"You're safe in the car," Silva said, manhandling the machinist. The man surrendered, and let himself be led.

"Wounded man here; beat it," Sonntag said to the pack of reporters and curiosity seekers. The man limped in, settled in the backseat, and Sonntag jammed the gears and yanked the car out of there. He circled around to the other side of the school, and parked.

"You need a doctor?"

"No, they just wanted to pound on me, not kill me."

"Yeah, but you'd better see someone," Silva said.

"We're Milwaukee cops, helping out over here."

"The detectives. I heard there were a couple looking into some shooting around here."

"I'm Joe Sonntag, and this is Frank Silva," he said. "You want to talk a little?"

"I want to talk a lot."

"Okay, you just go ahead," Silva said. "Maybe we can help."

"I don't think so. I don't think anyone outside of the union can help."

"And your name, sir?"

"Claude Kramer."

"And they just threw you out of a strike meeting?"

"The new guys, from the International in Pittsburgh. That's what they say."

"So, what's the deal? Maybe backtrack. We're just a couple of innocent bystanders."

Kramer laughed. "That's it, all right. Look, this local, it's being took over. I didn't like it, and began saying so."

"Okay, we'll back up," Silva said. "What was the local before this stuff started?"

"We were Metal Workers and Machinists Local 258. Every one of our officers was elected, guys we knew. Some of them, they were, they had ideas about how to help the working man."

"Like Stanley Argo?"

"No, he was a piece of crap. Like Wolf Yablonski. He was the most respected man in the local. You just knew he wanted the best for us all. He got us through the war and price controls and wages frozen up, he got us through and made us strong. He won two strikes after the war, but not this one. Someone's messing around with our local. Maybe Allis big shots, maybe not. But someone's wanting this local, three thousand men, lots of dues, and that someone's trying to sow trouble."

"Yablonski have enemies?"

"Even his enemies respected him."

"Who was that?"

"There's always some gripers and whiners around. It didn't matter what Yablonski did; he wasn't good enough for them."

"How about you, Kramer?"

"I was trying to make sure that Yablonski's legacy, all the stuff he put in place, is honored. He didn't like the new agreement with the company, not as good as before with all those scabs working, but we got to vote on an agreement. And then someone killed him, and now here's a bunch of men we don't know, with letters from the International Headquarters, and they're moving in."

"Who's they?"

"New president, sent to us, William Bagatelle, Billy Bags, and he cut a new deal with the company, and threw out the proposed contract, and the new deal's worse.. So I got up and said so, and kept saying so, and calling for a secret ballot, and next thing, two thugs I've never seen pick me up by the elbows and toss me out and land a few kidney punches, which haven't quit howling yet."

"So, was Billy Bags elected?"

"Sort of. The International said we had to take him, so we had a special session a couple days after the funeral, and we simply all say sure, that's what the International wants, so sure, we elect this fart president, but no one knows him."

"Did he throw you out?"

"I dunno. First I know, two thick guys are coming toward me, and they don't tell me to get up, they lift me up and haul me to the door."

"Can you identify them?"

"Jesus, I don't think I want to. I like my teeth, and I like my bones unbroke, and I like my eyes, and I like my nuts."

"If you sit here with us, and watch when this meeting ends, could you point them out to us?" Silva asked.

"There's two thousand guys in there."

"That's a no, right? How were they dressed?"

"Like the rest of us. Hey, you go after them and they'll pound me to pulp."

Sonntag grinned. "We won't let that happen. We're trying to identify who's doing what to your union. You have any ideas?"

"The Mob. Sometimes the mob's all tied up with management. The Mob owns the local, and the management likes it; they can deal with the Mob; they can't deal with a fiery guy like Wolf Yablonski. See it?"

"How do you know the Mob and management are in cahoots?" Silva asked.

"It always shows up on the floor. When there's trouble, the union steward is right there, between the member and the foreman. But when the steward's in the Mob, or bought by the Mob, a brother, he's got no rights on the assembly line. That and a lot of other stuff."

"So what are they voting on today?"

"Vote, ha! They're being told to forget the deal with the

company, and go for the new one that Billy Bags and the company put together in about ten minutes."

"And you objected?"

"Until I was escorted out."

"What are ya gonna do next?" Silva asked.

Claude Kramer went quiet. "I don't know who to trust," he said.

"That's rough company in there."

"No, most of those working stiffs I'd trust my life to. And they'd trust me with theirs. Someone's got to put this local back. Someone's got to defend organized labor. We're proud of our local. I guess that's me. I believe in it. I'm a union man. A real one, not just a card-carrier. This is what helps working people like me get a fair shake. I'm a union man to the day I die. So was Yablonski. You just keep on going, making a little headway, month after month. I'm going to get this brotherhood straightened out."

"You'll run for office?"

"It's too late for that."

"Do you know what you're up against?"

"Maybe better than you do, copper. How long has it been since you got beat up?"

"You could help us, Claude," Silva said.

"I'm for the local, and the rest isn't your business."

"Maybe we could help you," Sonntag said. "We're interested in your new president there, from Pittsburgh. The one no one around here ever heard of until the International sent him to you. Maybe we could sort of keep you posted about this guy."

"He's with the Mob."

"That might be more than you can deal with, sir," Sonntag said. "You may need to keep us informed."

"We solve our own problems," Kramer said. "Now, you guys done with me?"

"Not quite. Over on the other side of the building, there's a mob boss watching the doors. You want us to drop you somewhere far from here?"

"That would be chickenshit. No, I'll get out if you'll let me."

"You got a way we can reach you?"

"In the phone book."

"Okay, Claude, you be careful."

"Now I'm Claude, am I? I don't even know you. You can call me Claude after you've been pounded on for your beliefs. When they's shot a fist into you a few times, just because you want an honest union, then you can call me Claude."

The machinist slipped out, closed the door quietly, and hiked away.

"He sure is alone, isn't he?" Silva said.

"I'm going to worry about him."

"It doesn't do any good," Silva said. They watched the man hike eastward, and gradually diminish into nothing.

Sonntag fired up the Chevy and they eased back to the gym doors. The Nash was gone.

"That was smart," Silva said.

"They saw us," Sonntag said. "You want to go in?"

"Without backup?"

"Just to see what we can see."

"Worth a try, if we can get in."

There was no one guarding the door any more. They slid in, and chose to stand at the rear, surveying the steaming gym. A few men stared at them, but no one intervened.

They stepped in just in time to hear the result of the vote.

"It's unanimous. The strike is over," said a teller up front.

No dissenting votes. The one dissenter had been shown the doors.

No one seemed very happy. Most of them seemed to stare, their faces blank, their thoughts unknowable. This deal, if it was what it was reputed to be, wouldn't even pay back the strike losses for the duration of the two-year contract.

"We'll meet with management in an hour; you'll be working in the next day shift."

No one was cheering. The gym reeked of sweaty armpits.

"Hey, the scabs are dead meat," the boss said.

No one was amused.

A lot of machinists were in there, all of them silent. It was odd; the worst, most prolonged strike in local history had ground to a halt. The scabs would be discharged. The union men would start building tractors and generators and turbines. But all of that seemed to be drowned out by silence.

William Bagatelle stood at the makeshift podium underneath a basketball hoop. He was a baggy-eyed, pot-bellied bull of a man, but what interested Sonntag was the pair of thugs hovering around the new boss of the local.

"Those the guys?" Sonntag asked.

"It happened so fast, I don't know for sure," Silva said.

"Those are the guys," Sonntag said.

"Hey, we need backup," Silva said.

Neither of them was armed; neither had so much as a pair of cuffs.

"Don't you do it, Joe. There's ways of doing it right."

"We saw an assault; we've got the suspects."

"We're not even in Milwaukee!"

Sonntag was grinning.

The crowd was finally dissolving into knots of men. Sonntag saw a couple of reporters, who'd plunged in and were talking to men, or trying to. This vote would end up on the front pages of both papers.

He dodged bodies, and finally reached the two thugs, who were still hovering around Billy Bags.

Silva was not happy.

Sonntag approached one of the toughs, who eyed him as if he were dead fish.

"Lieutenant Sonntag here, Milwaukee police. I'm asking you and your friend there to follow us out. We've got a few things to talk to you about."

"Cops?"

"Detectives. Milwaukee police, yes. You can walk ahead of us. You and that gentleman."

The thug surveyed Sonntag and Silva, and eyed Bags.

"Hey, coppers, we're busy. Come back some other time, all right?"

Sonntag smiled easily. "Your choice; now without cuffs, or later, with a lot of bluecoats backing us up."

"Hey, Mickey, there here are cops, and they want to talk to us."

"About what?"

"About your behavior."

"Oh, that. I'm an altar boy. Aren't you an altar boy, Mickey?"

"Well, you come outside with us and tell us how to light the candles, all right?"

"Copper, you're a card."

"I knew we'd see eye to eye," Sonntag said.

The amazing thing was, the pair of thugs meandered through the mostly emptied gym, with Sonntag and Silva just behind. Silva looked like he'd sprung a leak, but the two thugs seemed peaceable enough.

They pierced the double metal doors, into a foyer area, and headed out to the unmarked Chevy.

"Hop in, gents," Sonntag said, opening the rear door.

Amazingly, both of the thugs did.

"You fellows carrying?" Sonntag asked.

"Carrying what, sir?"

"Smartass," Sonntag said. "Maybe we'll let you go if you sing like a pair of chickadees."

Chapter Twenty-Two

Sonntag slid into the driver's seat, and turned to talk to his pas sengers, behind the wire mesh dividing the seats.

"You fellows ready for a voluntary trip to the station house for a voluntary talk?"

"You mean us?" one asked.

"Yeah, I mean you. It's not every day that cops get to watch a little assault, and we'd like to learn a little bit about it."

"All voluntary, right?"

"So, what happens at the station house?" the other asked.

"You volunteer what you know, and we volunteer to listen."

"So where does that lead?"

"That depends on how good a voice you've got."

"How come this is all so polite?"

"We respect the union. You're union men, aren't you?"

"Well, we're gonna join."

"You don't have a card?" Silva asked.

"Well, we're from Cicero, and it takes a little time to get in. I mean, we have to get a job at the plant, and then we can get a card, but meanwhile we're friends of the working man, and organized labor."

"So what's your names?" Silva asked.

"What would you want that for?"

"Let's take a voluntary trip downtown," Sonntag said.

"I got rights," said one.

"Then volunteer your names," Silva said.

This one here, he's Sandy Sorrento, and me, I'm just called Big Duck."

"I've heard of you, Big Duck. You got web between your fingers, right?"

"How'd you know?"

"From wanted posters."

Sonntag eased the car into gear, and started toward the downtown station.

"You sure this is voluntary?" asked Big Duck.

"You can get out any time we volunteer to unlock," Sonntag said.

"How come you were misbehaving with that fellow?" Silva asked.

"Oh, him. He was in the way, A few knocks on the kidneys changed his mind."

"In whose way?"

"The local. The new president, William Bags, I mean Bagatelle."

"Where are you staying, Big Duck?" Silva asked, as Sonntag slid onto Greenfield Avenue and hurried east, past sleazy shops that sold wallpaper or garden supplies.

"Oh, we're at some friends of ours. Nice little place, all fixed up."

"Oh, sure, that's Fats's place, right?"

"Fats, yeah, he's a real nice man. He got this little house with two flats and fixed it up."

"Is Billy Bags there too?"

"Oh, yeah, Fats and his mother upstairs, and three of us downstairs. But as soon as Bags can find a place, he'll move out. He's looking to buy the Yablonski house."

"How come you pounded on that guy?" Silva asked.

"Who says we pounded on anyone?"

"We saw you."

"You didn't see us, you saw someone else."

Sonntag cut north on 27th, and then turned east on State Street.

"Hey, this isn't West Allis is it?"

"Milwaukee."

"I thought you were going to take us to the West Allis station."

'You volunteered to come here with us."

"Who'd that house belong to before Fats bought it?" Silva asked.

"There were a bunch of scabs in there; dead as pickles in brine now."

"What happened to them?"

"Mr. Parvenu, he got the place for a song."

"Yeah, from Anders Gropius. That guy work for Parvenu?"

"Never heard of him, " Big Duck said.

"How about Dimitri Karl?"

"Nope."

"How about Joseph Ginger?"

"Hey, am I a walking encyclopedia?"

"What about a Russian, Ilich Borovich?"

"Gropius, they disappeared him, I think," Big Duck said.

"How'd they do that?"

"Concrete collar, that's what I heard," Big Duck said. "Just a rumor. Nothing but scabs, not good union men."

"They weren't ordinary scabs; they were Fats Parvenu's own scabs," Silva said. "He was almost a scab employment agency. Why's that?"

"No one told us that," Big Duck said.

They reached the station, and Sonntag parked the car.

"You coming in for a voluntary talk?" he asked.

"I got no choice but voluntary," the hood replied.

"Good, then you'll volunteer out of the car, lift your arms while I volunteer to check you out, and then we'll all cooperate on going in."

"This doesn't seem voluntary enough," Big Duck said.

"You volunteered to assault a man in front of us," Silva said.

"I think we've been screwed," Sorrento said.

"You could volunteer to run, but you won't do a four-minute mile," Sonntag said.

"You could volunteer to punch us, but we would volunteer some additional felonies and misdemeanors," Silva said. "Good for a couple years, anyway."

"Then again, you could volunteer to walk sweetly inside, where there will be lots of smiling faces and lots of good conversation," Sonntag said. He slid a hand into his empty suit coat pocket.

The gas seemed to escape from the thugs, and they lumbered ahead and into the bullpen, where they immediately attracted attention. Some gents do that.

They settled in chairs at Sonntag's desk. There was a lot of meat in those chairs, and they groaned a little. Next thing, Captain Ackerman was boiling out of his office, and Eddy Walsh was looking for an excuse to join the party, and the two thick-bellied gents were basking in the admiration of the department.

"Well, what have we here?" the captain asked, aiming a plume of yellow smoke from his dogturd cigar at the visitors.

"Captain, this is Sandy Sorrento and Big Duck. They're independent contractors, who have volunteered to tell us about life in their hometown of Cicero."

"Pleased to meetcha," Sorrento said.

"This visit is entirely voluntary, captain. We asked them if they would enjoy a visit with us, which is preferable to an involuntary trip as a result of improving the kidneys of a dissenting machinist."

"You don't say! How do you do that, Mr. Sorrento?" the captain asked.

"You whack 'em from behind so they don't see it coming," Sorrento said.

"There's a better way," Ackerman said. "Do you know the most painful shot; the one that drops a man to the ground howling?"

"Aw, there's a dozen of those, cap," said Big Duck.

"Stand up and I'll show it to you," Ackerman said.

"Well, I'm here voluntary to help you fellows out."

"Get me a billy club, Silva, and I'll demonstrate."

Silva looked stricken, but soon produced a nice billy, polished to a fine sheen, and handed it to the captain.

"Now of course I'm not going to hurt you, seeing as how you've come in to help us here, but here's how it goes. There's a small area on the outside of each knee, right about here," he said, scraping the club over the vulnerable area of Big Duck's leg. "You have to know the exact place, and one sharp rap will do it. That's the miracle hit. One hit, just right, will drop a man and turn him into a howling lunatic. There's no pain that equals it."

"You don't say?" Sorrento said.

"Would you like to volunteer?" Ackerman asked. "You can try it on Big Duck, and he can try it on you."

"Cap, we'll take your word for it."

Ackerman smiled, leaked yellow smoke, and handed the billy back to Silva.

"These torpedoes know a lot about what's going on in West Allis, and they agreed to instruct us on the action over there," Sonntag said.

"Who's your boss?" Ackerman asked.

"We're self-employed, sir."

"Where do you live? I mean here, in Milwaukee?"

"We're residing temporary, guests of a friend of ours."

"They are acquainted with the labor leader William Bagatelle, Captain, and also colleagues of Mr. Anthony Parvenu. I believe they are all domiciled at a residence that last we knew was the property of a certain Anders Gropius."

"Oh, yes, a fine building, sawed into two flats, right?" Ackerman said.

"Yeah, Mr. Parvenu and his elderly mother occupy the top flat, with the view, while the rest of us are less fortunate," Big Duck said.

"It's temporary, sir. Mr. Bagatelle is looking for a residence in West Allis. The machinists union is honored to pick up the tab, now that he's its leading officer and chairman of the board."

"Mr. Parvenu is absolutely devoted to unions, cap. He believes in organized labor, in strong unions with lots of dues. That's what he's here for, to reform unions in Wisconsin. He's a visionary and a reformer, Cap," said Sorrento. "We're real proud to be a part of his labor reform movement."

"So what happened to the owner of that house? Gropius?"

"You know, that's a mystery. Fats wondered about it. No sooner did Gropius sell him the house but he vanished."

"Yeah, and what about Ginger? The scab that got shot? He was living there too, right?"

"There's a lot of troublemakers around, cap. They usually end up in a driveway somewhere," Big Duck said.

"Driveway?"

"Yeah, it's a fact of life. If there's a new concrete driveway around, there's gonna be someone under it," Big Duck said. "There's hardly a new driveway in Cicero, Illinois, that's not the resting place of someone who had trouble getting along with his friends. Driveways are hallowed ground."

"So is there a new driveway at Mr. Anthony Parvenu's current residence?" Captain Ackerman asked.

"Naw, just a gravel parking area. No one around there could afford garages– or cars. Who's got enough for a car? Cicero's more progressive than Milwaukee."

"You say Mr. Parvenu's old mother's there?"

"Yeah, she cooks, buys groceries, and visits the post office. A lot of people contribute to Mr. Parvenu's charities, and someone has to deposit the contributions," Big Duck said.

"Now, what happened to the other tenants there?" Silva asked.

"Oh, them. They left. Mr. Parvenu, he didn't want parasites around."

"They just left?"

"Hey, I don't run a travel service," Big Duck said.

"How'd you get the name Big Duck?"

"Because of my private parts. I've set records. I should be in Guinness. I've had a British countess look me up."

"How did Anthony Parvenu get to be called Fats?" Ackerman asked.

"Shh, he doesn't like that. It's his taste in women, but he don't want it advertised."

"Well, his friend Anastasia Case sure isn't fat," Sonntag said.

"She's not a, you know...she's just a friend. They make stuff happen."

"What does she want?" Silva asked.

"She wants one thing one day, something else the next. Drives Fats bananas."

"You mind explaining?"

"Hey, I'm just volunteering to help you coppers out, right?"

"She's the most beautiful woman in Milwaukee," Silva said. "She's a one-woman reform movement."

"Yeah, well, don't say that to Fats. He thinks she should get herself under a few feet of concrete and stay there."

"She must be very persuasive, right?"

"Hey, I don't talk about women," Big Duck said.

"She can buy half of Milwaukee," Sandy Sorrento said. "Man, can she snap her fingers. She says, 'Fats, hire scabs and keep the strike going,' so Fats hires scabs. She says 'Fats, end the strike, and ship the scabs out,' and he ends the strike and ships the scabs back to Arkansas."

"You puzzle me, Mr. Sorrento."

"Hell, she's got Fats on the run. I keep telling Fats, just get rid of her, just shut the door on her, but he likes palling around with a society babe."

"What's the strangest thing about her?" Silva asked.

"Gentleman, they don't talk about ladies," Sorrento said.

"You sure she's a lady?"

"I'm volunteering to keep my yap shut."

"What sort of hold does she have on Fats?" Ackerman asked.

"Well, for you, cap, I'll spill a few beans, but don't quote me. I worry because she's got Fats by the short hair. Like she's got some sort of lever. Like she's in control, like a Godfather, only she tells him what she wants and he jumps. I've never seen Fats act like that, kissing her big toe, doing whatever she wants. She doesn't even see him. She doesn't even see me or Big Duck or Billy Bags. It's like we're just wind-up soldiers to fight her wars. You know? She's no lady, if you want it straight from the horse's mouth. But one day she wants one thing, one day something else."

"You got any voluntary ideas?" Silva asked.

"She's like a robot. Wind her up and off she goes. And there's not a tender thought in her."

Silva looked saddened, momentarily, but Sonntag caught it.

The two muscleman volunteered all that they intended to volunteer, which was enough to avoid assault charges as far as

Sonntag was concerned. The rest of the hour was spent parrying various questions. Still, it had been valuable. The local was the prize, and various forces had vied to dominate it. The only real mystery was Anastasia Case. Her game was beyond fathoming.

Sonntag volunteered to take the mobsters back to West Allis, but they decided a taxicab would be just fine, and they walked out of the station house smiling.

But Silva wasn't smiling. He looked stricken.

Chapter Twenty-Three

Eddy Walsh coaxed it out. He was working through the photo copies of newspaper stories about Anastasia Case, with an occasional call to society editors for advice, when he finally tugged the right thread..

"That wedding caused a stir up on Lake Drive," Eddy said. "Here's the heir to a leather fortune, off to England to study economics, and he comes back engaged. Not to an Englishwoman, but to a local gal with a history of stirring the pot. Not some nice Episcopal gal, but a Milwaukee radical who claims to belong to the Socialist Workers Party, and calls herself a Wobbly, Industrial Workers of the World, and signed more petitions than a Chicago ward heeler. So she comes back here from England, and they have a big wedding, and none of her people show up, and she settles into life with Case, and now she's a cool progressive, and reformer."

Frank Silva listened dourly. "Or a Soviet agent," he said.

That all seemed bizarre to Joe Sonntag, who had not ventured into the world of ideology, subversion, and moles living quietly in a society they despised. This was a world in which people murdered one another for having the wrong beliefs, a world in which obsessed people tried to topple nations. He could understand the cruelty of an ordinary thug; it was hard to understand killers who destroyed anyone they deemed in the way of a great cause.

"It was always crawling through her, but a fifteen-year-old boy doesn't see that," Silva said. "She was romantic and fiery and obsessed; now she's a calculating and obedient slave of controllers somewhere."

"Which we can't prove," Eddy Walsh said.

"No, but we can foresee what happens next," Frank said. "At least sometimes."

"You want to talk a little? You're the only one here who had the faintest idea of what we've got on the hook, and what's coming."

"I've seen a little of it," Silva said. "But I could be as wrong as anyone else."

"Can you give us some idea how this connects to Anastasia Case?"

"Revolution is romantic. It's brimming with hope. It's radical and dangerous and exciting. It's powered by feverish dreams and ancient insults and injustices. But that's just romantics. The real revolution is operated by the most ruthless people on earth. They are a disciplined cadre of men without scruple. Marx is merely the excuse; Marx believed in things, but no seasoned revolutionary believes in good and evil. He believes in nothing. Anastasia was a romantic; now she's a bone-cold apparatchik."

"A spy?"

"A saboteur. An agent buried deep in a society he will try to destabilize or destroy."

"How?" Sonntag asked.

"Do her controllers want to own the machinists union? Do they want to weaken it? Do they want management to win the strike, increasing the bitterness of workers? Do they want to add to injustice, enraging ordinary people? Do they want to form progressive front groups pushing Soviet agendas? Do they want to see certain politicians elected? Like Henry Wallace? If Anastasia is actually such an agent, her instructions may vary day to day, and seem to contradict everything before. They may involve bringing scabs in to defeat the strike one day; killing Wolf Yablonski the next."

"Why would any rational person do that?"

"For the cause, Joe. The cause above all else. Once in a while, for money. Once in a while, for fear of exposure."

"So the controllers could want a scab shot one day, and a successful union leader shot the next?"

"Stalin has killed several million people, all for his own reasons. Including many of his allies and friends."

Something in all this troubled Sonntag. "This was a woman who paid her respects at the graves of men she cared about."

"Even saboteurs are poets, Joe."

"We have nothing on her except that she knew a couple of guys who were murdered," Eddy Walsh said.

Joe was grateful to Eddy for that. Joe liked evidence, not theory.

"We're looking at a woman who's got a Russian mother and a Russian name," Frank said. "And a woman who rebelled against her mother and everything her mother and father believed in."

"What's got to do with anything?"

"Let's go talk to that Marquette guy, Borovich, the White Russian," Frank said.

"You must know something I don't."

"Anastasia was a czar's daughter."

They headed for the university, and found Borovich tutoring someone in French in his cramped cubbyhole.

"Ah, the policemen. I will be with you shortly," the instructor said.

Joe and Frank studied the language department bulletin board for a few minutes, and then Borovich motioned them in.

"You have questions, gentlemen?" he asked.

Joe deferred to Frank. In truth, Joe scarcely knew why he was there.

"We're interested in a woman with a Russian mother. The woman's name is Anastasia; the mother's name is Natasha. What can you tell us about names?"

"Names? What's there to say, sir?"

"Could a woman named Anastasia behave in some way?"

"Are you well, officer? My name is Ilich. If it was Ivan would I be someone else?"

Joe was secretly agreeing with the professor.

"Yes," said Frank. "Tell us about Anastasia. The name. The Russian meaning."

Borovich settled in his swivel chair, eyed the standing officers. "It was a very popular name before the revolution," he said. "It was given to Grand Duchess Anastasia Nikolaevna, the Czar's youngest daughter. She's dead now. They're all dead. The Bolsheviks destroyed them. Regicide. Details unknown, place of burial unknown. That was nineteen eighteen."

The man seemed wistful, and his voice was reverent.

"Rumors persist that the girl escaped and lives. I sometimes catch myself yearning for that, but I know better. Any true Russian knows better."

"What else should we know?"

"Anastasia's a lesser saint."

"Suppose a girl's a rebel against her parents, her parents' church, and her parents' political and social views. Suppose her name's Anastasia."

"What are you asking me?"

"If you were named after a Czar's daughter, and you're a Red, how would you feel about your name? Anastasia?"

Borovich stared into the horizons of his mind. "I would fear that I am not trusted. The name betrays me. So I would try harder. If I were a Communist, I would be a fevered one, carrying the stigma of a sacred Russian name from the old days."

"It might radicalize her?"

Borovich shrugged. "Who am I to say such a thing?"

"Anastasia's mother Natasha hates the Reds; says they've destroyed her family. Made them disappear—either dead or in a gulag."

"Then there's a gulf between them, right?"

Sonntag nodded.

"You're chasing chimeras, sirs. I am simply a linguist of Russian inheritance, not Sigmund Freud."

"Actually, you've helped us," Silva said.

Sonntag couldn't imagine how, but he nodded. He was glad to get out of there. Icy undercurrents flowed from the Russian.

They retreated to the black Chevy, and sat in it. Sonntag didn't feel like driving, not yet,.

"I've been swept into some kind of whirlpool," he said.

"I almost drowned in it once," Silva said. "Here's what I got from this. Anastasia Case can't be a moderate, or progressive, or liberal. She can only be a radical."

"How do you know that?"

"I just do."

"I'm not getting it," Sonntag said.

"Joe, we're nibbling at the edges of something no one knows much about. There are armies marching in the night. They kill, they torture, they know no mercy. They killed a scab for some reason. They killed a respected labor union man for some reason. We don't know what those reasons are. We can't solve these crimes by knowing the motivations. Who can say what Ginger, or whoever he was, did to merit death? Or what a strong, incorruptible man like Yablonski did or did not do? I guess I'm saying we'll never understand why these men were executed. That's what happened. They were executed. They offended someone's religion."

"Me, I'm a city cop. I take the streetcar home. I eat the sandwich that Lizbeth wraps in wax paper and stuffs into my lunch bucket. I don't know a thing about conspiracies."

"Joe, I have an idea, and maybe I can sell it to you."

"Right now you can sell me anything."

"We should blow her cover."

"We should call up the State Department or the FBI, that's what we should do."

"No, Joe, give me this one. I know something about it."

"You're the kid she took to her bed."

"Yes, and I'm not the boy."

"So, what would blowing her cover do?"

"Things bust open. She panics. She has to talk to those who are controlling her. We keep an eye on her, and maybe apply some heat."

"You'd do that to the woman who... you're still half in love with?"

"That woman died somewhere in England."

"So you have a scheme?"

"Yeah. First, we go to Matt Dugan. He's always looking for stories. We tell him we're closing in on both killings, Ginger and Yablonski. There's some new stuff, international stuff. There are connections overseas. Get what I'm saying? Big hints that this is more than a domestic case. That's the first part."

"Frank, are you sure?"

"Here's the second. Harder for me, but I'm an adult. We go visit her. We tell her what we know. We tell her we have her history. We tell her we've got her living in England ahead of the war. We tell her we've watched her palling around with Fats Parvenu. We tell her we've put her tan Nash into the story. And would she like to come to the station and talk to us?"

Sonntag thought about that for a while, not liking it. "How do we get her to sit still while we tell her about her past?"

"She always did like me, when I was a kid."

"Would it work better if you did it alone, Frank? The leftwing cop, talking to her about stuff that's developing?"

Silva pondered it. "I'd feel better if you were with me, but I think I could get the job done better alone."

"And the job is?"

"To blow her cover so badly that she panics, and messes up, and we make a case."

"There's one thing you're not saying, Frank. If you go alone, there's risk."

"No, not if we give Dugan the story first. Then she knows it's not just me, her old lover, talking. It's the whole department."

"How would she respond?"

"She'll need to contact someone. She won't do it by phone. Not safe. She'll need to meet someone somewhere, and I'm thinking we'll be there."

Chapter Twenty-Four

Matt Dugan was wary.

"Hey, I spend my life trying to pry a story out of you, and now you've invited me into your parlor to hand me one. What gives?"

"Well, Matt, we think we're close to busting these labor union homicides wide open."

"Sure, and you want to tell me all about it."

Dugan was sitting on edge of Sonntag's battered desk, leaking skepticism.

"Well, we have a theory or two, anyway, and the best way for us to catch our fish is to tell the *Journal* what we suspect. If you print it, fine; if not, I'll have to leak stuff to the *Sentinel.*"

Dugan didn't budge. "I'll make that decision when I hear what you're playing with."

Joe nodded at Frank.

"These two homicides are connected. They're the work of someone trying to manipulate the strike. They're not motivated by anger or passion. They're motivated by someone's ideology. They probably are the work of some mobsters who showed up about when the strike started. The mobsters may have their own design, such as wanting to control the machinists union, but we think these killings were contract jobs, done for others. And we think the ones who are stirring the pot have connections outside of the United States, and have their own reasons to generate as much labor unrest as possible in this country."

"So you're chasing Reds now?" Dugan asked.

"It's a fair question. No, we're chasing whoever is stirring the unrest and violence; whoever kept the strike going much longer than it might have."

"We're out of cops and robbers, and into spies and the cold war."

"That's exactly what we'd like you to say."

"Huh? Say that?"

"Exactly."

"You're fishing. You don't know."

"We have a pretty good idea, and want to see what happens when a story like this hits the streets."

"The town's foremost liberal?"

"Maybe," Sonntag said. "Maybe not. We've placed a leftwing activist at or near both homicides. We're a bit puzzled about the shooting of the temporary, but it appears to be no accident. He was a loud anti-Communist and making a lot of noise about Red unions on the assembly line. He was stirring up the temporaries. The other, Wolf Yablonski, was resisting a proposed settlement. Then, he's shot, same type of shooting in the teeth, a trademark of a certain known killer, and the same person is hovering around. We know who that person is, and what the connection is, but we're a little hazy about the motives. This particular suspect apparently put out contracts, and we know who got the contracts and what he did, but we are still finding out about payments to him. You want to publish that? You can quote me. No anonymous sources."

"You're fishing. Theories aren't evidence."

"Take or leave it, Dugan. I hate to go to the *Sentinel* with it."

"I'm being used."

Sonntag nodded.

"You're going to be watching your suspect."

"We have several."

"The one I'm thinking about has a few thousand shares of the *Journal*."

Sonntag was smiling.

"The real story is that the company's unloading its temporaries, and going into full production today."

"No, Matt, it's that the new machinist president, Billy Bags, pushed the members into a worse deal than Yablonski's deal. And did it with muscle."

"I missed that."

"There was one serious protester. They threw him out of the strike vote, and punched him hard."

"You got a name? I want to talk to him."

"I'll ask him if he wants to talk to you. He's still hurting."

"All right, do that. I'm not giving you any promises. I'm not sure I'm going to write up your theories and start an international incident. Sending up balloons for the local cops isn't quite my style."

"Good to talk, Matt."

They watched the reporter head out of the bullpen. Sonntag was in no hurry. Reporters were known to read stuff on people's desks, even when the text was upside down. They were also good at catching conversations out of earshot, somehow.

But Dugan vanished, and Sonntag called Claude Kramer, reaching him at once.

"Matt Dugan of the *Journal* wants to talk to you but I didn't give him a name. If you want to talk to him, give him a call," Sonntag said.

"I'm ready to talk and talk and talk," Kramer said.

"You got anything more for us?"

"No, but I will. I decided that a pounding isn't going to stop me."

"Be careful, Claude."

"Whose maiden auntie are you, Lieutenant?"

Kramer hung up.

"Guess we'll see the story in the afternoon paper," Sonntag said.

Dugan's story missed the state edition, but made the city.

The story was all about the new president of Metal Worker and Machinists Local 258, William Bagatelle. The man, sent by the

International in Pittsburgh, had no credentials. He had never been a machinist, never paid dues to any union, and had previously, so far as anyone knew, been a bail bondsman before he was vaulted upward into the presidency of the largest local in the international union. The story quoted Claude Kramer, described as a dues-paying member of the local. Kramer was also quoted as saying the new contract was approved unanimously, and by open ballot, in spite of intense opposition, and that the strike settlement was poorer by far for the rank and file members than the one negotiated earlier.

And then, near the tail, was this: Milwaukee police say they have suspects and are closing in swiftly on the two homicides associated with the recent strike. One of the suspects had been loitering close to the victims and was known to both. The police report that both deaths had ideological motives. They follow a clear pattern and may have been grounded in the purposes of a foreign power. The police intend to question several political activists shortly, and have information pointing toward one in particular.

"Well, Dugan did it, his own way," Frank said.

"It's late. She'll need time to digest the news, or for someone to tell her about it," Sonntag said. "But in the morning, we might go disturb her breakfast."

"You take unfair advantage of people that early," Frank said.

"That's always my intent," Sonntag said. "There's nothing like knocking on a door at seven in the morning."

But it wasn't until around eight the next morning that Sonntag and Silva drove north on Lake Drive, enjoying the natural air conditioning. People who lived on the lakeshore enjoyed cooler summers. A lake breeze often comforted the wealthy residents while the inner city sweltered. The reverse was sometimes true in winter: the lake offered milder temperatures.

The Case mansion was a red granite rock pile, three-storied, turreted, and forbidding, at least on its landward side. Rich Milwaukeeans had ways of making their lakeshore grounds small havens.

A maid in a starchy black uniform with white collar and cuffs answered, eyed the detectives closely, and did not welcome them.

"I'm afraid Mr. And Mrs. Case aren't available," she said.

"We're Milwaukee Police. Detective Silva here and I'm Lieutenant Sonntag. We'd like to visit with Mrs. Case about some things she knows about. We're hoping she can help us."

"I don't think this is an appropriate moment," she said.

"We'll wait."

The maid vanished, while Sonntag studied the heavy foyer, badly lit and much too massive to be pleasant.

The maid did find her way back. "Mrs. Case says to tell you that if this is for the Policemen's Benefit Ball, she'll be pleased to buy six tickets."

"No, ma'am," Sonntag said. "We're hoping she'll help us find out the sources of some troubles in the Allis-Chalmers labor dispute. She took an active interest in it. We'll just wait here, and hope that she'll join us shortly."

They waited what seemed an interminable time, no doubt deliberate, but Sonntag knew he had his foot in the door, and the Cases would not be slamming it.

The maid didn't return, but a gentleman in a wine-colored silk robe appeared, looking much put out.

"I'm Anastasia's husband," he said. "She's still in dishabille, and won't be up and about until eleven or so. But if it's just a question or two, I'd be pleased to oblige. We're always interested in the wellbeing of our city."

"You're Herbert Case, then."

"Unfortunately, yes."

He didn't invite them in; so this was to be a doorway exchange, and the Milwaukee police might as well be Fuller Brush men. But Sonntag thought it was a good deal. He knew nothing at all about the heir to the leather fortune, and it just might be a right moment to find out a few things.

"Well, we're quite interested in whatever you can tell us. Mrs. Case was a close friend of the labor leader, and indeed, at the time of the funeral functioned as a hostess for the family. We were hoping she'd give us her impressions of Wolf Yablonski. You know. What sort of leader he was. What his purposes were. Things like that. We hope to make progress simply by looking closely into his life. And who could help us more?"

"Well, needless to say, I am not pleased with her various progressive activities. I have not only a large business to oversee, but a trust to manage, and it there's anything true about capital, it's timid. Rattle the place and capital flees, you know. I'm an economist, and I watch all this labor turmoil with deep dissatisfaction."

"What would give you satisfaction, sir?" Silva asked.

"Well, you're not economists, nor even businessmen, so it's a bit difficult for me to convey. Now, if there is anything specific, let me have it now. I was enjoying my orange juice and the *Sentinel*—a bit gaudy, right? But that's Hearst for you."

"I usually read the *Journal*, myself," Sonntag said. "It seems just the way to get the news before dinner. And of course it's not so, well, pro-Taft."

"Well, sir, we'd like to get some of Mrs. Case's insights about this labor situation. She was a friend of both the people who were shot, and we thought she could help us," Silva said.

"A friend? Surely you're mistaken."

"With her progressive politics, we can understand why she was close to Wolf Yablonski, but the other one is what puzzles us. You know, Joseph Ginger. Do you think she could tell us about him?"

"I have no idea what you're talking about," Case said.

"Well, you see, Ginger wasn't his name. He's been missing in action since the war, and we got his mother in, and she said it wasn't Ginger who got shot. That was a relief to her; it finally put his death behind her. But there was this guy Ginger, a friend of Mrs. Case, and he's not only a Temporary during the strike, he's a right-winger, telling everyone on the assembly line how rotten the Communists are, and how they should all fight the Red machinists union. We talked to guys who knew him, and they said he was a real rightist. So, of course, we got real curious. Was she trying to convert him?"

"I don't know anything about this, and surely you're mistaken."

"Nope, not mistaken, sir." Silva said. "She would meet Ginger when his shift was ending in the night, in her Nash. Now there's something else we'd like her help with. We did get some identification on this person, and it appears his real name was Dimitri Karl, and he was from overseas. He spoke good enough English, so maybe he was here a long time, but we can't quite find out where he was from. He was taking some lessons, which is how we found out a few things. He was staying in a place on the south side owned by Anders Gropius, and he's missing, and his place has fallen into the hands of some guys we think may be associated with organized crime. Now what we're thinking is that somehow, the Reds and the mob are lined up on some stuff, and we'd sure like the advice of Mrs. Case, because she knows all these people. I sure hope she wasn't getting too mixed up with people who don't have the best interests of organized labor at heart."

Herbert Case stared whitely at Silva, his hands slowly clenching.

Sonntag regarded Silva's discourse as a tour de force. It laid layer after layer of trouble on the Cases, without quite accusing anyone of anything. Something would have to give.

"You know, this is bizarre, officers. You are living in a fantasy world, and I'd suggest you stop harassing American citizens. You're sniffing around Anastasia as if she were somehow involved in all this. I shall take my complaint to the chief of police, as well as the mayor, and any other officials who might put a stop to this witch hunt of yours."

"Yeah, well, what do you know about it? I mean, she might have said a few things to you, sir," Silva said.

"I run a leather business. Good morning. Don't come back."

He swung the massive door shut, but not before Sonntag got a glimpse of Anastasia hovering in the shadows inside.

Chapter Twenty-Five

Sonntag drove quietly back downtown, mostly mulling the doorway confrontation.

"What do you think?" Silva asked.

"I want to know a lot more about Case," Sonntag said. "Where do I look?"

"Odd, but I don't know. Social registry of some sort? Chamber of Commerce?"

"Who knows him?"

"Most of the executives in Milwaukee."

"Let's try his tannery."

"Let's see what we can find out without alerting him," Silva said.

"Dorothea Blue," Sonntag said.

They laughed. The society editor was a great source, when she felt like cooperating.

"What do you think will happen up there on the lake front?"

"I think maybe he'll have a blue-nosed snit and chew her out, politely of course, for keeping bad company."

"You know, Joe, he has to know all about the company she keeps. If she was picking up Ginger after his shift in West Allis in the small hours of the morning, you'd better believe he knew about it. Same goes with her playing footsie with the mob."

"That's the most important thing. Whatever Anastasia Case is up to, so is Herbert Case."

"A tannery is a pretty quiet business. I've never heard of labor troubles in a leather works."

"That's perfect, isn't it?"

At the station house Sonntag called Dorothea Blue, Milwaukee's society maven. Sometimes she was helpful; more often, she told the cops to mind their own business. This time, she offered some help.

"Officer, call Mort Shriver. He does the obituaries."

"But Case is living."

"That just goes to show that you can learn a few things. A good obit writer stays ahead of the game. He's got files on all prominent or notorious people around town. He just collects stuff as the years go by; speeches, citations, family news, recognition, it all goes into a file, and when the guy dies, the obit writer's got the material right in front of him."

"I learn more from you every time I call, Dorothea."

"Yeah, we're all ghouls here. Waiting around for people to croak so we can write a yard of copy about them."

"Would Shriver share his trove?"

"Give him a ring."

That was good enough for Sonntag. He reached Shriver and identified himself.

"Who died?" Shriver asked.

"No one; we though you could help with the living."

"I prefer to deal with the dead, officer. It seems a little tacky to examine the living."

"Well, what we need is everything you've got about Herbert Case and his family."

"He'll live forever in the hearts of his countrymen."

"Do you have a file, and may we see it?"

"Oh, all right; this is very unusual."

"I'll be there in ten minutes."

Mr. Shriver proved to be gaunt man with gray-shot hair and a patina of dandruff on the shoulders of his baggy suit. He wore a white carnation.

"You going somewhere?" Sonntag asked.

"I wear a fresh carnation every day, sir. It's a way of greeting the bereaved."

"I'm grateful for the chance to look at your file."

"Here it is," he said, handing Sonntag a thin manilla folder. "Not much there. An uneventful life. They live longer than eventful lives. But their life is duller. I've never decided which is best. What's your option? An eventful but shorter life?"

"Ah..."

"You're not the type. When I write you up I'll avoid words like adventuresome."

"Ah...I guess I'll just read this if you can find a corner for me."

"Of course, it's different for women. The more adventuresome their lives, the longer they live. You take any ninety-year-old dowager and she's been to Fiji Island, swum with penguins, and met a few queens."

"But men are different, sir?"

"Oh, they divide into two classes. Those who do, and those who think. You take Harry Truman. He's not a thinker. He's a doer. You take Eleanor Roosevelt, she can't think at all. But she makes things happen. She's typical for a woman."

"How to you prove your case, Mr. Shriver?"

"Oh, it's obvious when you're in my cockpit, looking over finished lives. Men who are doers make money; men who are thinkers, like any novelist, don't make a dime. You might think lawyers are thinkers who make money, but no lawyer I've ever written an obit about is a thinker. Law is all rote, you know. Look up precedents. No original thinking there. But you take a doer, like Clark Gable, and he makes plenty of money. If I were to write an obit about Gable, sir, I'd say that he hunted and fished and chased women, but he didn't have a noodle in his kanoodle."

"I'd never given it a thought. My wife's a lot smarter than I am."

"Well, it's an illusion. After they've fed you a good meatloaf supper, sir, they seem smart but it's no different from forming a judgment while under the influence."

"Yes, well, is there a table where I can look at what you've got on Mr. Case?"

"Well, I thought I'd sit here and comment on each item. You can pull that chair up to the desk, and we'll dissect, gut, and sew up Herbert Case together."

Sonntag wondered why he got sidetracked into looking at the spouse of a suspect. He saw no escape, and settled in, while the obituary writer, who had long white fingers, opened the file as if it contained the secrets of all the major religions.

"There now. Here's a brief bio. He spoke to a United Fund black-tie dinner, and they ran a little portrait of him in the program."

Herbert Case was, it seemed, president and chief executive officer of a family-owned leather and footwear company. He was born in 1899, the second child of Hector and Agnes Fuller Case, the older child being a daughter, Hortense. He got his undergraduate degree in economics from the University of Wisconsin, and then spent two years in the family firm before heading for the London School of Economics for advanced work, before the war.

"Two years wandering around his family business, supposedly learning the trade," Shriver said. "Of course everyone knows what happened."

"I don't," Sonntag said.

"The son was full of new-fangled notions his father despised. The son picked up all those progressive notions in Madison, and wanted to turn the tannery into a cooperative, with everyone connected to the company owning a share of it. The old man blew up. The son, Herbert, blew a few fuses of his own, and stomped off to the London School of Economics to study whatever he felt like studying. Some said he was reading socialist texts."

That interested Sonntag.

"They say he met his wife over there," Shriver said. "The gossip was that things were rather torrid, you know." He grinned knowingly.

"Well, he returned, armed with a master's degree, and no sooner did he come back here than his father passed on to his reward, and there he was, still in his twenties, inheriting not just a big company, but also a job—if he forced the issue. The older gent, Hector, had left some able associates who might have run things. But Herbert would have none of it. He took over, practically before the last wreath was laid on his father's crypt in the mausoleum, and he's been an adequate manager. It's a private company, you know, so one can only guess, but Herbert doesn't seem wanting for money."

"How do you know all this, sir?"

"It's my business. I make no apologies. An obituary writer is more a gossip than a society columnist."

The rest of the material offered little that was out of the usual. Once young Herbert took over the tannery, he abandoned his idea of a cooperative, and ran his enterprise as any captain of industry might. He contributed to the Chamber of Commerce, made commencement speeches, donated to the United Fund, and largely stayed out of the limelight. Still, there were a few things that intrigued Sonntag. One was that his wife, Anastasia, was socially active, especially in various progressive and labor causes, her husband remained obscure. They were rarely seen together; indeed, she often attended civic events alone.

The other, which emerged only after Sonntag had pawed through various newspaper reports, was that Case spent unusual time traveling, always to England, usually on a Cunard steamship. He would abandon Milwaukee for six weeks at a time, cross the ocean, and engage in unknown activity in Europe. One account suggested he was a visiting lecturer at Cambridge. Maybe the erstwhile socialist had become an apostle of capitalism. Apart from those things, there seemed little about his life that raised any questions.

And yet Sonntag couldn't quite dismiss the man as unimportant. He made a lot of money, according to numerous articles on the company in the press. Where was it going?

"Thanks, Mr. Shriver," he said as the obituary writer stuffed his horde back into its manila jacket.

"He won't be dying for a while yet," Shriver said. "I usually get a sense of it a year or so in advance. I can sit here, and get a sense, and say this is Case's last year, and I'm always right."

"You really have that instinct?"

"Not instinct, sir. It's an occult knowledge. Only the best obituarists have experienced it. I check around, and there are only two or three of my acquaintance."

"You have any instincts about anyone now?"

Shriver turned very quiet. "None that I'm willing to share, officer."

"You have any instincts about someone who's recently died?"

Shriver slowly shook his head, and somehow Sonntag didn't believe him.

"I'll leave my card, and if you have any more psychic insights, sir, you could help the police department by giving me a call."

The obituary writer took the card gingerly.

Sonntag walked through a summer drizzle back to the station, feeling that he had gotten sidetracked once again. Two men were killed by the same killer during a violent labor dispute. How did he get lost in a maze of ideology and politics?

The moment he walked into the bullpen and dropped his wet fedora on a hat peg, Captain Ackerman boiled out of his office. The man always telegraphed his intent, and this time he was telegraphing a lot of hot water.

"I heard from Arthur Granger, esquire, attorney for the Cases. It seems the police have been maltreating them, treating the abusively, giving great offense, and even bullying the maid. He's taking the matter to the city council, the mayor, and maybe the city papers."

"I was pretty rough, captain, asking all those questions at his door before he was fully awake and dressed and powdered and puffed."

"Was it worth it?"

"I discovered that the place to go for stuff about prominent people is the obituary writer at the papers. The guy at the *Journal* might be the biggest asset we've got."

"And did you find out anything?"

"Herbert Case switched from a youthful progressive to a senile capitalist."

"Well, that's called growing up. Anything else?"

"He's in London two or three times a year."

"And who does Anastasia play with when he's gone?"

Sonntag sighed. Ackerman was as bad as J. Edgar Hoover sometimes. If there was one thing Joe Sonntag grasped about Anastasia Case, it was that she was empty of passion. She seemed not to have any female instincts at all. Maybe that wasn't what she was when Silva knew her, with another name and another life, but the present version was as bloodless as a porcelain doll. He wondered how he knew that about her; he was probably guessing.

"She plays with herself," he said.

"Anyway," Ackerman said, "you're in hot water with the city fathers–and I hope you stay there." He licked his gummy cigar and smiled.

There was one thing left to do that day: he drafted a teletype to Scotland Yard, seeking any information about Milwaukee businessman Herbert Case, who traveled regularly to England for month-long stays. Of interest would be activities, places visited, transfers of funds, and associations. He added that Case was not a suspect in a criminal inquiry at present.

He got Ackerman's permission, and sent the wire.

Another fruitless day. He collected his lunch bucket, with a sandwich he never got around to eating, pulled his fedora off the peg, and caught the Number Ten streetcar, settling into the tan wicker seats, and sniffing the familiar ozone odor of electric motors. He wasn't blue; just weary of plugging along without a break. Some cases were like that. Sometimes he never did get a break, no matter that he had pursued them hard and furiously. He wanted a break this time, but wishes wouldn't get him one. He would need to make his own breaks. The car ground across the terrifying 2,000-foot viaduct without landing on the Miller Brewing Company, and pretty soon he was greeting Lizbeth, who looked fresh in a sun suit, and settled into his chair to read the afternoon *Journal*.

The lead story in the second section, which focused on local news, was about the effect of the strike, now ended. There was a lot for the reporter to cover. Losses and gains for the machinists union; losses to Allis-Chalmers. The violence that left two people dead from unsolved shootings, and many others injured.

The reporter, Robert Karst, interviewed several people in company management, including a vice president in charge of the tractor division. The strike had forced the company to delay shipment of tractors overseas, where they would be put into service rebuilding European agriculture. In particular, the company had been unable to deliver more than two hundred of the five thousand tractors ordered by the Soviet Union. The Soviets had been unable to rebuild their war-torn steel mills, and such production as it had achieved in the postwar chaos went entirely into the armor of the Red Army. The Soviets were no longer able to buy arms from the United States, but tractors were another matter. The ruble was worthless, but the Soviets were willing to pay in gold, with the exchanges being brokered in London. And the Soviets were very angry because the long strike had crippled crop planting.

Joe Sonntag read and reread the story, wondering whether he had gotten his break after all.

Chapter Twenty-Six

It was like being handed the key to a locked door. Sonntag read and reread the long piece in the *Journal*, suddenly finding reasons, motives, possibilities. Were the Soviets messing around with a local strike? Were they pulling strings from far across the sea? They wanted tractors, right now, in time for the year's planting, especially winter wheat, which would be planted in the fall. And Allis-Chalmers had been paralyzed.

If so, was it espionage? No, it was manipulating domestic conflict. Was it sabotage? Yes, if its purpose was to weaken or destroy any domestic group—such as a labor union. Was it subversion, undermining the power and purpose of government? Well, sort of. It was the purpose of federal and state and local governments to protect lawful organizations.

And there is where Sonntag's busy mind stopped. Two people had been killed by bullets fired into their face. And so far there wasn't any thread connecting those murders to domestic criminals, and even less a thread tying them to a foreign power. Even so, the article scorched his mind. Suddenly, an entire scenario presented itself.

He would start in the morning with a long talk with the tractor division vice president, and anyone else who'd talk about the company's commitment to deliver.

Since the war, the Soviet Union had been truculent, blotting up its neighbors, terrorizing its own citizens, and actively engaged in a global enterprise. Did that include manipulating a strike?

It seemed absurd, actually. He would talk to a few company executives and probably end up shelving the whole notion.

"You've been sitting there, staring at the ceiling," Lizbeth said.

"I do that when I'm adding two and two and getting three," he said.

"You drink's half melted."

"Oh, how did that happen?"

She settled on the sofa. "Okay, the whole nine yards," she said.

"Oh, I was inventing crimes."

She smiled wryly. She knew she had him.

"Never read the newspaper when you're stumped," he said.

"The Allis Chalmers story. I read it before you wandered in, looking dazed, as if the streetcar had finally landed in the valley."

"The Soviet Union had reason to end the strike as fast as possible."

"No wonder you're looking fevered," she said. "Your imagination leads you down primrose paths."

"That's mostly what you do," he said, sipping the cool bourbon.

"I have a headache," she said, "but you might cure it."

He didn't know how the hell to interpret that. She was smirking. The evening was opening up.

"I have to talk to some tractor people tomorrow, just to put my nutty ideas to bed."

"I can see what's on your mind," she said.

"I don't know how many tractors the temporary employees got out. Not many. They have to be trained. They were mostly hired to bust the union," he said.

"Where do you think they went? I mean, they were paid off and sent out the door yesterday."

"Back to Arkansas," Sonntag said.

"Except for the dead man whose name you don't know."

"Maybe you could do better," he said.

She stared at him, stricken, rose, and began putting the meal together in deep silence. That's how it went through the dinner, through the evening, and through the night. He was sorry, but didn't know how to say it to her. The Allis-Chalmers homicides had worn him down. He was full of theories and lacking the most basic facts. He didn't even have any ballistic evidence, and could not link a gun to the killings, other than caliber.

He got to work early the next morning, checked out a Nash, and left word with the dispatcher. He arrived just ahead of the day shift, when union machinists were hurrying in, punching a time card, and heading into the great barns of the factory. They weren't rejoicing. They'd see their first pay envelope in a week. Many were living hand to mouth. A whistle announced the hour, and he sensed, rather than heard, a quickening within.

He approached the gateman. "Where would I find Art Coffin?" he asked.

"Who's that?"

"In charge of the tractor division."

"He doesn't see salesman."

"Milwaukee police."

"You're still snooping around here. Go around the block to the main offices, and ask there."

The watchman pulled out a *Captain Marvel* comic.

Sonntag worked his way to the offices, inquired, was told that Mr. Coffin was busy, and to come back some other time.

"I'll find him. Steer me," Sonntag said.

There must have been something in the way he said it. He was so tired of this factory and its labor problems that it showed. The male receptionist pointed, and Sonntag headed down a hallway, found the office and entered.

"Milwaukee police," he said, trumping any objections from a stenographer.

He pushed straight in, found the man in his shirtsleeves, looking thoroughly ticked, and flashed his badge.

"Lieutenant Sonntag. I need five minutes, sir. It'll help us resolve some troubles here. Now, what's the deal with the Soviet Union?"

"I'm supposed to tell you all that in five minutes?"

"Yes, sir, three if possible."

Somehow, Coffin decided to abide with this invader, and even smiled slightly.

"They need tractors. We were supposed to deliver two thousand this spring, and the rest by August. It took a lot of doing; their ruble isn't worth a plugged nickel, but we finally got it worked out. And then came several wildcat stoppages in the spring, and the two-month strike."

"What did they do?"

"Bears get nasty."

"Did they threaten the company?"

"They told us to stop the strike and deliver on schedule or they'd cancel."

"And what did you reply?"

"We said go to hell. We've got a good domestic market, still backed up because of the war, and price controls, and all the rest."

"So they tried to break the strike themselves?"

"Where did you get that strange idea?"

"We buried two reasons a few weeks ago."

"Get outa here. Cops are nuts," he said.

"What did they do to put some heat on you?"

"They said we should end the strike."

"And what did you say?'

"Just like that?"

"Did they bust the union?"

"Of course they did."

"How?"

"They bought some help from the mob. Say, I'm busy around here. Okay?"

"Were you glad to see the mob? Billy Bags, is it?"

"Whatever gets the job done, Sonntag. Now, if you'll excuse me."

He picked up a briefcase and walked out.

It wasn't even five minutes.

Sonntag found the company treasurer, Hal Stoltz, on a different floor, and found a much more cooperative man.

"Milwaukee PD, are you? Still looking into those tragedies?"

"Yes, sir, at the request of your local police. I just learned that the company was unable to deliver tractors to the Soviets on time."

"The Soviets don't have labor troubles. They shoot people."

"Are you being paid?"

"We got a large sum in advance; the rest contingent on delivery."

"Which didn't happen?"

"The strike slowed us."

Swiftly, Sonntag got the whole picture. The first shipment of tractors was due in April, but had been delayed by work stoppages and wildcat strikes. A thousand more were due June 1, but the strike stopped delivery. Two thousand more would be due August 1, in time for fall plowing and planting. The rest were to be delivered before year's end. It looked like the first three deadlines were or would be blown. Labor trouble had been at the heart of most of it; not only in the Allis-Chalmers plant, but in steel mills and parts suppliers. It was as if the industrial sector of the whole American economy was paralyzed. And the company was starving for cash because the bulk of the payments were to be made upon delivery. What's more, the whole industrial sector was still trying to meet pent-up demand for goods now that the war was over and price controls were eased or stopped.

The tractors themselves had all been shipped through the Great Lakes and St. Lawrence Seaway, to Kronstadt on the Baltic Sea near Leningrad. From there, they were shipped to communes across the Soviet. The historic port of Kronstadt was icebound a third or more of each year, which added to the urgency. The tractors could arrive only in the warmer months.

"So what did the commissars do about the strike?" Sonntag asked.

Stoltz shrugged. "It's not their country here."

"Do you think they were stirring the pot here?"

"Lieutenant, my business is finance."

"Well, did they put financial pressure on you? When you didn't deliver?"

"They were the souls of politeness, officer."

"No threats? Did they try to cancel the contract? Or penalize you?"

"They made frequent inquiry, through the Soviet embassy, about delays, and how soon they might expect the product."

"But nothing else?"

"Not us, sir, but the union. First the Reds were supporting the strike, and then they weren't, and then there were those violent moments."

"The Communists supported the machinists strike?"

"At first. Solidarity and all that. Then there was some sort of change. Management didn't know what the devil it was, and the Communists were fighting the machinists union. We got a few rumors, but that's all. Something happened."

"Like maybe at first the Reds were doing their old Solidarity routine, but then Moscow wanted to shut down the strike because it wanted tractors fast?"

Stoltz stared into space. "That's as good a theory as any," he said. "We're sure not going to know what went on. I don't suppose I've helped much."

"Actually, Mr. Stoltz, you've give me something to work with."

"That's the first compliment I've gotten in a year. You want to know what people usually say when they enter my office? Why aren't you paying the bills?"

Sonntag left a card, and headed into the morning. He still couldn't finger anyone for the killings, but he had a working theory; something that mostly fit, though he still couldn't quite put the man who called himself Ginger into the picture. He cranked up the unmarked Nash, and headed into town, oddly elated.

Maybe he could find some machinists union guy who'd tell him what really was going on inside that local. He wondered if maybe Claude Kramer, the dissenter, might open up a little, not about the mob, but about union politics. Worth a try.

He found a payphone, parked, and called in, and got the address from Frank Silva.

Kramer lived on the near north side, a long commute to Allis-Chalmers. Actually, not too far from the station. Milwaukee often gave the impression of being sleepy, and never more so than on this chill summer morning. You never heard a car honk in Milwaukee. Traffic moved silently, drivers shifted gears, and were often able to go through five or six green lights in a row before being halted. Maybe the traffic engineers had worked something out pretty well.

Kramer lived in a worn duplex that had carefully pruned shrubbery around it and a bird house hanging from the tree in the side yard. Milwaukee houses had a little space around them. Its working classes had a little comfort in most neighborhoods.

The mailbox, which was stuffed, indicated he lived on the second floor. Sonntag climbed, knocked, and got no answer. Well of course. Kramer was at work. The strike was over. Sonntag eyed the mail, stuffed in the upright bin, and noticed a Wisconsin Electric bill, and a *Model Railroader* magazine, published in Milwaukee. There were a lot of guys in town who built model railroads, and belonged to clubs that ran them.

Sonntag headed back to the station, called Allis-Chalmers personnel, and asked about Claude Kramer. It took them forever, but finally a nasty clerk informed him that Kramer hadn't shown up, and was replaced by another union hire, and no, Kramer had given no reason or notice, but that's what you expect from the union.

Sonntag filed all that away. He would check on Kramer after a few days, if he remembered it. He found Silva studying the Milwaukee port news. A small steamer, the William Berg, actually a wartime Liberty Ship, was scheduled to depart for Kronstadt in the morning, laden with fifty-seven tractors, largely built by the temporary help during the strike, and plows, harrows, and spare parts. It was a paltry shipment, but one to appease the Kremlin.

"Why do I want to go watch that little ship depart?" Silva asked.

"Tell me. I sure don't know."

"Why are all the bells ringing?" Silva asked.

"We've got more important things to do," Sonntag said. "Like putting two mobsters in the lockup. You want to come with me to Fats' house?"

"I want to inspect the William Berg, stem to stern, is what."

"We don't have that power. What do you expect to find, apart from a lot of agricultural machinery?"

"Oh, a killer or two," Silva said.

But Sonntag laughed it off.

Chapter Twenty-Seven

They stared at the big south side house. Fats hadn't quit remodeling it. There were new segments of concrete on the front walk, but the most interesting thing was new windows, all of the lower ones pebbled glass.

"No one sees in at night," Frank Silva said.

"But does anyone see out?" Sonntag said.

They eyed the place warily. Both detectives were carrying this morning. You didn't go visit Fats Parvenu and Billy Bags without some persuasion. Sonntag hated to carry. The compact automatic under the left side of his suit coat weighed, and was bulky, and wasn't much good in a pinch.

They had an unmarked black Ford with a wire screen separating the back seat, and doors that could lock tight with the press of a dashboard button. Fancy stuff this time.

They headed up the new walk, climbed the three steps to the porch, and rang.

Nothing happened.

They rang again. This time the door opened slightly, and that elderly woman they had seen here before peered out, from behind a door chain.

"Milwaukee police," Sonntag said. "We'd like to talk to Mr. Parvenu. And also Mr. Bagatelle."

"I don't think they're here," she said.

"We'll wait. Or we can call for help. Or we can put a few units here and in the alley for the next few hours or days or weeks, until you decide that they're here."

She eyed them, turned, and they could see her climbing the stairs. The front door remained chained.

Eventually, Parvenu showed up in his undershirt and khaki pants.

"Milwaukee police. We'd like to talk to you, here or at the station, your choice."

"You got some kind of papers or something?"

"We thought you'd prefer that we didn't get search warrants."

"This is just a friendly little visit, is it?"

"Is Bagatelle here?" Sonntag asked. "We'd like to talk to both of you."

"Never heard of him," Parvenu said.

"So that's how it's going to go. All right, come on out, and we'll drive you to town for some talk."

"I want a shirt."

"Tell her to bring it."

She was hovering behind him, and heard it. Wordlessly she ascended the shadowed stairs, and returned with a pink shirt.

That made Parvenu guilty as hell, Sonntag thought. Any male who wore a pink shirt was automatically someone to send up the river.

Parvenu stuffed the shirt into his pants, which the detectives watched. Only then did he undo the chain.

"How long?" Fats asked.

"The more you sing, the faster it'll go."

Sonntag had a sense that other eyes were studying them as they headed down the walkway to the street, and they ushered Fats into the rear seat of the Ford. The rear doors locked with a resounding click.

"You guys aren't very smart," Fats said.

"That's what they say," Silva said, through the wire mesh.

Sonntag drove carefully, an eye on the rearview mirror. They were not being followed. A quiet summer's day was evolving. It always struck Sonntag as peculiar: a very busy and toiling city, baking in silence. Did anyone in town ever blow a horn?

They released Fats from his cage and escorted him into the station house. Fats was looking pretty fruity in his pink shirt. He needed a Hawaiian straw hat with a gaudy band on it to complete his ensemble.

Sonntag led Fats to a small interrogation room, but not before the entourage caught the eye of Captain Ackerman, who erupted from his office.

"Well, look what the cat dragged in," Ackerman said. "How many felonies did you commit today?"

"I can give you my name, rank and serial number," Fats said, settling in for the duration. "Anything more is a war crime."

"Okay, Fats, why are you in Milwaukee?" Sonntag asked.

"I want a cup a coffee. You get a man up, you need to give him some coffee."

Silva headed for the coffee pot. Once Fats had a sip, he would be demanding not to have any more.

"I like golfing," Fats said. "You got the best courses. Better than Cicero. You take Brown Deer, and that's a famous eighteen."

"Who are your friends here, Fats?"

"The trouble is, I don't have any."

"Who are your enemies, Fats?"

"Sometimes I think everyone on earth hates me," Fats said. "Even my mother."

"What about your tenant, Billy Bags?"

"Who's that? Never heard of him."

"You know anyone over at the Machinists Local in West Allis?"

"West Allis, where's that?"

"You've been hobnobbing with Anastasia Case. That's tall corn, Fats."

"Never heard of her. I' like short, fat women with big hips."

"Who'd you buy your house from, Fats?"

"I didn't buy any house. I don't own any real estate."

"How come you're living in a house owned by a man named Gropius?"

"Never heard of him."

"So, do you own the place?"

"What place?"

"So who's paying for all the improvements? You got fresh paint, new gutters, new sidewalks, and new windows. You must have a real nice landlord, Fats."

"Yeah, I told him I'd invite him to church if he fixed it up. We attend together, you know?"

"You and Gropius?"

"I never asked his name. Some guy who's the landlord."

"That your dear old ma living there?"

"Naw, that gal, she's an Albanian I bought on the black market."

"She shops. She's got all the streetcar routes figured out. Straight to the banks. You got some accounts in town, Fats?"

"No, I bank with First Chicago, but mostly I'm overdrawn."

"So, Fats, are you armed? You got a few lethal items in there?"

"I'm a pacifist, lieutenant. Live and let live, that's my motto."

"Who did you let live, Fats?"

"I have a real bad time killing an ant."

"Whose aunt?"

"Aren't you the comic, Lieutenant."

"Why did you shoot Yablonski?"

"I swear on my mother's sewing basket, officer, I don't know who you're talking about."

"Why did you shoot the scab? What was his name?"

"What's a scab, officer? I never heard the term."

"How do you make your living, Fats?"

"I don't, officer. I don't own more than the shirt on my back."

"Who's Wolf Yablonski?"

"I think I've heard the name somewhere, maybe on the nightly news."

"How's your friend Anastasia?"

"Everyone in the Yellow Pages is my friend, officer."

"What's the caliber of your pistol?"

"I didn't know I have one."

"What are the Soviets paying you?"

"Not enough."

"What's Billy Bags' cut of the dues?"

"He's a dedicated steward, working for nothing."

"Did I hear that from your very own mouth, Fats?"

"Are we done, pal?"

"Just getting started, Fats. You might as well make yourself comfortable."

It was going well. Fats was sparring, and slowly contradicting himself. The secret was to go after him from all angles. And do it so fast that he could hardly get one answer out before hitting him with other questions. He was already less cocky, and showing signs of slowing down. Sonntag thought that another hour or so would yield something of value. Both Frank and Captain Ackerman had subsided, watching Sonntag pile on the heat. Sonntag knew he was the best man in the department for that. And in fact, he was enjoying himself.

"Fats, tell me about Cicero. Is it true that they hide bodies under driveways there?"

"I never heard of it," Fats said. "And I got no driveways around here."

Silva's eyes met Sonntag's.

"Yeah, you're right, Fats," Sonntag said.

That was worth the whole effort. "Hey, how long has it been since you've seen Anastasia Case?"

"Who's that?" Fats said.

"Your girlfriend."

"Oh, is that her name? I got about ten girlfriends."

"She's a pretty one. You must feel lucky."

"In the dark, they're all the same," Fats said.

"She sure has an agenda," Sonntag said.

"What's that mean?"

"She's a pretty busy lady, don't you think? Her name's in the paper a lot. You see it there?"

"I don't read the society pages."

"Were you with her when she went to pick up Joseph Ginger after his night shift?"

"Huh? Who's that?"

"The scab that got shot at about one in the morning."

"I never heard of it. Must have been before I came up here. Milwaukee's real quiet at night. Now Cicero, we've got clubs; Milwaukee, it sleeps all night."

"What did she say when Ginger got shot?"

"How should I know? I wasn't there."

"Where were you? You got an alibi, Fats?"

"I musta been sound asleep, if you'll pardon the expression. Me, I got bad eyes. I got amnesia. I got senile dementia. Hey, are you turds done with me?"

"You've already spilled a lot of beans, Fats," Sonntag said. "Man, are you in trouble. You got nothing but prison bars in front of you."

"Who says? You say? Man, what an outfit up here. Now, Chicago, they got real cops, and you can talk to them, and they talk to you."

"What do you talk about with Chicago cops, Fats?"

"Wouldn't you like to know."

"Maybe you cut deals down there. Is that it?"

"Chicago, it's one big city, lieutenant. Milwaukee, it's the sticks."

It was time for Silva to edge in. "Well, Mr. Parvenu, I guess no one got anything done with this little visit," he said. "I guess you could call it ping pong. We hit the ball, you hit it back, and no one scores, right?"

Silva was so gentle and peaceful that Fats stared.

"You talk about cutting a deal down there in Cook County; that's the sort of thing we're interested in. You know how it goes. You help us a little, we help you a little. We got a problem here; two bodies, and we've got no real leads. You keep showing up whenever we look into it. So you're our best lead. I mean, there you are in the middle of it. So, we think you know things, and we're looking for a favor or two from you, and maybe you'll want to help us a little."

"I don't know a thing, pal."

"Okay, okay, we'll keep on until we get the story. If you don't know a thing, then we're barking up the wrong tree. If you know a few things, Mr. Parvenu, I think you'll enjoy wearing black and white stripes up in central Wisconsin."

"You done? Take me outa here? You had it with old Fats?"

"You want streetcar money, or should we drive you back?"

"You drive me back, every inch, and you set me loose in front of my house."

"I'm disappointed, sir. I really thought you'd help us," Frank said.

"What's the deal?"

"We don't deal. We like favors."

"This is a Red deal," he said. "You should learn all about Reds."

"Why do you say that?"

"Take me home. My mouth is buttoned tighter than a fly."

And so it was. He went mum. Like the Berlin Wall.

Sonntag and Silva escorted Fats to a patrol car, put him in the back, and wound through rush hour traffic until they got to Fats' duplex.

"Drop me down the street. I don't want no one seeing cops cut me loose."

But Sonntag simply parked in front of Fats' place, unlocked the rear doors, and waited.

Fats didn't hesitate. He bailed out, beelined for the front porch, and soon vanished inside, behind the pebbled glass windows.

Sonntag and Silva sat and watched for a while. Sometimes there were great third acts or encores playing, and all it took was a little watching. But the house went dark and silent.

"Want to dig it up?" Silva asked.

"I hope we've got enough to get the warrant," Sonntag said.

It would be dicey, persuading the judge. But Sonntag was pretty sure he'd get the search warrant. And then Fats might sing a different tune.

"He pushed out a blue chip at the last," Silva said. "Reds."

"You think he'll talk?"

"Not without some encouragement. I think we're best off just going for the bodies."

When they got back to the station, they laid it out to Ackerman. There wasn't a whole lot, but maybe enough. Sonntag wanted search warrants for Fats' domicile; Billy Bags' domicile; and the yard, including the front walk.

"If we get the warrants, we'll need a jackhammer and crew, and a few cops," Sonntag said. "And maybe a hearse."

Ackerman gummed his cigar, enjoying the thought. "We get to dig up Fats Parvenu's brand new concrete," he said. "I think I'll go watch. I can't get all this tomorrow. It may take a few days," he said.

"We can wait," Sonntag said. "Old habits have a way of solving crimes."

Chapter Twenty-Eight

Sonntag stopped at Claude Kramer's upstairs flat, and found no one home. A few more letters were stuffed in the mail receptacle.

Sonntag rang the bell downstairs, and a woman with a baby in her arms answered, stared uneasily, and started to close the door.

"Just a minute. I'm Lieutenant Sonntag, Milwaukee Police. I'm trying to locate Claude Kramer, upstairs."

"Police? What did he do?"

"I'm worried about him. I can't find him. He isn't showing up for work."

"I haven't seen him," she said.

"Are you his landlady?"

"No, Mr. Bork owns the building. We rent."

"I don't suppose you'd have a key to Kramer's place."

"I do, but I wouldn't let you go there, I mean, it's not okay."

"But it's okay for you to check it out?"

She nodded.

"Would you take a look? Just make sure things are all right?"

"Why do you think they aren't?"

Sonntag smiled. "They probably are fine, ma'am. He's someone I admire. Maybe he's sick."

She thought a moment, nodded, and disappeared, returning with the key.

"You hold Angus," she said, thrusting the squirming boy at Sonntag.

The lieutenant accepted the wiggling child, who didn't like that one bit and began whining. But Angus's mom sailed up the stairs, while the kid squirmed like an angry octopus.

The pants were suspiciously damp.

He hated to expose her to possible tragedy, but sometimes you do what you have to do. The smell of piss increased, and he thought of lowering the kid to the floor, but he grimly held on until the weary mother returned. He was only too glad to hand her the kid.

"Not there. Not sick. Just not there."

"Anything disturbed?"

She eyed him warily. "Should there be?"

"Has that mail been there long?"

"I haven't paid any attention."

"Okay, here's my card. When he returns, please have him call me."

She studied it. "You an officer? I mean, an *officer* officer?"

"I'm in charge of investigations."

"I hope he's okay."

"We do too, ma'am."

She seemed relieved to get back to her child-tending; Sonntag was relieved to let her.

When he got back to the station, Ackerman had news. "Here's two search warrants. You can search Parvenu's flat for weapons. The other lets you dig up Parvenu's yard, including walk. Get a city street crew, and take some armed men. And take Gorilla Meyers."

Meyers was the department photographer, a wizard of the Speed Graflex.

"There better be bodies in there, Sonntag, or I'll turn you into one."

Sonntag laughed. He'd heard that item about once a month for a few years.

He called the city public works people, and they groused and whined, but promised to show up the next morning at seven with a compressor, jackhammer, and three guys with picks and shovels. They he got four cops in two cars, plus himself and Silva.

Seven was a nice summer hour when the sound of jackhammers would lift residents out of their beds, and some cops on the front lawn would draw a crowd. He thought about alerting Matt Dugan, but thought better of it. There might be nothing but dirt under those sidewalks. At the last minute he added a forensic pathologist, a genius of his acquaintance named Doctor Stoppl, who'd helped him in another case.

By six the next summer's dawn, he had his entire crew assembled at the station house, and they quietly paraded south and west until they reach Fats' strange duplex. The sun was just peeking over Lake Michigan.

Silva was grinning. He hadn't enjoyed this labor case, but now he was awaiting some entertainment.

"You want to, or should I?" he asked.

"We'll need a couple of blues to keep Fats and his ma corralled," Sonntag said.

So there were four at the door at seven sharp. Sonntag rang the bell, which clanged within. For a long while no one showed. Finally, the old gal showed up in a white robe and hair full of silver colored curlers.

"Police," Sonntag said. "We've a search warrant to search the premises of Anthony Parvenu, upstairs, right?"

"You can't come in here; he ain't here." She eyed the two detectives and the two uniforms behind them, and started to shut the door, but Sonntag's foot stopped the door. "Here's the warrant," he said.

"He's not here."

"He doesn't have to be."

"Where is he?" asked Silva.

"He's gone."

"Ma'am, you step aside. We also have a warrant to search the grounds, and we're going to make a lot of noise. Is William Bagatelle in there?" he asked, nodding toward the lower unit.

"He's gone."

"Where'd he go?" Silva asked.

She stared at him, suddenly going quiet.

"You step outside, ma'am. These officers will look after you here on the porch."

She did.

"I'll tell them to start in," Sonntag said. He motioned them to the four rectangles of fresh concrete in the walkway. He thought for a moment he'd end up looking like a damned fool. He'd had that happen plenty of times.

The city crew powered up the diesel air compressor, and eyed the fresh, smooth concrete. Dr. Stoppl sat stoically in a cop car, watching the show. So far, there had been no neighborhood ruckus. People slept on, or read the *Sentinel.*

"We're going upstairs, ma'am," he told the lady. "Where did you say Mr. Parvenu is?"

"He left. I don't know."

"Was it after we drove him back here?"

"Then? Yes. He got Billy and a car and went."

Sonntag turned to Silva. "Our little conversation drove him out of town."

They headed up the stairs. Sonntag withdrew his automatic, just in case. There were dead cops who didn't take basic precautions. The door was open.

"Fats, you come on out," he said.

But there was only silence. He waved his fedora at the doorway, but no one shot it. He and Silva rushed in. The place was immaculate. The old lady kept a clean house. Too clean, Sonntag thought. As if she had been scrubbing ever since her son– if that's who he was– hastened away two evenings earlier.

He knew what he'd find: not a damned thing.

Outside, the diesel droned, and then he heard jackhammers batter the walkway. It wouldn't take long. About fifteen or sixteen feet of walkway. Sonntag headed immediately toward the bedroom, unloaded drawers of underwear and socks and flannel shirts. Nothing. Nothing in the closet. Nothing under the bed or under the mattress.

Silva was working the kitchen and bathroom, and they worked the clothes closets and the stuffed furniture, and the storage. The place was clean; deliberately clean. Fats knew well enugh how to leave a place as spotless as an altar. They did not forget the wastebaskets or clothes hamper or the linen closet or the electrical utility box.

The flat was clean.

Out in the front yard, the street crew had broken up the new concrete and was dragging the pieces out of the ground. There was a bed of thick gravel beneath. The uniforms watched; so did the pathologist, who sat on the front porch. A silent crowd had collected at the sidewalk. The cops weren't letting anyone close. The street crew began shoveling gravel, and then into a layer of rough rubble, the four of them unhappy about this assignment. They struck canvas about four feet down, and gradually cleared rubble away from a war surplus pup tent half. A rank odor crept out of the diggings.

Sonntag watched, dourly. The only question was which missing man was in that stained, maggoty canvas. This was murder being unveiled, shovelful by shovelful. This wasn't some abstract death, such as one found in mysteries, but a foul, maggoty corpse, its life and breath and dreams and hopes driven out of it. Sonntag had seen plenty of it; men in war had seen more of it. But anyone who had seen death wrought by violence felt an abiding hatred of it.

Sonntag eyed Frank Silva, who was looking a little green around the gills. But Frank, the eternal idealist, would weather it.

Gorilla Meyers photographed the graves from several angles.

Stoppl stared in to the shadowed pit where the canvas stretched. "I think we'd better get some help," he said. "Call the Health Department. We need a chlorinator and a couple of men in gear."

That took an hour, but the street crew completed its excavation of the second canvas-wrapped body, this one much newer and not fouling the air. Sonntag was pretty sure it would shroud Claude Kramer. The Health Department crew arrived in rubberized canvas bib overalls, and long rubber gloves, and activated carbon gas masks. Onlookers turned very quiet as the newcomers sprayed the canvas with the chlorinated spray, and then slowly lifted the first body out, and pulled aside the canvas. There wasn't much left of Anders Gropius. He had been shot through the mouth; his spinal column had been destroyed. It took only a glance to identify him. The hair, the eaten-away jaw.

Claude Kramer had met the same fate, but was intact. A bullet had punched his teeth out and destroyed his neck. Sonntag stared, saddened. A brave man, Kramer. The trademark killing now extended to four bodies, all associated with the strike. A shot in the mouth was the calling card.

"Are you surprised?" Frank asked.

"We'll want warrants for Fats, and for Billy Bags, and we're going to need to find the mob foot soldiers. These two were buried by crews at night, who dug, wrapped and lowered the bodies, poured rubble and gravel over them, and maybe the concrete contractors were involved too, but I doubt it."

"Where do we start?" Silva asked.

"Some guys in leather aviator jackets."

Silva grinned. "Signatures."

"Some people like to advertise."

At Stoppl's nod, the Health Department guys lifted the canvas and lowered Gropius into a sheet metal carrier. Kramer followed. The remains would be frozen pending further identification if necessary. There wasn't much left of teeth for dental records. The rest would be a stinking, ugly job at the morgue.

The spectators watched in hooded silence.

Sonntag noticed Matt Dugan standing just outside of the police line. He'd be wanting answers, and Sonntag didn't feel like answering them. In any case, the department wasn't about to release the names of the dead until more work had been done, and some effort had been made to locate survivors.

Sonntag corralled a cop. "Tell Matt Dugan, there, that the PD has uncovered two bodies, that I can't release names yet, and that both bodies are victims of homicide. Tell him he can call the case the walkway killings. In Cicero, Illinois, they use driveways. I'll talk to him later at the station, but I can't say when. You can give him a clue: one of the dead is the owner of the property."

The cop grinned. "I love feeding tidbits to reporters," he said, and headed toward the street.

One of the Chevy black and whites had a working radio. Sonntag made use of it, asked the dispatcher to get Ackerman, and after describing the find, asked permission, on pursuit grounds, to search William Bagatelle's place too.

"You got a key?" Ackerman asked.

"Anybody in the attorney's office going to be unhappy?" Sonntag asked.

"You told me that Kramer was thrown out when he began objecting to Billy Bags?"

"Something like that."

"Bust in. I'll take the heat if there is any."

But it wasn't necessary. The old gal had a key for the lower flat, too. She let Sonntag and Silva into the lower flat. They looked around, seeing nothing but an orderly room in the light streaming through the pebbled glass. The glass let light in, but kept the world out, and kept the world from seeing anything at all within. It was like living behind prison walls, Sonntag thought. A very strange life.

He knew little about Billy Bags, and the room revealed almost nothing more. Everything was empty. Nothing in closets, nothing in the kitchen, nothing in the bathroom, not even towels. The place had been abandoned, carefully, completely, so that it was ready for the next tenant. So William Bagatelle, the new boss of the machinists local, had fled too. And the big union out at the Allis-Chalmers plant would require a new president, another election. Or at least it seemed that way.

"Nothing in the toilet tank," Silva said. He never missed a trick.

Both residents, upstairs and down, had left town, it seemed. And had left town just after Sonntag and Silva had grilled Fats hard. Fats had been a good match, parrying every surprise question, but not good enough. And he knew it. And those bodies, being loaded into a city vehicle outside, were the proof of it.

The strike had cost four deaths. Or maybe that wasn't the way to say it. The struggle to own the local had triggered four deaths. But this time it had gotten too hot for the mob, and the two pigeons flew.

Then again, maybe not. There were accomplices who dug those graves, carried and wrapped the bodies. And buried them right there under a front walk from the sidewalk to the front door.

Those accomplices probably were around, and quite possibly keeping the local under the

thumb of the mob. Sonntag thought it was time to look for guys in leather aviator jackets.

Chapter Twenty-Nine

The man standing at Sonntag's desk so early that morning had iron hair, cut short the way so many veterans of the war wore it. He had stern eyes, a pocked face with a war wound along one cheek-bone, and he wore a gray suit and blue tie, all of it conservative.

"You're the head of investigations?" he asked.

"Sonntag, sir."

"I'm William Bagatelle."

Sonntag eyed the man, sure he had never seen him. He bore no resemblance to the man of the same name Sonntag saw briefly at the time of the strike vote.

"Have a seat, sir."

"I arrived last evening from Pittsburgh, and discovered in the morning paper that's I'm a wanted man. So, if you want me, here I am."

"I wonder, sir, if you can identify yourself."

Bagatelle withdrew a breast wallet, and a passport with a photo in it. This man was William Bagatelle of Pittsburgh. One by one, Bagatelle added to the pile. Drivers license, a credential letter stating he was the executive vice president of the International Brotherhood of Metal Workers and Machinists; a member of Pittsburgh Local 27; a card identifying him as a Veterans Administration patient; and a small photo folder with black and white prints of a wife and two children.

"I am here to straighten out some irregularities in the West Allis local," he said. "We weren't aware of all of it. A man named Claude Kramer wrote us, and now it turns out that I am a wanted man for the homicide of this same machinist. What shall I do about this, sir?"

"You've been in Pittsburgh these last three or four months?"

"I can assure you–I was working. There are many who'd vouch for it."

"You're a veteran?"

"Wounded in forty-four, discharged, purple heart, distinguished service cross. I returned to my local, helped build armored personnel carriers, advanced to my present office. I'm a machinist. I can run any lathe. And now I discover I'm a wanted man here."

"Have you Mr. Kramer's letter, sir?"

"I do." Bagatelle produced the opened letter, still in its envelope, addressed to Bagatelle at the international headquarters. He pulled the letter and handed it to Sonntag.

It was addressed to the International Union headquarters, a carefully wrought account of the mob takeover of the local, with emphasis on the a mob-imposed new president, with the familiar name of William Bagatelle. The letter requested help. It was signed by Claude Kramer. It was dated ten days earlier.

"I came as swiftly as a trip could be arranged, sir."

"We found two bodies buried in a style familiar to the Cicero mob, in a house sawed into two flats, the lower being occupied by someone with your name, the upper being occupied by a known mob figure called Fats Parvenu."

"I seem to be in trouble."

Sonntag smiled. "That's unlikely at this point. But there's a lot you can do to help us. The mob gentlemen have taken their leave of us, but we believe they left confederates in control of the local. Probably accomplices. Someone had to dig those graves, load in the rubble and gravel, arrange for the paving, as well as shoot those two men mob-style."

"Mob style?"

"The trademark is a bullet through the mouth."

"How will I help?"

"Finger the confederates. But before you accept, you should know you're a marked man the moment you arrive in West Allis."

"I took care of myself during the war."

"These people don't fight according to the Geneva conventions."

"Neither do I."

"Let's go talk to my superior, Captain Ackerman, and my top detective, Frank Silva," Sonntag said.

Moments later, Bagatelle was showing his credentials, his letter from Kramer, and telling his story, and volunteering his help.

Ackerman stared. "We don't want to hand out another purple heart," he said. There was an odd tenderness in his voice. Ackerman was a sucker for any wounded veteran.

"There's a warrant on me," Bagatelle said.

"It's yours," Sonntag said. He handed Bagatelle the warrant.

"That doesn't end it. The county has to quash it."

Ackerman called the county attorney. Two minutes later the warrant was as dead as the victims.

"Who do I talk to in the local?"

"We don't know. They've thrown us out. It's a private organization."

"I have my ways," Bagatelle said. "Done here?"

"You need a ride somewhere?"

"Not in a cop car."

Bagatelle stepped out, and vanished down the stairs.

"I'd like to be a fly on the wall over there," Silva said.

"So who was the guy calling himself Bagatelle? Who maybe pulled the triggers?" Ackerman asked.

"Do you think we could slide someone in, give Bagatelle some security?" Silva asked.

"I have one of my usual brilliant hunches that the real Billy is going to clean house," Ackerman said.

Ackerman was famous for his lousy hunches.

"I know these guys," Silva said. "He'll get a regular job. The company's looking for any skilled machinist it can get. Remember, plenty of machinists headed out. That was a long strike. They moved to California. He'll get a job, and join the local, and then we'll see some stuff."

"Meanwhile, we're looking for some killers," Sonntag said.

The strike cases were growing cold by the hour. The union had rolled up its sleeve and gone back to work. The papers were complaining that there was no progress on the killings, and questioning the competence of the police. Sonntag tried one or another angle, including staking out the union hall, but no one in war-surplus leather jackets showed up. Not in late summer, at any rate. They heard nothing from Bagatelle, either, except that he was working at the plant, he was screwing tractors together, and keeping his mouth shut.

Then one morning he walked into the station. He was wearing work dungarees this time, and somehow gave the impression he was solid, tough, and not a man to mess with.

"Okay, here's the deal," he said. "I work the second shift. I hang around the union hall. There's no one notices I've got the same name as the president who vanished. I'm just another guy, blue shirt, but I'm keeping my ears open. The guy using my name, he's back in Cicero; so is one of his thugs. The other one, a Cuban contract killer named Fulgencio Fuentes, is all that's left of the mob in West Allis. That's his name but he's called Muy Bueno because that's all he says. You ask him to do something, he says Muy Bueno. You ask him who he is, he says Muy Bueno. You ask him how he feels, he says Muy Bueno. So that's his name. Now get this. You ask him to kill someone, and he says Muy Bueno. You want the man who killed those two you dug up, you arrest Muy Bueno."

"How do we prove it?" Sonntag asked.

"Muy's always armed."

"With what?"

"A snub-nose."

"That's not going to knock teeth out at any distance."

Bagatelle looked annoyed. "That's what he carries, not what he uses."

"How do you know that?"

"Guys talk on the assembly line. They're scared of him"

"Where does he live?"

"In the flat above the union hall. There's a covered stairwell at the rear. He has an arsenal up there."

"His task is to keep the local quiet until the heat's off?"

"His itch is to shoot cops, lieutenant. Maybe it's good that you're locked out of there."

"Muy Bueno eats, he lives, he doesn't spend much time in the flat."

"Muy Bueno had a girlfriend, but he hasn't seen her in a couple of weeks. He spent a lot of time with her, I'm told."

"Have a name?"

"No, but she's rich."

"Anastasia Case. She's been very quiet lately."

"They say Muy's gotten real mean. She hasn't shown up, and Muy's ready to quit. He needs a woman a night. That's what the gossip is."

"You've been busy."

"I've been in combat. Italy, North Africa, France. It's a strange thing, what war does to a man."

"Doesn't anyone wonder why a man with the same name as the mob president is working the line?"

"Certainly, and they stay very, very quiet."

"If we were to raid Muy's flat, when and how?"

"He goes out to eat."

"Is it booby-trapped or rigged?"

"Nothing is beyond Muy Bueno."

"What about accomplices? The ones who dug those walkway graves?"

"You grilled Fats, right? Within an hour or two afterward, there wasn't a one of the mob in Wisconsin. Except Muy. He's the only pigeon around. The brothers are afraid of him. As long as he's around, the mob still owns the local."

"You think he did the shooting?"

"Hey, I'm just a new guy on the assembly line."

"Let's get him," Ackerman said. "What do we need?"

"Stealth, I think," Sonntag said. "Any show of uniforms, and Fulgencio would be back in Havana."

Ackerman puffed, and finally said, "you know what you're saying? You plain clothes guys? We could send in a riot squad."

They all knew.

"Mr. Bagatelle, you've opened the door for us."

"I came out of the war wanting to set the world right. It was a mistake," he said.

"What are your plans when this is over, sir?"

"They elected me president, even if they didn't know it. I'll take that office. I'll put the local in order, and turn it over to its executive committee, and go back to my family and my job at U.S. Steel."

"You got any advice for us, sir?"

"Yes. Getting Fuentes out of there doesn't end it. The rich woman knows the rest of the story."

"We're working on that," Silva said.

Bagatelle left, walking into a late summer morning.

"Well, what are we waiting for?" Sonntag asked.

"I'm ready," Silva said.

Ackerman chewed on his cigar, and said nothing. It was obviously an effort for him to keep his yap shut.

Sonntag and Silva strapped on underarm holsters, armed themselves, slipped into baggy suit coats, and headed out. They checked out a rattletrap Ford F100 pickup truck. Not that they could keep from looking like cops. Sonntag swore that he looked like a cop off-duty, wearing a swimming suit on a beach.

Silva drove out to the west side They cruised past the storefront union hall, drove the alley behind the hall, noted the green wooden stairwell leading to the upstairs flat, which had no door at its base; found a spot down the alley a bit, parked and waited. The day heated up, then cooled under a cloud cover, but no one entered or left the stairwell.

"We'll see what we need," Sonntag said.

They left the truck, walked gingerly up the dark stairwell, lit only by a small window where the stair reached door to the flat. Silva had his service pistol out. Sonntag gently tried the door; it was locked. The lock was modern and well made, and not easily jimmied. They would need to call in a locksmith to breach it.

So Sonntag knocked. No one responded. He knocked again. They heard no shuffling of feet. Then Silva pointed upward. A key hung on a small nail. Sonntag lifted it off the nail, gently slid it into the lock, and turned the handle. The bolt snapped back noisily. Sonntag waited, half expecting the door to swing open, or someone to start shooting through the door. It didn't happen.

There were legal protocols required here.

He knocked, and flattened himself against the wall.

"Police," he said. "Open up, and hands up."

They pushed the door open, and pushed in. A gauzy curtain at an open window ballooned, and then settled back.

Muy Bueno was out.

A swift survey of the flat eliminated the presence of the Cuban. But he was not far away. He had an odd altar set up, the image of someone Sonntag didn't know, but maybe a patron saint of Cubans. An array of silk flowers decked the frame. In a small bowl, as if an offering, were a dozen or so spent shells, a pile of empty brass. There were two alligator-hide weapons cases. Sonntag pulled a handkerchief and opened one. It contained an odd weapon, best described as a revolver with a lengthy barrel, a silencer, and cross-hair sights. If an assassin were planning to shoot someone through the teeth at a medium distance, it would do nicely. It appeared to be custom made.

"Jesus," Silva said. "What a thing to lay before an altar."

Sonntag wished he knew the name of the saint. A golden halo encircled its head. The saint held two lightning bolts. He wore a purple loincloth.

They did a thorough survey of the rest of the flat, finding a hideout revolver in the archaic bathroom, and another, a Derringer, in a niche at the door, behind more silk flowers in a vase. The rest of the flat was nearly empty. The man was not settling in.

People who laid spent cartridges before a saint would be far more dangerous than any routine thug, he thought.

"What saint is that?" he asked. Silva always knew stuff.

"Beats me," Silva said. "Maybe Santeria, Voodoo, African, Latin mix."

"We've got everything but our pigeon," Sonntag said. "Do we pull out and lock up and wait?"

"Muy Bueno," said Muy Bueno, standing in the door frame, a shining revolver in each hand.

Chapter Thirty

Sonntag kicked the altar. The gilded image went sailing. The bowl with the spent brass spewed its cartridges. The silk flowers flew every which way.

Some guttural scream ripped out of Muy Bueno. Silva drew, aimed, fired a shot that knocked one revolver out of Fuente's hand which bloomed with blood. He dropped the other revolver, which discharged, sending the bullet straight through the mouth of the image.

The Cuban howled. Sonntag landed on him, patted him down, and pinned him while Silva found a towel and wrapped the hand. The shot had torn open the thumb.

Fuentes moaned, and then began howling, some eerie wail that sent chills through Sonntag. Fuentes was staring at the image with the hole through the teeth, and groaning.

"There, you see? Your saint's dead," Silva said. "His teeth knocked out."

Fuentes's cry strangled in his throat. He had seen the end of the world.

"Who'd you shoot?" Sonntag asked.

"They are like the seashells on a beach," Fuente said. "I am done. I am dead."

"Did you shoot the scab, coming out of the plant?"

"Ah, who can say?"

"Who was with you?"

"The rich lady."

"Did you shoot Wolf Yablonski?"

"It was asked of me by the rich lady."

"Was she there?"

"She was always there, and afterward, we came here and I added a brass casing to the bowl, and she took off her clothes."

"Why did she want these people dead?"

"She worked for a secret government."

"Government?"

"She had masters; she did what they bid. We always did it."

"Who did you work for?"

"I employ myself."

"You a blood brother of Fats?"

"We do not share blood."

"But he brought you here?"

"I brought myself here, at his request."

"He sent for you? And you came, to work for him?"

"Always myself. I choose. I work for nothing. It is not money. It is reputation. For me, the fear is everything. They whisper Muy Bueno, and I own the world."

"That made you a big man?"

"No, senor, very small. I am like a little spider."

"What was the name of the rich lady?" Sonntag asked.

"She was la senora. I do not speak her name."

"She hired Fats who hired you?"

"I am not for hire. If the spider stings, it is his choice. If the spider doesn't feel like it, he doesn't sting."

"Did you feel like stinging la senora?"

"Si, sometimes, after we had slept. When she was soft and warm. I say to myself, now is the moment."

"She targeted people and you shot them with this device?"

"It is very sad, senores, a bullet in the teeth. A person cannot lie in his coffin and no one can weep for the dead. Very sad."

The towel over his hand was reddening. There were shouts down below.

"Fuentes, we're charging you. You walk ahead of us, and we'll get an ambulance for you and get you patched up."

"You will carry me. I will not move a muscle. I will not be your mechanical toy."

"Your choice," Sonntag said.

Silva headed for the door. "Police here; call an ambulance. Man's hurt. Don't come up here."

"You hurt? Cops hurt?" someone down there shouted.

"No, we're Milwaukee detectives. Get your West Allis cops in; we're on a case for them."

It took a while. Sirens, the rush of boots.

"Up there, who are you?"

"Lieutenant Sonntag. Detective Silva, Milwaukee PD. We've an injured man. We're charging him."

"Safe to come up there?"

"Yes, the injured man's down."

Two uniforms appeared in the door, weapons drawn, eyed Muy Bueno, and holstered their revolvers.

"Meet Muy Bueno," Sonntag said.

"We already know him," a cop said. He eyed the odd weapon in its case. "Tools of the trade," he said.

"Has he been frisked?" the cop said.

"Go ahead," Sonntag said.

They frisked the man, found nothing more.

The ambulance pulled up outside, and two medics arrived, studied the bleeding hand, and applied a tourniquet while Muy Bueno moaned.

He's being held on homicide charges. We're coming with you," Sonntag said.

They got the contract killer to Milwaukee Hospital, where he was patched up and put under guard.

Sonntag collected Gorilla Meyers to photograph the upstairs

flat, the ruined altar, and Muy Bueno's weapons before they were removed from the scene. Gorilla burnt a few flashbulbs.

There were a lot of spectators crowding the street when Sonntag and Silva began removing the stuff, most of them machinists. They watched silently, their eyes on the gun cases. The West Allis cops studied the crowd, and the Milwaukee detectives, uncertain about all of it.

Then Sonntag and Silva brought all that stuff to the station. There would be prints taken of the weapons and cases, and ballistic samples done on all of the weapons. There were reports to be written. There would be long interrogations by Captain Ackerman.

They'd nabbed the trigger man; they hadn't nabbed the mob, or Anastasia Case, whose fate was growing darker by the minute.

Once Fuentes was treated and his hand sewn together, there would be some interrogations. For the moment, he was so heavily sedated that nothing more could be gotten from him. But there were two witnesses; the man's confession of two homicides, and maybe many more, was enough to seal the case. The case was beginning to resolve itself.

It wasn't until later in the day that Ackerman finally corralled his investigators.

"Tell me," he said.

"We've got the man who pulled the trigger, and we know why he did it; Anastasia Case was his muse, if that's the right word," Sonntag said.

Silva was looking solemn. This was a woman he had loved, back when she was using a different surname. And was an impassioned radical. "What we don't know is why. She's working for someone or something. My instinct is that she's going to go so quiet that we'll hardly get her name out of her."

"Do we want to talk some more to Fuentes before we go visiting?" Sonntag asked.

"There's a lot we don't know," Silva said.

They headed out State Street in an old Ford, and found Fuentes's room. A cop sat in a folding chair in front of the door, reading a Batman comic.

"I have to sign you in and out. Also, you don't go in armed."

"We're not," Silva said.

Fuente's hand was clean and bandaged, and he was staring at the ceiling.

"Muy Bueno," he mumbled.

"I hope you're not hurting so much," Sonntag said.

"Morphine," the man mumbled.

"Let's get the whole story," Silva said. "We'll go slow. You take your time, okay?"

"I want to sleep."

"Well, the faster we do this, the sooner you can."

"Go away."

"Your santo was shot in the mouth," Silva said. "There's nothing left for you. Except maybe you tell us about it. Who was the woman?"

"Lots of dinero."

"What did she give you?"

"She said I would die for the revolution and be a hero of the U.S.S.R."

"Is that why you shot the ones she wanted killed?"

"It is a good thing to die for the revolution. I don't know one from another, but all revolutions are good. Caromba! The first one, the scab, he didn't want a revolution. The second one, the union jefe, he didn't want the revolution."

"So she said you should shoot them?"

"She just say, you want a night with me, and then I knew. One bullet, one night, mi corizon. It was a bargain. A bullet is easy. A night, never easy. I will sleep now."

"Who did you kill we don't know about?"

"Quatro, cinco."

"You shoot Anders Gropius?"

"Who knows their name? I don't know. They point; I shoot."

"Who's they?"

"Antonio Parvenu."

"He had you shoot the man who owned that house?"

"He was in the way. He was renting rooms to scabs. Then the jefe wanted it. The place was good for the jefe."

He talked, he dozed, he held his bandaged hand beside him, he asked a nurse for more morphine. Sometimes Sonntag and Silva filled in the picture; other times they waited patiently, while Fulgencio Fuentes decided whether or not to say anything. It wasn't a good, clear picture, but it was a picture.

The mob wanted the local. The Soviet wanted tractors. It also wanted the local if it could. The Soviets saw labor as the key to the revolution. Own the locals, and some day they would bring the United States to its knees. All of this was too grand and abstract for Sonntag, but Silva was devouring it, understanding it, asking Muy Bueno all the right things. All Sonntag wanted was leads, hard evidence, stuff that would stand up, bringing criminals to justice. And that meant, in the end, bringing reserved, slim, privileged Anastasia Case to court. Her fevered dreams had somehow whitewashed homicide— all for the cause, of course. Anything for the cause.

Finally a nurse chased them out. "Let him rest; he needs rest," she said. The look in her eye hinted of vast disapproval. Her patient was suffering, and the police were abusing him.

Well, okay.

The cop at the door was reading Superman now.

"Lois Lane's pretty cute, but dumb," Silva said. "Superman's a sucker."

"Yeah," said the cop.

There was time to go get her. Ackerman would want to send in the riot troops, but this was Sonntag and Silva's deal, and wordlessly they set out to do it. This would close an era of turbulence and trouble, when beliefs and ideals got out of hand, and led to murder and mayhem. Sonntag drove. Milwaukee's core was always peaceful, never more so now, as Sonntag traced his way into the city's heart, and then cut north to the red granite pile on the shore of Lake Michigan.

Silva was particularly somber. The woman they would arrest was a woman he had loved as a boy, a woman who had fevered him and given him dreams and a vision during the Depression, when capitalism seemed dead, and socialism shone like a beacon. There she was, casually breaking the rules and enjoying it, and lifting Frank Silva into a new world.

"You must hate this," Sonntag said.

Silva didn't respond for a moment. "If we were taking the Anastasia I remember, yes, I would hate it. I'd almost turn in my badge. But we're not going for that woman. We're going for a thin, cold, calculating woman I don't know and don't care to know."

"You any idea what changed her?"

"Yes," Silva said shortly.

"I'm not good with this case," Sonntag said. "I'm missing something."

"When people have differing versions of heaven," Silva said, "they kill each other."

Sonntag turned into the looped driveway that led to the front portico, and parked. The place seemed oddly forlorn.

"You okay, Frank?" Sonntag asked.

"We're carrying," Silva said.

Sonntag pushed the button. They heard a bell. After a lengthy period, the maid opened.

"We're here to see Mrs. Case," Sonntag said.

"You're the police again?" she asked.

"Yes. Please take us to Mrs. Case."

"She's not here, sirs."

"Where might we find her?"

"I—I wish I knew, sirs. Mr. Case left three weeks ago, and never said a word. I take care of things. I have my own quarters, and I take care of things, No one has opened the mail, the bills are piling up, and frankly, sirs, I fear something's quite, well, not right."

"You're in charge, ma'am?"

"No, I'm the housekeeper. There's no one."

"May we have permission to look around? Maybe we can help you."

"It's not my, I mean, well, I find comfort in it. Please come in, sirs."

Sonntag hoped she would find the comfort she needed but somehow he doubted it.

They walked gingerly through silent stately rooms, each dusted and clean. It was a place of velvet drapes and wing chairs and a dining table that could seat twelve. She had collected the mail each day, and now it rested on the dining table, unopened. They peered into the spacious kitchen and pantry with a chest freezer, a utility room, a foyer with french doors that led to a lakeside patio that would be a choice place in the summers. She accompanied them as they probed each bedroom, peered into closets, studied the baronial bathroom, and finally, her own small quarters, not at all humble; a pleasant apartment.

"May we see the basement, ma'am?"

She nodded. Down gloomy stairs they found a coal-fed boiler, cold now; a utility and tool room; and a lot of somber spaces that held an array of garden furniture.

"Did he say when he'd be back?" Sonntag asked.

"He didn't say anything, sir. He vanished. She's gone. I keep waiting for, I don't know what."

"Flew the coop," Sonntag said.

Chapter Thirty-One

This needed looking into.

"Ma'am, have you Mr. Case's office number?" Sonntag asked.

She supplied it. He called, ending up with a male assistant whose response astonished him.

"I'm sorry, sir. Mr. Case is no longer with us. He left the company."

"Left? But his family owns it."

"He sold it, sir. It was privately owned, you know. We're a division of Grosvenor Leather now, sir."

"Sold it? When was this?"

"I'm not sure, sir. About three weeks."

"Where did he go? How can I reach him?"

"Mr. Case didn't convey his plans, sir. If you'd like to talk to our acting manager, Mr. Coggswell, I'll put him on. But he's an employee of Grosvenor, brought in."

"What about Case's personal mail? Where are you forwarding it?"

"To his home, sir."

"He left no address?"

"None. He did say he would be traveling. That's all anyone knows, sir."

So that was that. Sonntag hung up and stared at the wall.

"Do you mind if I look at his mail, ma'am?"

"Is that proper, sir?"

"We're not opening it. We'd like to see what it is, where it's from."

"Well, you're the police," she said.

There was a lot of it. Bills, mostly. He and Silva studied the pile. Some, addressed to Anastasia, were newsletters from various progressive groups and the Henry Wallace campaign committee. Wallace was taking on Harry Truman, from the left.

One envelope caught Sonntag's eye. It was addressed to Case; it was from the Baltic and Northern Shipping Company.

He showed it to Silva, who nodded.

"Ma'am, we're going to open this," he said.

"You're the police," she said.

The police were breaking postal law, but he didn't say it. He slit open the envelope with his fingernail, and extracted a receipt. It was for the passage of one person on the William Berg to Kronstadt, U.S.S.R.

"Did Mr. Case talk about going overseas, ma'am?"

"He was very agitated just before he left here; no, he didn't."

"Did Mrs. Case discuss it with him?"

"She left before he did, sir."

"How much ahead?"

"Oh, how can I say? You're making me very nervous. One day earlier, that's when I didn't see her."

"Is there anything, anything, that's different now that they're gone?'

"Oh, sirs, may I sit down? I've been so worried. There is something different. I have lost their trust."

They waited. She struggled, her eyes filled with dread. Then she rose, led them to the pantry and the oversized freezer chest, and pointed to the lock. It was simply a padlock, linking the hasp, which had been screwed to the sheet metal lid.

"That was not there before he left?"

She shook her head. "Why didn't he trust me?" she asked. "I am so ashamed; he locked it from me. I can't bear it, the shame." Tears welled up.

"All I need is a screwdriver," Silva said.

She produced one.

He unscrewed the hasp one sheet metal screw at a time, until it fell loose. The hasp and lock no longer pinned the lid. Silva lifted it. A gust of icy air eddied out as he swung it open.

She was lying there, frozen solid, her eyes seeing nothing, stretched across frozen meat. She was wearing a white cotton dressing gown. She had been shot in the heart, a small, almost bloodless perforation in her bosom. An automatic lay on her stomach, no doubt the murder weapon, heavily frosted. She was perfectly preserved, her icy countenance perfect, her face serene.

The housekeeper groaned, and fainted.

Sonntag caught her as she collapsed, and laid her gently across the pantry floor. They would let her lie there for the moment. Anastasia Case, dead, frozen into perfection, hidden in a locked freezer. Herbert Case gone, his business sold, his passage to the Soviet Union probably completed by now, if indeed he was on that little freighter. It puzzled him, at least until Silva enlightened him.

"He was the controller, the Soviet agent, Joe. We blew her cover; he knew that when we confronted him at the front door. It was only a matter of time. He was not so much Anastasia's spouse as her spymaster. She bought into Stalinism, she bought the package, she was turned into an agent in England, she and her spouse and controller, upper crust people, returned here, valuable assets to the Soviets."

But then he couldn't talk. Sonntag knew that Silva was staring not at the dead Anastasia Case, but at the warm, passionate, daring, golden Anastasia Ryan, his lover and mentor and muse.

The housekeeper was stirring. "Call in; I'll get her up," Sonntag said.

The woman opened her eyes, stared up into the faces of two detectives, and closed her eyes again.

"There's a couch in there, ma'am," he said. He helped her up and supported her while she shuffled into the parlor, and a yellow silk sofa.

"We'll have a doctor for you in a minute," he said.

"I don't need a doctor," she said. "I need...there's nothing that I need."

Silva called, explained, and then stared bitterly into the freezer chest.

"It's religions," he said. "We get religions, and we kill for them."

They heard the sirens well before they saw the black and whites. Sonntag felt oddly morose. Usually, when he'd resolved a tough case and some lethal and dangerous mortal had been salted away, he felt a certain satisfaction. This time, staring into Anastasia Case's frozen face, he felt an odd sorrow.

They swarmed in, half a dozen uniforms, Gorilla Meyers, with his big Speed Graflex and a pocketful of flashbulbs. And not least, Captain Ackerman, bustling through the door, terrifying the housekeeper, whose name Sonntag had not yet gotten. Moments later they were grouped around the freezer chest, peering down upon Anastasia Case.

"Subversives," said Ackerman.

"Romantics," said Silva.

Ackerman stared at him as if he were fodder for J. Edgar Hoover.

"You touch the gun?" the captain asked.

The question annoyed Sonntag, and he didn't respond.

"It'll be clean," Eddy Walsh said.

"This was Herbert's work?"

"He was on the Robert Berg, that ex-Liberty Ship that sailed from the Milwaukee Port three weeks ago," Silva said. "It reached the U.S.S.R. yesterday."

"Why would he do it?" Ackerman asked.

"We blew her cover. He was the spymaster. Only they weren't collecting intelligence so much as manipulating events. Like the strike."

"Disloyal bastards, and killers."

Sonntag waited for Silva to erupt, but he didn't. "We've got most of the story; not all," Silva said. "There's going to be a few holes. Maybe we'll get more if we can grab Fats Parvenu."

"I'll talk to the FBI," Ackerman said. "I want him on the Wanted list."

Sonntag thought that Fats would enjoy being there.

"Do we wait for a medic?" Silva asked.

"She's a block of ice. They can do it all at the morgue."

Which meant they'd move Anastasia, as soon as Gorilla got done. He was already frying flashbulbs, covering all angles.

"The press wants in," said a uniform.

"I'll talk to them later," Sonntag said.

"No, I'll talk to them," Ackerman said. He smelled glory.

Sonntag grinned. "Just wait," he said. Ackerman scowled, and nodded.

The county's ambulance pulled up. It would do for a hearse this time.

Eddy Walsh waited until Gorilla was done, found a towel, and lifted the automatic from Anastasia's midriff. He dropped it into a cloth sack. There was nothing else of interest visible. The ambulance guys came in with a stretcher, got the nod, and lifted frozen Anastasia out of the chest. They all peered in, looking for blood underneath, but there was none. She had been shot somewhere else. There were packages of frozen elk, moose, and deer underneath. They lifted these out, looking for whatever might be found, and found nothing.

"Where do we get shipping information?" Ackerman asked. "Get me the company. If that tub hasn't reached Russia, I want the navy to move in."

No one leapt to Ackerman's command. He chewed on his gummy cigar, and grinned, knowing full well what a panic he's started.

Miss Willoughby, the spinster housekeeper, was so distraught that they summoned a physician and he sedated her in her apartment, but not before they'd done a swift search of the quarters, finding nothing of interest.

The rest of the house required attention. Cops and detectives spread out, looking at everything. They finally discovered, from specks of blood and spilled coffee, that Anastasia had been shot out on the lakeside patio, early one morning, while she was taking coffee and watching the sun rise up from the quiet lake.

There were things to go through, mail, deeds to the house and other property, and in particular the shadowy web of communication that connected Case to his Soviet controllers. But that was going to be a task for the FBI. Sonntag knew that this would be taken from his hands, fast, and he and the Milwaukee PD might never be privy to the details.

Sure enough, the Milwaukee agent in charge, showed up even before Sonntag and Silva had completed their survey, and insisted that the detectives stop, now. Sonntag replied, with some heat, that it was a murder case, and murder was his jurisdiction, not the FBI's, and he was going to continue to investigate until he was forbidden to do so.

The agent simply smiled, made a phone call, and Ackerman uneasily told Sonntag and Silva they were off the case, and to cease tampering with the evidence.

Tampering with the evidence. Sonntag fumed.

But it wasn't over. The agent, one Jack Slate, told Sonntag to keep his trap shut; it was all confidential. And by God get out of the way and don't touch a damned thing.

That was too much for Sonntag, orders issuing from some other organization. The hell with that.

He found the *Journal's* Matt Dugan waiting patiently in the drive, barred by police lines.

"Come on, Matt," he said, opening the door to his unmarked car.

"Here's the story, as much of it as I have; we've been yanked off the case by the FBI," he said. "Anastasia Case was found in a locked chest freezer in the pantry, shot in the chest, the apparent murder weapon lying on top of her frozen body. Her husband sailed out on the William Berg, full of tractors, and has now reached the Soviet Union. It appears he shot her out on the patio, while she was enjoying the sunrise and reading the *Sentinel.* Before he fled, he sold the tannery– it was not a corporation, but a privately owned business."

"If Hoover's got this, I'll never know what the rest of it is."

Sonntag continued with what he knew, and sometimes with what he surmised, carefully making distinctions. They were Soviet agents. He was her controller. Sonntag's murder investigations had edged closer and closer to them. But she was dead and he had shipped out before they caught Fulgencio Fuentes, who confirmed her role in the strike violence. The rest would be theory: the Soviets wanted the strike to end fast; they needed tractors fast; they employed the mob to stop the strike any way it could; Anastasia Case, born Anastasia Ryan, oversaw the swift termination of the strike. She had gone from Socialist romantic to Soviet agent, working with her husband and controller, Herbert Case.

"That's the story, Matt. There's holes in it. We don't know why the temporary employee was killed, and we're sure only that his name isn't Joseph Ginger. We may never know. But Fuentes killed him, and has confessed to it. And tells us that Anastasia was with him, pointed the man out, and Fuentes murdered him."

Dugan made notes, and then sagged into the seat. "You know what? I'm depressed," he said.

"You're not the only one. This is off the record. Frank Silva had a fling with her, when he was a boy and the Depression seemed like the end of the world. The end of capitalism. She was a fabulous woman, Anastasia Ryan, back then. A romantic socialist rebel. But later she sold her soul and became a slave of men with very large designs."

"Case fascinates me. He owned a large business, and yet turned himself into a spymaster for the Communists."

"Belief's a funny thing, Matt. There's people who'll kill in the name of God and consider they are doing the world a favor."

"How'm I going to write this up, Joe? I've got two hours before deadline."

"I'll give you the headline; it'll go nicely in the *Journal.* Rich Communist Shot Reading the *Sentinel.* How does that sound, Dugan?"

"Hey, Sonntag, you're in the wrong profession," Dugan said.

About the Author

Axel Brand has clerked in a record store, worked on an assembly line, written newspaper stories and editorials, edited fiction and non-fiction books, taught writing, and raised and trained saddle horses. He says:

"The Milwaukee where I grew up in the forties was a place where English was often a second language, and each neighborhood had its own tongue. It was a place with corner taverns, where families collected, and a place of churches, many of them transplanted from the old country. I remember the orange streetcars and the motormen in dark blue who watched the fare money drop into the glass box and then gave you a transfer. I remember the Big Band music that played on WTMJ and WEMP, along with *Charlie McCarthy and Edgar Bergen*, or *Fibber McGee and Molly*. And I remember it as a safe and solid place, run by a socialist mayor, with four seasons and a settled way of life. So I set my mysteries there, in a big industrial town that had amenities, a town that I fondly remember."

Visit his page online. http://axelbrand.blogger.com

Joe's World

The Joe Sonntag mysteries are set in the late 1940s in Milwaukee, Wisconsin. At that time, Milwaukee, noted for its breweries and manufacturing, was experiencing a population growth that continued into the early 1970s.

The Allis-Chalmers plant is a focal point in this story. While the strike in *The Saboteur* is not based on an actual occurrence, the plant suffered several post-war labor disputes. The tractor company was founded in West Allis, Wisconsin, a suburb of Milwaukee, in the early 19th century. It produced military machinery during World War II.

http://en.wikipedia.org/wiki/Allis-Chalmers_Manufacturing_Company

Joe always has great trepidation about taking the streetcar to and from work because of the Wells Street viaduct. One look at this photo on the "Remember When" site will show why he gets white-knuckled.

http://content.mpl.org/u?/RememberWhe,8

Gorilla Meyers, the police photographer in Joe's division, uses a Speed Graflex camera. This press camera was at its height of popularity in the late 1940s.

In post-war Milwaukee and other cities, the major shopping centers were situated downtown. In 1948 Gimbels Department Store, founded in Milwaukee, was one of the largest chain department stores in the country, with premiere stores in New York City, Philadelphia and Pittsburgh.

Learn more about Gimbels at
http://en.wikipedia.org/wiki/Gimbels

This was Joe Sonntag's world. I hope you enjoy this dip into the past.

—Axel Brand

Made in the USA
Charleston, SC
20 September 2015